Silver Moon Books of Leeds and New York are in no way connected with
Silver Moon Books of London

If you like one of our books you will probably like them all!

Write for our free 32 page booklet of extracts from early books
- surely the most erotic feebie yet - and, if you wish to be on
our confidential mailing list, from forthcoming monthly titles
as they are published:-

Silver Moon Reader Services
109A Roundhay Road
Leeds
LS8 5AJ
United Kingdom

http://www.adultbookshops.com

or leave details on our 24hr UK answerphone
08700 10 90 60
International acces code then +44 08700 10 90 60

<u>**New authors welcome**</u>
Please send submissions to
Silver Moon Books Ltd.
PO Box 5663
Nottingham
NG3 6PJ
or
editor@electronicbookshops.com

PAINFUL PRIZE
by
Stephen Rawlings

Also by Stephen Rawlings in Silver Moon Books:
Eve in Eden.

CONTENTS

PART ONE: HUNTED

The man and the girl sat in a car in a country lane, consulting a small sheet of paper he held up for them both to read. He was well-built, about mid-thirties one would suppose, successful in some way obviously, his clothes, the car, his air of assurance spelt it out clearly. Though not classically handsome, women would find him attractive, even without the trappings of success. With them he was a dangerous man to have around.

She was some years younger, perhaps twenty-five or six, tall for her sex, a mass of auburn hair tied back with a simple elastic ring, leaving her pretty face free. Its prettiness at this moment, however, had to be assumed to some extent, for she seemed to have had an accident of some sort. Her cheeks were heavily smeared with thick wet matter, greenish brown and reeking of cow. She might well have tried to clean herself up before going further, had her hands not been secured behind her back.

As it was, she disregarded the state of her features to concentrate on an apparent problem with the message on the paper, a concentration interrupted from time to time by a grimace of pain, and a certain uneasiness in her posture, since she writhed her buttocks on the seat, and shifted her weight from side to side.

Suddenly she said, "Axwell, the river there. Georgina said old Major Grange has a boathouse on the river he hardly uses. How about that?"

"Brilliant," the man replied, "that's it for sure. We used to play there as kids. Martin knows the place, he's bound to have chosen it. Now no more talking, we have to get there fast. Open wide."

For some reason he held in his other hand a small wad of pale blue nylon. A curved section of narrow lace even suggested it might be part of the girl's underwear. Though it

7

may have started the journey embracing the girl's smooth bottom cheeks, and the moist channel between them, it was now sodden with saliva from prolonged insertion in her mouth to keep her silent. He'd slipped it out to enable her to contribute to the solving of the clue to their next destination but, now, he returned the wad of flimsy nylon to her obediently parted lips.

"Clever girl," he cried, and impulsively pulled her towards him, regardless of her filthy face, to kiss her warmly on her panty-stuffed mouth.

She winced as the fresh burning stripes on her bottom made contact with the cruel needle-sharp projections of the wicker mat she was sitting on, without benefit of underpants, nor dress come to that, since it was deliberately pulled up behind her to allow her bare bruised flesh to rest on the unfinished weave of the basket-work. Still, she did not resist him, responding avidly to his kiss, in as much as her nylon crammed mouth would allow. She would have flung her arms around him but her wrists being secured behind her prevented that, so she tried to press her breasts against him instead, though their position in the car made it difficult and, additionally, they and their sensitive nipples had problems of their own to contend with. All her reservations had fled now. She gave herself up completely to the adventure.

There had been moments up to this point when she'd wondered what she had got herself into, and just why she was putting up with it. For instance, when she had hung over the gate waiting for him to begin her thrashing. She'd felt the rough timber of the top rail pressing into her bare unprotected belly, the print dress, a Versace number and a touch over the top for such rural ramblings, hiked up to her waist, her panties round her nylon-clad knees. She could just take her weight on the toes of her medium heeled sandals, her only real concession to this ride into the country, replacing the expensive Italian heels that were her usual wear in the city.

Behind her she could hear him making experimental cuts of the air with the terrifying birch switch he had just cut from the hedge. As it sliced the air with a sound like ripping silk, she had flinched at the thought of it cutting into her virgin buttocks that had never felt the cruel kiss of rod or cane before.

She was suffering even before he began. The harsh wooden gate bit painfully into her naked belly and the tops of her thighs as she bent over it, her bare buttocks jutting out behind, smooth pink half globes.

Their deep divide, normally closed demurely over the secrets within, was now wide-spread by the painful pose, so that she could feel the air on the tightly furled anal dimple. She could sense his eyes dwelling on the fatted vulva where it pouted its plump lips through the lozenge gap at the top of her thighs, its pert prominence only slightly softened by the delicate fringe of auburn curls that vied for space between the smooth columns of her legs. She was strangely disturbed by the knowledge.

It wasn't as if it was the first time she had been naked before him. God knows he had taken her there often enough, and she had no secrets from him, but this seemed different in some deep meaningful way; an invasion of her deeper than mere sex. Now he was to whip her and she felt both fear and excitement, apprehension and a vagina-wetting tingling in her crotch. What was happening to her? What was she doing, bent three parts naked over a five-barred gate in an open field, without even the shelter of the birch tree from which he had cut that frighteningly swishy rod he was practicing with? That was shortly going to fall on those tender bare pink buttocks she was now so conscious of, as if her whole being resided in them, and leave them as barred as the gate.

She certainly hadn't expected anything like this when they had left home that morning. Home was a charming cottage

9

in truly rural England, as opposed to the nominally rural character of the estate houses constructed in what were no more than disguised dormitory towns serving the great conurbations. Sexton Hinds had retained its flavour of the genuine English country village, still no larger than it had been left when the last developers had put up the Georgian pub two centuries before.

Not that the inhabitants were exclusively bucolic. There were plenty of people living there whose Great-grandfathers - and their Great-grandfathers - had occupied cottages in the vicinity, but there was a tidy proportion of folk who had come in from the city seeking peace and quiet. They had themselves. Henry had always talked of returning to the village where he'd been raised, since they had first shared an apartment together two years before and then, three months ago, he had suddenly swept Jenny off her feet by a flying visit to Sexton, when he'd walked her into Withy Cottage and announced that it could be theirs, but she'd have to say yes or no on the spot. It was hardly fair, on a beautiful Spring day, the birds singing, the trees coming into their first leaf, wild flowers in every field and spinney. She had said yes on the spot, and here they were. Well not quite here; not bent over a gate waiting to be flogged. That had come later.

At first she'd found it difficult to fit in. Although there seemed to be plenty of people like themselves, with whom to make friends, indeed Henry seemed to know everyone in sight already, she found a certain reserve among the women; a sense of not fitting in. It was not as if they were hostile but in some strange way they gave her a sense that she was on the outside and had not yet been elected to the club. As time went by she tried harder and harder to crack the ice but, although they were politeness itself, she never seemed to get close, seemed always to be on the outside looking in, and that through gauze curtains.

That was how they had come to be here really. It had all

started a couple of weeks back, during a Saturday night drinking session at the Trident, their local pub. They had fallen into the way of meeting there regularly with a group of youngish people, most of whom Henry seemed to have known from before they had met. The women were all attractive and confident beings who seemed to get on with their partners very well, and she enjoyed the happy atmosphere which carried more than a slight hint of sex, though little overt evidence; just a certain eroticism about the way the women dressed and carried themselves, some fetish wear, chains and leather collars occasionally on show, sometimes little games, where they would be commanded to remain silent, until allowed to speak again. Once she saw a couple in a restaurant, where the woman was not allowed to eat or drink for herself, but only had what her partner offered her on his fork, or from his glass. She suspected that quite a bit more went on in private, but that her presence might be an inhibiting factor. After all, she was the newcomer; Henry had only brought her to live in the village three months ago, while he had lived there for years, before he moved to the city. Woman-like, her curiosity was aroused... and she felt an irrational urge to join in their games.

Her chance came when the talk turned to the forth-coming treasure hunt.

"You're coming of course?" one of the women said to her, more a statement than a question. She looked at Henry for guidance.

"'Course we are darling. Wouldn't miss it for the world," he assured her.

Later that night, comfortably curled in each other's arms in the big old-fashioned bed, she asked him about the treasure hunt.

"Actually," he said, "I'm glad that Renee asked you like that. You've always said you wanted to get to know the other girls better, and this is your chance. Mind you," he added

11

with a hint of seriousness in his voice, "you'll need to accept the local traditions, if you want them to accept you. Be a good sport and all that."

"You mean we've got to win."

"That would certainly be a good start, but there's other things as well."

"What sort of things?" she wanted to know.

"Well, for a start it's a bit different from your usual pub treasure hunt. Not just a case of solving the clues to find your way round the course. There are things to be... collected."

"You mean, like a scavenge hunt? A pair of corsets, a policeman's helmet, the vicar's wife's knickers, that sort of thing?"

"Well, sort of. Actually more in the way of forfeits," he answered vaguely.

"What sort of forfeits?"

"I don't know really," he replied, again a little evasively. "They're different each time. I warn you, you may find them a bit embarrassing, or even a little uncomfortable at times."

"I don't care," she retorted emphatically, "I want to be accepted by the other girls, and I'm prepared to put up with quite a lot to get that."

"Good girl," Henry replied approvingly, turning over and pulling her down onto a stiff and vigorous token of his esteem.

Later, after a second hot and belly-filling satisfaction, she lay, warm semen still trickling from her pouting gash, speculating drowsily about the nature of these trials. Well, they couldn't be all that bad, she thought, all the other girls seemed quite delighted by the idea of a treasure hunt.

Came the day she was determined that not only was she going to put up a good show, but that they'd make their mark by winning outright, so, when Henry, gasping a bunch of clues in their sealed envelopes, grabbed her arm and whispered, "Let's not hang about chatting with the others. If we get a good start, we can probably stay ahead and be first

12

home," she had gone with him eagerly to get the car on to what passed for a main road in those parts and open the first clue:

CLUE 1

Biddy kept her complexion pure
And you must do the same.
In her belfry seek the cure.
And play the maidens' game.

"Biddy?" he pondered, then inspiration came, "Bridget the Fair; one of our local Saints, and that explains the belfry. There's a church dedicated to her near the next village."

As he engaged gear and set off for the place, she asked why she was known as 'the Fair'.

"Not too sure how it all started," he admitted, "but she's been the patron Saint of local girls for centuries. Follow her and you're assured of beautiful skin and a rich husband."

"I not sure how to take that," she joked. "Do I need to improve my skin, and do I want a husband? I'm quite content with you as you are."

"Rich, you mean?" he laughed back.

"Well it's not something I object to," she admitted.

St. Bridget's church stood in a small field set apart from the village, sharing it with a small stream and a group of friendly cows. To reach it they had to cross the water on stepping stones, and she teetered unsteadily on her heels for a moment, looking down into the mixture of mud and slime where the cattle had mangled the bank when they came down to drink. It began to dawn on her that in order to impress the other girls, she might have over dressed for the occasion, in her designer dress, stockings and leather shoes.

"Ugh!" she exclaimed, as the gentle breeze brought a pungent whiff of cow to her delicate nostrils. "Real country air."

It wasn't hard to find the clue. Inside the tiny church an even tinier stair spiralled up one floor of the tower to where the bell-ringers had their room below the belfry itself. Half a dozen ropes hung slackly from the ceiling, each furnished with a brightly coloured wool handgrip. Pinned to one was a large envelope. Henry reached in and extracted a slip of paper:

'You must do as Bridget's maidens do.
Side to side and up and down, or you won't have face
enough to win.'

"And what on earth does that gibberish mean?" she wanted to know.

"That's easy," he assured her, "I told you there were local customs associated with our Biddy. To make your skin fair as hers it needs a mud pack."

She looked at him, wide eyed as the penny dropped.

"Oh no!" she exclaimed, hand to mouth. "No, you can't mean what I think you mean. No way."

"Oh, yes, darling. Told you the girls had a way here. Nice coating of that delicious mud from the stream and the instructions are quite clear. You have to smear it all over. Up and down, side to side. Remember?"

"I can't Henry. It stinks," she wailed.

"So where's all the determination gone?" he asked. "Where's the girl who said she'd do anything to get in with the crowd? Failed at the first fence. Do you think the others would hesitate? Do you think Renee hesitated when George put a bowl of soup on the floor for her, and she had to go down and lap it all up in front of the whole restaurant, or Penny refused when Fred told her to wear her knickers round her knees all evening? Besides," he softened his tone a little; "you'd do it like a shot if a Chelsea beauty salon charged you a hundred guineas for the privilege."

14

"You're right," she said, tilting up her chin, "I'm being a wimp. I'll show them I'm as good as them," and she headed for the stairs.

It took some puffing and blowing, squeals, moans and flinching from the noxious goo, as she knelt on her nyloned knees, putting a hesitant hand into the stinking black gloop. She raised it to her disgusted nostrils.

"Oh, yuck!" she exclaimed, "It's gross."

"The local girls wouldn't make a fuss like that," Henry said scornfully.

For answer she raised the bovine-scented goo to her delicate features and slapped it home, as if not daring to hang about or her courage would fail her, smearing it onto her cheeks, spreading more across her smooth brow and onto her rounded chin. A generous portion found its way onto her wrinkling nose. By the time she scrambled to her sandalled feet and headed for the car again she looked like a circus clown, or some kind of urban terrorist. She carefully avoided looking in the vanity mirror in front of her seat.

"God!" she prayed aloud, "Don't let us meet anyone I know."

"Then we'd better get going, before the others catch us up," Henry advised. "What's the next clue?"

CLUE 2

Cherries are red
In Back-End lane.
If your man is handy,
Yours should be the same.

"Well, the first part's easy," she said, "Everybody knows there's a cherry orchard in Back Lane, Overton, but what's all this about the man's hands? Doesn't make sense to me."

Henry grinned.

"I think I know what's up," he replied, "but better wait until we get there, and see if it's what I think."

"So what is it then?" she insisted.

"Just you sit quietly on your pretty little arse," he said infuriatingly, "and it will all become clear."

He wasn't saying any more, so she had to sit as he had suggested, while they drove the two or three miles to Overton. Since he wasn't saying any more about what the clue might mean, she reverted to the other topic uppermost in her mind at the time, their chances of winning and the close knit group of couples that represented the opposition.

"Do they do this sort of thing often?" she asked.

"Who?" he asked in return. "Oh you mean the Group," he never referred to them by any other name, so she assumed they were just an informal gathering, "well not treasure hunts, they only come round once in a while."

"What sort of other things then?" she persisted. "Do they have other competitions and so on?"

"Yes, well in a way. It's mainly a social thing," he explained, "parties at each others' houses, meals out together, once or twice they've arranged holidays where we've all stayed in someone's villa, that sort of thing"

"They all seem very close. The women are always talking in half sentences, never quite completing anything, as if they share a code, and don't need to spell it out exactly."

"They do in a way; lots of shared experiences, and that sort of thing. Makes them very close."

"I think I'd like to be like that, be one of the circle I mean," she said almost wistfully. Then, "What sort of secrets do they share? What sort of experiences?"

"You know, you ask altogether too many questions," Henry said. "Remember, curiosity killed the cat. Anyway, we're nearly there now, so let's concentrate on finding the next clue. If you really want to find out their secrets, the best way is to come out the winner in the treasure hunt, and be accepted into the circle. Then you'll be able to chew the rag with them all night long."

Back Lane, and its little orchard of leafy trees came in sight. In the spring, tourists by the drove flocked to the area to see the splendid vistas of pink and white blossom that filled the vale, but now the blossom had been replaced by clusters of fruit, not yet ripe, but beginning to turn colour. Next month the pickers would come and the tourists return to buy from wayside stalls, but for now the area was deserted. Up Back Lane the gate stood open into a yard, where the baskets were assembled for transport to market, the sheds now empty and closed, all save one whose door stood invitingly open.

"Pound to a penny that one's for us," Henry declared, and led the way into the cool shade of the interior.

The shed, like the others, was empty, or almost so. To one side was a simple wooden bench. It was painted white with a large black cross at its exact centre, where someone sitting on it would place their bottom while, pinned to the timber of the wall was a neatly printed white card:

'X marks the spot' it read, and then, underneath...
'Red hot not just pink, to win the prize!'

"What on earth is that meant to mean?" she asked, puzzled. "It doesn't make any sense to me."

"Clear as daylight to me," Henry replied, sitting down on the bench, and patting his lap, "take your knickers down, and come over here."

"What do you mean?" she said, suspiciously, hanging back.

"Just that. Take your pants down, and come over my knee for a good old fashioned bare-bottomed spanking. Cherry red those cheeks will be, when my handy hand has finished with them."

17

"Henry Travers, don't you dare," she squeaked in alarm, "I'll do no such thing."

"Then we might as well pack up now and go home," he told her making as if to rise from the bench.

That checked her.

"What do you mean? Nobody else is going to stand for this either. None of the other women would let a man spank their bare bottoms."

"Oh no? Calm down and try to think straight for a moment," Henry advised. "Do you mean to say you haven't seen the signs? The little secrets they have between them, the way they pat each other's bottoms sometimes and grin, and occasionally wince as if they're a bit sore down there? Can you really say you haven't suspected there's something like that going on around here?"

It was true. She had noticed things, a red patch on Georgina's bottom one day, when she was doing a hurried change in the ladies room at the club, Jenny's bikini riding up and showing a strange double track on the top of her thigh, girls sucking in their breath fiercely, and twisting up their faces as they took their place on a barstool. She'd speculated about these things to herself, and even mentioned it to Henry on one occasion. He hadn't mocked her suspicions, but he'd tactfully turned the conversation, and she'd got nowhere at the time. What she had got was a strange thrill from thinking that some of her new friends might have had their bottoms spanked or caned. Now that thrill came back in spades. Just what would it be like to lie over a man's knee and have her bare bottom spanked? Sore, she was sure, but exciting. She would never dare suggest such a thing, probably never agree to submit to it under any other circumstances, but this was the perfect opportunity, the ultimate cop out. She could pretend to herself that she was only doing it to be a good sport, and support her partner in the competition; classic feminine self-deception.

"Alright," she said, "but not too hard mind you, I'm very sensitive down there."

Henry repeated his invitation to bare her pretty bottom, and this time she obliged, putting her hands under her skirt and her thumbs into the elastic waist. She pulled them smoothly down over the firm rounds of her shapely buttocks, and left them dangling round her knees, then draped herself carefully over his lap.

He flipped up the back of her dress, exposing the taut bare flesh, the cheeks tightly clenched in fearful anticipation, and put his left hand on the small of her back to keep her down.

"You're clenching," he accused. "Relax, let your cheeks go slack. It will be better that way."

He omitted to mention that it would be better for him, not her. His sensual pleasure would be maximised if his hand slapped onto soft slack flesh, while she would feel the sting even more, but she'd have to learn that for herself.

She did her best to let her cheeks soften, some of the tension going out of them, and he raised his hand and brought the palm down hard on her left buttock.

"Ouch!" she squealed. "That's too hard. You can't expect a girl to take it like that."

"I can and I do," Henry replied firmly. "You think that stings? Just wait until I take my belt, or a cane, to you."

A belt or a cane! What did he mean? Henry cut off her panicky speculation by bringing his hand down again, this time on the quivering right mound, leaving a clear handprint to match that already glowing on the left cheek.

"The other women take it much harder than that," he assured her, "Besides, your cheeks have got to be cherry red, pink's not good enough, you saw the note yourself, and its kinder to get them red hot with a few good ones, than go on spanking you all afternoon. Not that I wouldn't enjoy doing just that," he added cheerfully.

19

"You beast," she squealed, wriggling under the stinging blows that now fell in a steady procession on her reddening cheeks, "I hate you."

Secretly, though, she had to admit that it was rather exciting, trapped over the knee of a strong man, with her knickers round her knees, and a horny hand smacking her bare backside. She bit her lip and lay still, only jumping a little each time his palm cracked across her flaming cheeks.

After a dozen on each buttock she was beginning to get seriously sore.

"That's enough," she gasped, and put her hands behind her, trying to protect her battered bottom.

She might as well not have bothered. With swift movements he captured each wrist, forced them up between her shoulder blades, and gripped them there with his left hand, pressing tightly down. Now, when his right resumed its business of painting her pretty pink buttocks a deep cherry red, as they writhed and bucked under his flailing palm, she was truly helpless. For a second or so she fought him silently, then opened her mouth to threaten all sorts of dire consequences if he didn't let her go, but the words never came. Instead a strange weakness came over her, it was the magic of being held helpless by a strong man, the fire growing as hot in her belly as on her bottom, and she surrendered to it, regardless of, or was it because of, the hot throbbing pain in her backside which somehow had got all mixed up with warm wet feelings in her belly and weeping pussy. Whatever it was, she went slack and submitted utterly to him.

Henry felt her surrender and gave her a half dozen more, as hard as he could lay them on, just for luck, then pulled her to her feet, turning her so that she faced away from him. While she stood, quite docile now, he lifted the hem which had fallen down over the roasted rump and admired his handiwork. Both orbs glowed a bright red. Cherry it was, just as prescribed, and she subdued into the bargain. He

20

dropped the flap of cloth over the glowing mounds and turned her back towards him. She let herself be handled like a tailor's dummy and when he drew her to him and kissed her on the mouth, opened her lips and responded warmly.

"That's my girl," he said, "I'm proud of you. You took that like a good'un. Keep this up, and you'll win the treasure hunt, and acceptance into the group into the bargain. They'll all want to have you around if you're such a good sport."

It was only later, when the turmoil of the day was over, and she was beginning to think straight about what had happened, that she noticed that he had kept talking about her winning the hunt, not them, but at the time she was too absorbed in her burning feelings, not all in her bruised buttocks, to make any sense of it.

When they walked back to the car she hung on his arm with both hands, clinging to him as if she'd never let him go.

The spell was lifted, if not broken, when she sat, and the pressure on her seat reminded her that she was well spanked below, and her tender bum well bruised.

"Ouch," she cried. "You're a beast to treat a girl like that. I won't be able to sit for weeks."

"You'll have to sit right now if you want to win this competition," he told her, "just try and keep still, while we open the next clue."

CLUE 3

Where the Pilgrims walked in pain,
You must follow too.
Fill your stocking with the grain,
Six pieces in each shoe.

"I don't understand a word of that," she said in a tone of deepest foreboding," but I'm quite sure I'm not going to like it. Your idea that I might find things a touch uncomfortable

21

seems like a gross understatement form my point of view," she added, wriggling on her burning seat.

"Don't exaggerate," Henry advised, "a little bum warming never did a girl any harm. Besides admit it, you were getting quite turned on by the end."

Before she could utter the indignant denial that sprang to her lips he continued.

"The clue's quite simple really. The ancient Pilgrim's way crosses the downs just above here, and there's a memorial on the crest of the hill," he informed her. "Odds on it'll be up there."

The lane petered out a little short of the memorial and they had to abandon the car and walk the last few hundred yards to the little shrine with its ancient carvings, showing pilgrims passing in all forms of penitential guises; women on their hands and knees, a man hopping with one foot tied up behind his back, a woman, bent under an enormous pack, naked from the waist up as far as she could make out, and looking surprisingly like a modern day back-packer, she thought. Above the worn stone figures an inscription in Latin recorded their passing. A more modern inscription adorned a card wedged in a jar set neatly on a ledge:

'Six in each shoe.'

She opened the screw top to reveal the contents; hard grains of Patna rice.

"I still don't get it," she complained.

"Quite simple," Henry assured her. "In the old days the value of a pilgrimage was much enhanced if one paid a penance along the way; going on hands and knees like these ladies here, carrying a burden like this lass. One of the commonest was to walk with grains of rice or corn in one's shoes. There's a story that one wanton wench was condemned by her confessor to walk the way with dried peas in her shoes.

She obeyed, but took the precaution of boiling them first. Mushy but painless. However there'll be nothing like that today," he warned. "You just have to put six grains in each shoe but, since you're wearing sandals, I think they'd better go inside your stockings, so that there's no chance of them falling out. You wouldn't want that, would you?"

Privately she thought that was just what she wanted, but decided it would be inappropriate to express her views on the matter. Instead, she sat on the stone bench that was part of the memorial, presumably for the pilgrims of old to rest on at the summit of their walk, and reached under her dress to unhook a garter tab from the dark nylon welt of one stocking.

Henry looked on admiringly. He always took pleasure from watching her perform this ritual. The baring of the long slim thigh, with the exciting band of white flesh above the stocking top, the symbolic admittance offered by the release of the grips, the sensuous motion of her hands stroking down the shapely leg, rolling down the flimsy covering producing a part nakedness almost more arousing than if she had stripped altogether.

She pulled the last few inches off her foot, the toe of the stocking reluctantly releasing the painted pink nail, then turned the last few inches inside-out, to form a cup to receive the six bitterly hard grains Henry counted out for her.

Now the process was reversed, the stocking carefully fitted over the arching foot, and round the slim shapely ankle, then rolled back up again above the dimpled knee. Finally Henry's favourite part, the slow sensuous stroking again, to fit it smoothly as far up the thigh as it could go before securing it safely back in place with the garter-tabs. By the time she had completed the same feminine rite on her other leg, Henry was becoming acutely conscious of a familiar hardening in his pants.

Finally it was done, and he held out his hand to help her

stand again. For a moment it seemed as if nothing had happened, and then one knee gave way and she almost doubled over, as her weight came on one of the hard pieces under her tender toes.

"Come on," Henry urged, "we haven't time to hang about if we're going to stay ahead of the game."

Biting her lip, she forced herself to ignore the discomfort in her foot. Once she had got over the first shock it didn't seem so bad. Just a stone in her shoe and she gritted her teeth and tried to ignore it, but it was quite a walk to the car, on an uneven track, and a downward slope that threw her weight heavily on her foot with each step. By the time she reached the car she was hobbling painfully, and subsided into her seat, grateful to take her weight off her tortured toes, no longer mindful of the soreness in her bottom, which, in any case, was now no more than a pleasant warmth. 'Pleasant', she thought with a shock, what was coming over her? Further speculation was cut short by Henry handing her the next envelope to open:

CLUE 4

"Naughty Nancy's pegged out her knickers,
And left the bag for you.
Help yourself to four tight clickers,
You'll know just what to do.

"There's more than one Nancy in the village," Henry observed, "but I think we can cut down the candidates fairly easily. Nancy Brigham is nearly seventy and, although they say she was quite a goer in her heyday, I suspect she tends to flannel bloomers, or at best, old fashioned Directoires. Nancy Giles is the right age, but no one would call her naughty. Bit of a prig really, and I would expect some very unexciting underwear if you lifted her skirt," he offered.

24

"As to the rest," he said, "Nancy Acton probably never wears anything but white cottons, and Nancy Chater's would have to be bloomers as big as bin sacks to take in her huge butt. Nancy Brookes would certainly qualify as 'naughty' but it's a question whether she ever wears knickers at all. No, he announced firmly, "it has to be Nancy Logan. She's bold as brass, and as attractive as sin. I think we'll try there first."

In the event Nancy turned out to have a line of delicate little numbers in black, red or gold and, as if to signal that she was the one, even a couple of G strings fluttering in the breeze. Whatever message these flags spelt out, it was probably close to Nelson's famous signal; Perhaps 'Nancy expects that every man this day will do his duty.'

Also on the line was the peg basket, a sewn up Tee shirt on a hanger with a slot to receive the pegs. There was no message that she could see but, printed on the front of the tee shirt, in the appropriate place, was a drawing of a half cup bra, the breasts within spilling over the edge, the nipples boldly picked out in scarlet. She gulped. She was beginning to get the message, but, this far on, she wasn't going to give up. She pulled down the front of her dress, lifted a breast until one rosy nipple found itself unexpectedly exposed to light and air, and held out her hand for a peg.

It cost her a grunt or two to get it in place, her fingers reluctant to let go and allow the full pressure to grip on the tender teat but eventually she managed it. Then the other. After the first twinge it didn't seem so bad. As with everything so far, she was finding a girl could accommodate herself to such levels of pain quite easily.

"Aren't you forgetting something?" Henry asked, as she made to return the pegged tits to their habitual snug resting place, "the clue said four."

"If you don't mind," she retorted, "I only have two. I'm a girl, not a cow," she added, with a flash of spirit.

25

"I can count," Henry shot back, "but you can put one peg over another. Double the grip, that sort of thing."

For a moment she looked at him in disbelief, then set her mouth and held out her hand for 'afters'.

They hurt like hell, but she wasn't going to let him know she was suffering. This was turning into a challenge and accepting challenges was what had lifted her to the considerable success she had achieved on her own, before falling so helplessly for Henry's charm. Mercifully, by the time they got back to the car, the worst of the additional hurt from the doubled peg pressure was subsiding into a dull, but inescapable, ache, though she found it difficult to ignore it, even in the process of opening the next clue:

CLUE 5

On Crockford's farm
You'll find a barn,
And something good for heating.
Set Crockies jaws
On lips of yours,
But not those meant for eating.

Henry gave a smug smile.

"That's easy. Ginger Harris lives at Crockford's farm, so its got to be there, and I know where there's an unused barn, too."

The barn proved to be more a workshop than a forage store, with a black iron stove in the centre. In its iron belly, cold now, they found a box with a card taped to it bearing the legend:

'Don't be greedy, only three per twat, but keep your balance please.'

26

She opened the box and looked with distaste at the contents; electrical clips, serrated crocodile jaws designed to ensure a good grip on battery terminals and murder on genitals, for by now she had absolutely no doubt about where they should go. Well perhaps one query.

"What do I do with the third one?" she asked, slipping down her panties and tucking the dress up round her waist.

He gave a slow ironic grin.

"Middle for diddle. You saw what the note said, keep it balanced, and what's the middle of your middle eh? Just clip it on your clit and you'll be in perfect balance."

She gulped. Perfect balance indeed; more like perfect hell, but she kept her legs open and fished out a clip.

It hurt more than she had imagined. She could hardly bear to let go of the handles and let the full bite sink in. The fat labia bulged out either side of the jaws as they bit into the tender girl meat and she hissed with pain, but she had made up her mind to go through with it and wasn't going to be deflected now. She gave herself a few moments for the worst of the bite to dull and reached for the second. Again a hissing intake of breath, teeth set hard in her lower lip, and the deed was done. She straightened a moment to get on top of the pain, then bent her legs slightly again to open her thighs and reached for the third beastly biter.

With two fingers of her left hand she parted the labia where they drew together at the top of her unaccountably sopping slot, exposing the engorged pink bud of her clitoris, protruding fattily from its sheath. It was a very definite organ, no shrinking violet, a tomato red, pea-sized gland which when, as now, aroused from its soft warm fleshy nest, was as big as the top joint of her little finger. No difficulty in applying one of these savage little clips to this significant presence except, of course, finding the courage to place it there and face the anguish she knew for certain it would cause. She rubbed the waking bud a second to bring it fully erect

27

and placed the cold hostile metal against its tender and vulnerable bulge.

At first she couldn't do it. She let the jaws close over the throbbing piece of sexual tissue and opened her fingers slightly to let the teeth take hold, but she couldn't bring herself to go all the way, and squeezed down on the clip again to relieve the pressure. Henry watched her struggle fascinated at the sight of her fighting herself to achieve the victory she so desperately craved.

"You're wasting time," he said at last, "the others will be here any minute. Just count to three and let it go."

She closed her eyes and began to count, a half sob punctuating each numeral.

"One... Two... Three... Aaahh!"

She danced from foot to foot, bent half double for a few moments, her fists beating the air while the teeth sank into the delicate morsel between her legs, and she tried to contain the pain. It was nearly a minute before she could straighten, red faced under the degrading coating of cow mud and follow him back to the car, waddling with her legs wide parted. Henry gave her a moment to recover then passed the next envelope:

CLUE 6

At Six Mile Bottom a six barred gate,
Look low and left to find your fate.
The gate has six bars like miles to bottom
Make certain yours has also got'em

"Well, you can take a short rest," Henry informed her, "Six Mile Bottom is way the other side of the valley, past the next village. It'll take all of twenty minutes I would say. Can't get up any speed on these lanes, so you can lie back and nurse your wounds."

As she accepted the invitation to lie back while she could, she realised that things were getting serious. It didn't take a genius to work out what was happening here. Strangely she found her strongest reaction was not rebellion, or even fear of what sounded unmistakably like an invitation to a beating, but fear that she might not be able to take it and would disgrace herself.

The twenty minutes passed all too fast, but at least, by the time they reached the spot Henry had sought out, the worst of her pangs from the cruel jaws in her tenderest flesh had subsided to numbness. The gate was like any other, a solid timber construction between sturdy posts, five horizontal bars with a sixth running diagonally across it to brace the whole structure. It led off a little lane at the bottom of the valley, where a copse of birches stood near the little river that ran through it. Low and left, fastened to the timber with a thumbtack, was a plastic envelope with the inevitable neat white card advising:

'Cut a rod from the hedge.
Lay them on the bare, one for each bar. Only strong
clear welts will count.'

She gulped at the stark message. One last protest seemed in order.

"Don't you think it's a bit risky, beating a girl's bottom? You never know what damage you might do," she said hesitantly.

Henry was unimpressed.

"That just goes to show how much you have still to learn," he remarked. "Provided you stick to the old tradition, a rod as thick as a man's finger, you can't go wrong," he assured her. "A healthy girl's bottom is a sound well-padded structure, with all the muscles and sinews nicely wrapped in fatty tissue with plenty of nerve endings near the surface to guarantee its sensitivity. It's so perfectly designed for the purpose that one can only suppose that it has evolved that way for the better regulation of relations between the sexes."

She wasn't sure she was convinced by this original application of Darwin's theory, but thought it better not to argue at this sensitive juncture, when it seemed her bottom might be on the line.

"Anyway, no time to worry about that now," Henry said briskly. "You've got a rod to cut; a rod for your own backside, as the saying goes," and he led the way to the birches, taking a large clasp knife from his pocket as he went.

"Right," he said, as they reached the gently swaying trees, "select your rod. You can gauge it against this," and he held out his hand with the fingers outstretched.

She looked doubtfully at it. Normally she thrilled to the strength of the man, and his solid build, but now even the least of his fingers seemed frighteningly thick. A rod that thick would be a tree trunk!

"Eh. How long?" she asked nervously.

"Nothing very great," he said casually. "Just a bit longer than my arm will do."

She looked again at the long sinewy limb he extended and gulped.

"Come on, don't hang about," he urged, "I want to get this over with and be on our way."

Not half as much as I do, she thought mutinously, but reached up into the tree and began to select her rod.

"No," Henry called, "much too thin," as she gripped her first selection, "That'd only tickle you. We have to raise real welts, remember. Ah, that's better," he approved, as in panic she grabbed the thickest, whippiest limb in reach, "I can do some real work with that. Cut it off near the trunk and then trim off any buds and twigs. It's in your own best interest. Don't want any broken skin do we."

She did not, and worked hard to ensure that the rod was

as smooth and free from projections as she could make it, conscious every moment she held it that this would soon be lashing into her unprotected buttock flesh.

They scrambled back to the gate, Henry absently swishing the rod through the air with a menacing hissing noise as they went. Her hinds clenched beneath her flimsy dress at every cut.

"Right," he said, as they reached the gate, "knickers to your knees, and hike that dress well up off your rump and tuck it into your belt," then, when she was bare behind, with the air caressing her naked hinds, "step up on the bottom bar, with your legs a couple of feet apart and bend over the top rail. You can reach down and grip one of the middle rails to steady yourself."

And that was how she had come to be bending over the gate in this awkward and uncomfortable position, fearful that, at any moment, someone might come along the lane and see her there, bare-arsed and bent, though what their reaction might be she could not guess. This was a very strange valley, where women's lives were very different from those in the 'outside' world, as she was discovering with every minute that went by. She flinched again as Henry made the rod sing in the air again.

"Get ready," he warned, and she tightened her grip on the rail below her.

There was a pause that seemed to last for ever and then the air sang before the rod again. This time though it did not end in silence, but in a loud thuck as the limber stick sank deep into her stretched bottom.

A feeling almost of cold flashed across the bent hinds then the full fury of the cut burst and she let out a strangled shriek of shocked pain. It was awful, far worse than she had expected, a flaming burning in her seat that swept through her whole body below the waist. She let go of the rail and arched up clasping her wounded bottom in both hands as she teetered on the lowest rail.

"Get back," he ordered sternly. "I'll let you off this time, seeing as it's your first, and you're not used to this sort of thing but, I warn you, let go of the rail again and the stroke won't count."

With the tears starting to burn at the corners of her eyes, as much from shame at her weakness as from the throbbing pain in her backside, she went dumbly back over the bar, feeling it pressing into her bare belly again, stretching the skin of her bent buttocks, where the livid line of the welt had now darkened and started to rise above the surrounding flesh. Her body rigid, she awaited the next.

When it came she was better prepared. The element of surprise was gone and there was the fear of earning more than the necessary tariff to hold her in position. She grunted at the impact, and hissed through her teeth at the rising after-tide of agony, but kept down. Henry looked on with knowing approval. As he had thought she was promising material for this sport. She just needed handling right.

Three crashed in just above the parallel tracks of the first two, and she took it well but, before he gave her the next there was something to attend to; a reinforcing of the control he was imposing on her.

"You're clenching," he told her, "let you buttocks hang loose. The rod works best when it can swing up into slack flesh. Relax your thigh muscles and stop clenching your bum."

She moaned but obeyed, and again Henry gave a nod of satisfaction. He hadn't misjudged her; she was going to be alright. She was made of the right stuff. He swept in the fifth with an added turn of his wrist that had her gasping and rising on her toes, her buttocks swinging from side to side, as if to shake off the pain. As she steadied, she pushed herself up from the awkward bent position, but kept her hands from her welted bum with its five blatant purple line.

"I thought I told you to stay down," he said accusingly.

"B... but it's over," she blurted, "that was five, and the gate only has five bars."

"You need to brush up your arithmetic," Henry advised. "What about the brace? Now get back down at once, or I'll add extra."

With a sob she obeyed, The two half globes spread and open, the vulva once more peering back at him through its russet fringe, the cruel brass jaws still firmly embedded in the tender tissues of labia and clit. Stepping a little back, and to the side, Henry measured his mark, then sprang forward onto one foot and dropped his wrist, laying the thick bendy switch diagonally across the five parallel burning bars on her bottom, in perfect imitation of the pattern of the gate. She gave a small gargling screech as the rod's track crossed each of her earlier, and now throbbingly tender, welts.

"Now you can get up," Henry said, with the satisfaction of a man who knows his work has been well done.

He gave her a few moments to recover, holding her close in his arms, while she sniffed against his chest.

"Your first beating ever?" he asked, gently stroking her hair.

She nodded dumbly.

"Well I don't suppose it will be the last," he said. She didn't reply.

By now she had quietened and he led the way back to the car and pulled out the next envelope:

CLUE 7

In the silent woman's room,
Number three will spell your doom.
In the china box appears
How to save your partner's ears.

33

Once again she could make nothing of it, but Henry had no doubts.

"The Silent Woman," he said. "Pub in Handy Birches. Got a great inn sign, a woman with her head under her arm."

"But what's all this about China boxes and number three?" she wanted to know.

"I'm not sure but unless I'm very much mistaken, I'd say you're looking for the ladies, and the third cubicle, where you'll have to look in the cistern for the rest of the clue."

"Hmm. I think that makes sense. Drive on," she said in mock resignation, "and take me to my fate."

He glanced across at her. She was shaping up nicely.

She noticed that Henry seemed to know the pub quite well.

"You can get to the ladies without going through the bar," he said, as they pulled up in the car park. "See that door in the corner? Go through there and it's on your right. No place for a gentleman. I'll wait here for you."

She climbed out of the car, grateful that she wouldn't have to go through the bar with her dung-smeared face, and shuffled off to the side entrance. Her teats ached, the teeth in her labia was still sore enough to make her walk spraddle-legged, while the clip on her clit was a torment, even though it had numbed a little. Her movements in getting out of the car seemed to have twisted it somehow, and she doubled up momentarily before forcing herself to straighten and get on with the task in hand. Her bottom throbbed and her feet ached as she crossed the yard. With all her other problems she had forgotten about those cruelly hard grains in the toes of her stockings until she put her weight on them again, and she was thankful to reach cubicle number three at last.

She bolted the door behind her, so as not to be disturbed, and cautiously lifted the lid of the china cistern. Sure enough there was a plastic bag in there with a half dozen old stockings and the usual card:

34

'Fold your panties and push them in your mouth...
then tie a stocking round your head to keep it in place.'

She stared in disgust at the card for a moment. She was expected to gag herself in this humiliating fashion, and then go out in public. Yuck. She would have been less concerned if she'd been ordered to inflict yet more pain on herself, provided it was not obvious to all, but you couldn't disguise a nylon knotted round your head. Suppose she ran into another woman on her way out? She'd die! She bent and lifted the hem of her dress.

Seconds later the air was cool on her heated bottom and the knickers were wadded in her mouth. With trembling hands she wound one of the stockings round her head over the impromptu gag and tied it firmly behind. It seemed like an act of final and irrevocable surrender.

All the time she was frightened someone would come in and trap her in her hide, but the coast was clear. Even the car park was empty of humans and she was able to slip into the car unobserved.

"Very nice," Henry observed, taking in the gag, "just what every woman needs, I'd say. Except of course when she giving head." She glared at him indignantly, but was unable to reply. Henry reached for a new envelope.

CLUE 8

There's help for you, keep you out of temptation.
Hanging up in the Brock's plantation.
Behind your back they'll be good to use,
To stop you getting rid of clues.

He gave it to her to read, but was aware she could make little contribution in her present state.

"I think I get the location," he said, "Badger's Copse would

35

fit for the Brock's plantation. As for the rest, let's go and see," and he swung the car off the car park and back the way they had come.

This time it was only a short ride before he pulled off into an even narrower track that finally came to a halt just inside a small wood in front of a weather beaten hut.

"Gamekeeper's hut," Henry explained. "A few weeks ago it would be really busy round here; chicks and wire runs in all directions. Old Mellors, the keeper, would probably blow your head off if you trespassed then.

"But the chicks are long grown up and taken to their summer homes, ready to be driven out and blasted from the sky, come the glorious twelfth, so we'll be quite safe now."

He led the way into the bare little structure. Mellors seemed to be almost obsessively tidy for nothing remained but a clean swept table and shut cupboards. And a bunch of plastic cable ties hanging on a hook in the low ceiling with the inevitable white card stating:

'Help yourself.'

"That seems pretty explicit," Henry noted in a one-sided conversation, "Just put your wrists together behind your back for a minute please, and we'll have you fixed up in a trice."

Reluctantly she crossed her wrists behind her, and flinched slightly at the feel of the tough plastic strip wrapping round them and being pulled taut. This was something different again. Different and strangely thrilling. Up till now she had retained physical control of her person, even if she had surrendered it mentally. She could have torn the gag from her mouth, taken the fiendish clip from off her suffering clit, even cleaned her disgustingly soiled face. Now she was truly helpless, and filled with excitement. She could feel a hot flower blooming in her belly, and thick sticky secretions gathering in her vagina, ready to overflow and trickle down

36

her legs. Her heightened colour and obvious arousal did not escape Henry's knowing gaze as he led her back to the car once more, and opened yet another clue.

Since it was meant to be her hunt, and her triumph if she could beat the other women to the finish line, it seemed only fair that she should be able to contribute, so he tugged open the knot on the back of her head, and tapped her on the lips with his forefinger, saying, "Open up, sweetie. Let's see if you can guess the next."

She opened up obediently, only too glad to have the load taken off her tongue and the power of speech returned, however temporarily. She'd found it curiously unnerving to be unable to communicate, especially so as she was used to giving pert answers to any observations her partner might make. Now she had had to listen in respectful silence, and she didn't know whether she hated or enjoyed it. It was certainly different; there was something quite comforting in being helpless, she was finding.

She flexed her cheeks gratefully, and licked her darting red tongue over parched lips, working her jaw, which was sore from the pressure of the wadded panties.

"What do you make of this then?" Henry asked, holding up the new piece of paper.

CLUE 9

'Where maidens nine were wont to sit,
Reclining at their leisure,
You'll find a seat entirely fit,
Though not to give you pleasure.'

"Not a lot," she replied, "though I'd have thought it would take a little while to round up nine maidens round these parts. As far as I can tell, the little bitches drop their pants as soon as they start their periods round here."

'Well,' he thought, 'nothing's depressed her spirits... so far, so good.' Aloud he said, "Don't judge them all by your own randy standards. If you're going to talk dirty I'd better put those knickers back where they came from. Anyway, I'm surprised you didn't think of the Nine Maidens, the stone circle up on the Downs."

"Of course, "she cried. "How stupid of me!"

"You're forgiven. I have the advantage over you in that I've not only been there more than once but not so long ago, was treated to a scene up there that most men wouldn't forget in a hurry."

"What was that then?" she asked, full of curiosity, woman like. "Something sexy I should think, if it stayed in your mind."

"Just for that you can have your rag back in right now," he replied. "It'll give my ears a rest."

He pinched the sides of her jaw between a strong finger and thumb, so that she had to open, and stuffed the sodden plug of panty material back into her mouth. Once again she made no resistance, though she looked both disappointed and still curious, as far as her puffed out cheeks allowed her feelings to appear at all. He took pity on her.

"Sit back and behave, and I'll tell you all about it as we go," he promised. "It's the other side of the county and it will help to pass the time."

***

The men were obviously up to something. They exchanged cryptic remarks, talked about being ready when they met up that evening, and generally showed signs of hatching a plot. The wiser women knew better than to betray their curiosity, but one or two earned themselves a smart spanking for being too inquisitive, or were sentenced to minor humiliations, having to go round with a table tennis ball in their mouths, wear their knickers round their knees, or similar familiar disciplinary measures, for asking too many questions.

At first it seemed it was going to be a pleasant but very tame evening; they went to the pub for a few drinks, moved on to the Box Tree restaurant at Layiton to be wined and dined in some style. Rachel apparently, hadn't learned her lesson, despite having spent the evening with a clothes peg on her clit for undue curiosity. She could not resist pressing her partner once again for a clue as to what was to happen, and was made to kneel on the floor, with her hands behind her back, and bend forward to eat her meal from a bowl set down for her like a dog. Not that the others actually got to feed themselves. The party was well known and tolerated at the Box Tree, and each girl knelt by her 'master' and was fed by his hand, and from his glass. They all found it a source of great intimacy and affection, rather than just humiliating as more 'liberated', that is to say, lost, women might have done.

Only the men had places laid for them and each kneeling girl, her hands held behind her, raised her pretty mouth to delicately take the morsels donated to them by their masters.

Henry gave the lead. He was on one of his periodic visits to his birthplace and, since urgent business had meant that Chris couldn't attend the dinner himself, he had asked Henry if he would be so kind as to take Georgina, so that the girl would not miss out on the event; a duty he was more than happy to accept. He took a little avocado on a spoon, and held it out towards Georgina's mouth. Her lush red lips parted obediently, and she took the morsel onto her tongue tasting it with obvious pleasure. In their turn the other men offered their women titbits from their plates.

Rachel did not share in the 'starter', being in disgrace but Bill asked one of the waitresses to bring him a shallow bowl, into which he placed some of the potato served him, a little minced beef, some peas and a generous helping of thick brown gravy. He took a fork and mashed the mixture into a viscous paste, then set it on the floor by Jenny's knees.

"Eat," he commanded.

She knew better than to protest, or to use her hands. She bent forward, straining to reach down to the bowl, and pushed her face into it until she could lick up the mush little by little with her flickering pink tongue. It was a strain to bend like that, and humiliating to eat like a dog, especially with the waitresses, in their smart black and white uniforms, and black patent leather pumps, passing by every few minutes, and catching a view of her nearly bare bum, her mini skirt drawn onto her back by the head-down pose, and her thong panties disappearing into her crack. Also she couldn't avoid getting her face smeared, especially as she worked her way down the bowl, and her hair kept falling over her face and sticking to the viscous mush. Altogether she was degraded and humiliated enough to suit even her masochistic spirit, by the time her meal was done.

Meanwhile the other girls enjoyed their masters' affectionate attentions. There is something very intimate about the act of feeding a submissive woman, and the feeling is reciprocated since the dependence on another for food is one of the strongest bonds known to man, or woman. What did it matter if an ill-judged movement left a smear of grease on cheek or chin, the sensation of being owned and cared for compensated for everything. Such meals are much more than games. They represent an intimacy only exceeded by that of a shared bed, and not always then. Two people can lie in a bed together, with little warmth in their contact, but the passing and receiving of food, the choosing and acceptance of a choice morsel, the offering of a glass to lips parted to sip from the rim, all these are bonds of affection, based on submission and control, that the mere fact of sleeping together does not always approach.

Rachel's punishment was much more severe than it appeared since, besides humiliating and soiling her, it

40

deprived her of the bonds of intimacy that the others were enjoying.

When the meal was over, the women were permitted to retire to the ladies room and 'freshen up', cleaning their faces and repairing their make-up, not to speak of giving their tongues a chance to wag, that the intimate atmosphere at dinner had tended to inhibit. Rachel though, was not allowed to go with them, even to relieve her bladder, let alone to wash or straighten her sticky hair. It was a cruel sentence and Georgina pleaded on her behalf and gained her a modest concession. She couldn't wash or tend herself, but the other women could, if they wished, lick her clean.

The waitresses had left the room by then, but one returned to collect the coffee things. She had looked on unconcerned when the women had been fed, but now stopped, open-mouthed. Rachel still knelt on the floor, where she had been joined by all the others, who knelt round her, each licking carefully whatever part of her face and hair they could reach, like a group of mother cats all cleaning the one kitten. Their tongues curled under her chin, stroked into the lobes of her ears, her dish had managed to get even there, wriggled into her nostrils, gently laved around her moist eyes, combed through her gravy glued hair. When they had finished she was pink and clean all over, and almost purring at the loving, intimate attentions she had received. The waitress came back to earth with a jolt, and almost fled from the room.

Time passed. The party stayed until late, the men sharing sips of their brandies and liqueurs with their women, who knelt again docilely by their sides. It was the early hours before they finally left, a sleepy but complaisant restaurateur letting them out personally, the over-excited waitresses being dismissed long before to find what release they could in their own or in others' beds.

To the women's surprise, they did not turn for home, but towards the high ridge of the downs, climbing steadily. There

41

were one or two attempts to ask what was happening but, when asked if they had forgotten already just why Jenny had been punished, they held their tongues and waited with what patience they could manage to see what happened. They had little doubt it would concern them personally and would call for some price in suffering, humiliation or embarrassment for them all.

They drew up on the top of a ridge, where a stile led through a fence into a grassy area, where dark shapes could be made out by the light of the nearing dawn that lit the eastern sky.

"The Nine Maidens," Poppy exclaimed, "I should have known from the way we were heading."

"You should have guessed from the date too," George contributed.

"The date? What's that... Oh no!"

"Oh yes. It's Midsummer morning, and the dawn is almost here. Strip off girls. You're about to be sacrificed."

"But it's freezing!" they cried, almost as one woman.

"You'll be warm enough in a minute, I promise you," George assured them. "Everything off, down to your pretty panties. Bare bums and tits are the order of the day for maiden sacrifices."

"We're hardly maidens, after you men have had your wicked way with us so often," Laura reminded him.

He laughed. "But you're still very tasty, and I don't remember you protesting much at the time. We'll just have to use our imaginations. Come on; get 'em off."

With shudders and protests they obeyed as usual, six pinkly naked forms soon standing bare-foot in the dew. The light was strengthening by the minute revealing the ring of great upright stones set in a circle thousands of years ago for some lost ceremony of sex and fertility.

"We have to get the sun to rise for us," Bill cried. "The maidens must circle the stones to bring him up."

42

"They'll certainly bring something up," Henry remarked to his neighbour, "I can feel it in my trousers right now."

Hesitatingly the girls began to walk round the outside of the circle, the growing light gleaming on their pink and shivering flesh.

"Faster!" George cried. "The maidens ran until they dropped. I told you you'd get warm soon."

Even as he spoke, there was a yelp from the leading girl in the pack. Unnoticed by the girls, while they had been peeling off their clothes to offer their shuddering nakedness to the chilly dawn air and dewy grass, the men had been busy cutting hazel switches from the hedge that ran along one side of the compound around the standing stones. Now they used them to cut shrinking buttocks, extra sensitised by the cold, sending the girls speeding round the ring, stretched out in a scattered line, leaving each vulnerable to the stinging rods. They yelped and squealed as the swishy sticks found thighs and bottoms, running as fast as they could now, hair flying, breasts bouncing. The cold air on their teats had hardened them until they stood out like tiny pink and red thumbs, but the breasts they adorned were still full of bounce, and rode up and down their chests delightfully as they ran, desperately trying to avoid the cuts of the supple rods. It had been a clear night and the temperature had dropped suddenly, the grass glittering with diamond drops of dew that their bare feet would have cringed from if they had not been concentrating so desperately on running fast enough to avoid the slashing hazel twigs.

The men drove them to near exhaustion, and until the sun lifted itself in a red ball over the horizon. As its blood red rays turned to gold George shouted, "The sacrifice! The sacrifice!" and seized the nearest woman in the racing circle, throwing her to the cold wet grass, forcing her thighs apart and plunging into her warm inner depths. One by one the other men caught the nearest exhausted 'maiden' and served

43

her as vigorously. In minutes their rasping breaths from their forced run had changed to panting pleas for more, more, and then to a cacophony of sounds as each gave voice to her orgasm in her own distinctive style, one honking helplessly, another shrieking her passion, a third simply going "Ooooh, oooh, oooh," as if she had never made any other sound in her life, and would make no other in the future. The sacrifice was complete!

***

She had listened in bursting silence. Her eyes had opened wide at some of the revelations, the semi-public nature of the visits to the Box Tree, especially Rachel's degrading meal and her humiliation in front of the waitresses. Was it worse to be fouled and degraded in this way before other women? She thought, deep down, this might be so. To be seen thus by men, women's natural masters, seemed somehow appropriate but in front of strange women? No that would be a hundred times worse.

And the others, kept helpless to feed themselves, dependent on their men to feed them. Ah that was something altogether different and exciting. Rachel's ordeal had set her pulses racing strangely, imagining, even in a way wishing, herself in the same position. She felt herself positively melting, and not just mentally. She had been in a state of arousal for some time now, but this sent her juices down her thighs. If her knickers had not been in her mouth, they would have become just as sopping by now, clinging to her groin. She'd not only seethed with a desperate need to ask questions, but with her sexual needs as well.

Under the combined pressure she felt as if she might explode, and, as they reached the top of the down, which Henry had so graphically described, she grunted through her gag to draw his attention. She knew better than to try and

44

spit it out. In the first place it was not as easy as it seemed, the wet rag clinging round her teeth. In the second her experiences of the afternoon reinforced by all the details she had been learning about the way of life of the group she was now even more keen to be accepted into, made it very clear that an unguarded curiosity was a sure way for a woman to find herself with a sore bottom. So, although her female nature meant she could not resist giving vent to her feelings by urgent little noises through the fold of her panties, she was careful not to be too insistent.

Henry was very well aware of her needs, he'd handled women before at this point in their progress towards self-fulfilment, and decided that it would be excellent discipline for her to have them unsatisfied for a little longer.

As she almost steamed in her excitement and frustration, he left the slimy pad of panties firmly embedded between her teeth and her tongue, and led her by the arm to the stile, supporting her as she lifted each long stockinged leg in turn, giving flashes of pantyless crotch, and flaming bottom in the process. She hardly seemed to notice, despite the feel of cool air on her bare wet vulva, and equally naked, but burning, buttocks, more concerned with the freshly wakened painful sensations in her clamped genitals, and pegged nipples. As they walked to the centre of the enclosure that surrounded the Maidens, she groaned afresh. Six grains of rice trapped in a stocking sounded harmless enough but, by the time she had walked the three or four hundred yards from the car park, they felt like nails driven into her tender feet.

They stood upright, nine dark ancient stones of irregular shape, in a circle like the maidens of the legend, and seeming to look towards one side of the ring. There a set of stones formed a kind of throne, with three or four uprights framing and supporting a flat horizontal stone that formed the 'seat'. Deeming it was time for her to play her part in the hunt again, he made picking movements with finger and thumb, and she

45

gratefully opened her mouth and let him pull out her gag.

"Ooh, thanks," she said, gratefully, once she'd worked her jaws a bit to loosen them, "I could get to dislike being gagged. Oh Henry, I've been bursting to ask. Was it all true, or did you just make it up about Georgina and the others? I can't believe that women like that would allow themselves to be ordered around, made to kneel in front of waitresses, have no food of their own. It's just not like them."

"You think not? Just what are they like, do you think? Or, put another way, what sort of women would submit to that sort of thing, as you put it? Think about it," he suggested, "but not now. You've work to do to find this clue and get on with the hunt. Unless you'd prefer I put your panties back in your mouth to quieten you," he threatened.

Wisely she contained her curiosity and her comments, although she did put some thought into what he'd said. Was it possible that, as he'd hinted, it was the intelligent high-achieving women who were most likely to succumb to the temptation to hand themselves over to another's will? She thought about what she'd accepted that afternoon already and began to think she might be close to the answer, but was called away from further consideration by Henry taking her arm and leading her firmly towards the Maidens Seat, ignoring her groans, but giving her the support she needed as she hobbled painfully on the wickedly hard grains in her stockings. Rather than feel resentment at being made to suffer like this she felt instead, gratitude and security in his hold.

The Seat was formed of flat stones arranged to form quite a sophisticated bench, with sides, back, seat and a space beneath. In that space she could see something white, which turned out to be a card:

'Take your pick and take your seat... nothing but the bare essentials mind.'

Beneath the card was a stack of woven wicker mats. They were on sale in all the local craft shops, just the thing to put under hot plates to protect the table, except that these particular examples were not fully finished. Where the mats sold to visitors would have the ends of each length of stripped withy tucked neatly into the weave, these had their ends left protruding, stone hard, and needle sharp, forming a set of porcupine spikes on one side of the mat.

"Which would you like?" Henry asked.

She looked at them with distaste. She could hazard a guess at to how these contraptions might be employed and didn't care for the thought.

"Just give me the top one," she said resignedly, "I don't think it will make much difference."

Henry obliged and held it up for her inspection. She looked at the forest of short sharp points that adorned one surface and groaned.

"I've a horrid feeling I know what I've got to do with this," she sighed, as she regarded the pointy mat without enthusiasm, "and I believe the rhyme when it says it will be no pleasure. My bottom's sore enough already, after you beat me so cruelly, and sitting on this is going to be no fun."

"But you'll do it because you want to beat the other girls, and be accepted into the club?"

"True," she admitted, "I must be mad to do it."

They set off towards the stile and the waiting car. After he had helped her over, he stopped her.

"Here, you can carry your own mat," he said with a grin, "open your legs."

She had been about to protest that she couldn't hold it with her hands tied behind her, but remembered in time not to answer back, but to do as she was told. It was becoming surprisingly easy for her already to obey the commands he gave. Besides, if she were quiet, he might just forget about the gag, and it would be worth a lot not to have her knickers forced back between her teeth.

She stood with legs apart, waiting patiently as he rolled up the mat, the spikes on the outside, and pushed the tight cylinder high up between her thighs, until she could grip it with her soft white flesh, then dropped her dress back into place.

"How am I meant to walk like this?" she protested, then shut up quickly as she realised her mistake. Perhaps he might have let her off the panty gag, if she'd held her peace, but now he opened her jaws with the usual irresistible pressure on the corners of her mouth and stuffed the tight wad back in place once more.

Unable to do anything else but try her best, and not caring to think about what he might do if she were to drop the uncomfortable studded wedge between her thighs, she set off at a shuffle down the lane.

When they had arrived, the car park had been empty, and they had mercifully had the place to themselves. Now there was another car near theirs, and a large and boisterous family preparing to march off to view the Maidens, mother, father, two teenage children, and an older girl, maybe eighteen. She hoped Henry would turn aside and wait inconspicuously by the hedge until the family had passed, but he held on his way and she had no choice but to follow, trying to walk as naturally as possible, but hampered badly her sore feet and the roll between her bare thighs which she gripped tightly to stop it slipping. Her waddling gait was duck-like, and they couldn't help but know there was something wrong with her, while she was terrible conscious of the gag in her mouth, and her pinioned wrists.

At least Henry moved to cover her back, walking just a little to one side, and slightly behind, with his hand on her arm so that it looked as if they were simply in a rather romantic embrace.

"Come on," he said, "they won't be able to tell. They'll

48

probably think you've been caught short and dumped in your knickers. As for the gag, if you keep your mouth shut and your eyes on the road, they'll be certain you've done something disgusting and can't meet their eyes."

Hardly reassuring, she thought. She wondered if she wouldn't really have felt better if they'd been able to know just what her state was; the thick blazing welts across her buttocks, the horrid mat she'd have to set those same throbbing stripes on in just a minute, her bound wrists, and the wet panties in her mouth. Her mud smeared face, and the painful intruders in her hose. And the clips on her teats and vulva, although, with the passing of time their hurt had subsided into a dull numbness, pushed out of mind by the accumulation of her other discomforts. She wondered how the girl would react, and had a sudden insane wish to show her; to shout out, 'look, you could be like this. This is how a woman should be.'

The moment and the family passed, and they were at the car. The younger children hurrying to the stile and the waiting Maidens but, she noticed, the girl lagged behind watching her with an abstracted look. Had she sensed something? She was roused from her speculation by Henry tugging at her arm as he turned her into the open door of the car. Without ceremony he hauled up her dress behind.

"Open!" and she obediently relaxed her thighs so that he could remove the mat and set it on the leather of the seat.

"Bare essentials, remember?" he said, as he pushed her sore striped buttocks onto the cruel spikes, without even the thin fabric of the dress to protect them.

She gasped and tried to adjust herself to minimise the discomfort, as he closed the door and got into the driver's seat. The last thing she saw as they left the car park was the girl gazing in open wonder. She couldn't tell at that distance if the look on her face was one of horror or envy.

They opened the next clue as soon as they were safely

out of her sight:

CLUE 10

Where the hatchet has done good work
You'll need to find a punt.
The pole has somewhat to insert,
In bottom, not in c***.

So now they were on the river at Axwell. The old
boathouse was easy enough to find, with a punt tied up
outside. The pole neatly in the straps alongside and, taped to
it, another plastic bag. He had left her in the same parlous
condition of painful restraint, but once again relented enough
to relieve her of the gag, at least for the moment. She had no
confidence that she would be left with the power of speech
for long. Stepping into the flat-bottomed boat he lifted out
the contents of the bag; the usual card and, her eyes widened
in speculation, a large bubble pack of a dozen thick brown
torpedo-shaped objects, each as big as a man's thumb.

"What on earth are those?" she demanded, not at all sure
she wanted to know.

"I knew I should have left those panties in place," Henry
said resignedly, "you really must learn to control your
curiosity," and he turned the card over without giving her an
answer.

The card proclaimed:

*'Double dose, and keep it fast.
This cleansing draught is meant to last.'*

Henry grinned evilly.

"Feet apart, and bend over tight," he ordered.

"But what are they?" she begged. "What are you going
to do with them?"

50

"Veterinary suppositories," he informed her. "They'll flush you out and get you clean, all the way up your lovely bowels."

"Oh God, I couldn't take one of those," she wailed. "They're made for horses, not girls."

"'Fraid you'll have to unless you want to cry off. Pity though," he added. "This is the last, and you're so near home now."

"Oh shit! All right, but careful how you stuff that in. I'm only small behind."

She placed her legs firmly apart and bent over as far as she could and still preserve her balance, hampered as she was by her pinioned wrists. Henry drew her dress onto her back, and prised her swollen buttock cheeks apart with one hand. The air on her anal dimple reminded her how exposed she was. There was a towpath along the river that might at any minute bring a walker in sight of her half-naked body bent so humiliatingly over.

"Oh, hurry please," she gasped, "let's get it over with before someone comes."

She grunted as she felt the tough gelatin capsule forcing her sphincter open, and lodging in her rectal tube. She gasped again as he rammed it all the way home with his thumb, then tried to rise.

"Get down," he barked. "Double dose, remember?"

She moaned, but went down again. The second torpedo penetrated her unwilling anus and was stuffed deeply up to join the first.

"Now you can get up," Henry said, slapping her playfully on one sore haunch. "Better get back to the car quickly, if you know what's good for you. Those little beauties will melt and begin their work any moment now."

She looked at him in horror.

"But I can't get back in the car. I'll have to go here. Let me go behind the boat house, please Henry."

"No way, you have to keep those there until we get back to the Trident, or you lose the race," he informed her.

"But I can't, I can't," she wailed, "I can feel it coming now. Oh Henry, please. I won't be able to hold it."

"I said it was a mistake, letting you speak," was all the reply she got, and in seconds the panty gag was back in place, with the stocking tied tightly round her head to ensure it stayed there. She looked at him with pleading eyes, but he was adamant. Lifting her dress behind again, he forced her firmly down on the spiked mat.

"Perhaps a little prickle in your bum will take your mind off your belly," he speculated.

The ride was a torment that got worse with every passing minute. Almost as soon as she was back on her painful seat, the gelatin began to leak its contents, a strong caustic laxative fluid she could feel first as a slight burning sensation but which, far too rapidly for her peace of mind, began to fill her whole lower bowel. The motion of the car did nothing for her comfort, and soon she was in the grip of belly cramps, that had her moaning through her gag as she strained to keep her sphincter from giving way. Every bit of her bottom cried out for release, and her anus writhed and clenched in her attempts to prevent it turning itself inside out under the imperative to void her guts. Tears rolled down her face as the spasms rocked her.

Mercifully Major Grange's boathouse was only minutes from their destination. Moaning and grunting in her retentive endeavours, she stumbled from the car to see Tom standing in the doorway to the pub. Hope took over. He seemed to be welcoming them as winners.

"rrr...nng...arrr...uuurt?" she tried to ask, as she hobbled painfully up to him, her wrists still fastened behind her, the dress caught up at her waist, revealing a bruised and battered bottom, the half dozen stripes now over-laid by a painful looking rash of angry spots, a few of which had penetrated the tender skin.

"Just a minute, my dear," Tom said kindly," I think you'll make more sense without this," and relieved her of her gag.

"Are we the first? Have we won?" she croaked, as soon as she could get her tongue to form the words properly.

"Well, you've won," he conceded," but you're the last home. Come and meet your friends."

Dumbstruck, not understanding what he meant, she followed him into the bar. To her amazement every one of the people she knew, even by sight, was there to greet her.

"Oh darling," Renee cried, coming forward with a knot of other women. "Well done. We knew you could do it. Welcome to Sexton."

Not one of the women crowding round her, giving her congratulations and kisses, despite her still fouled face, showed the slightest sing of having been through even a part of the ordeal she had just endured, and she realised with a shock that she had been the only one to take that terrible trail from clue to loathsome clue.

"Give her room," Renee cried, as the other girls pressed her close, "the poor darling will want to shit. Off to the ladies room everybody."

They swept her off between them, her knees almost unable to support her as she writhed and clenched under the suppositories' evil influence. In the powder-room, Renee flung open the door of a cubicle and, without ceremony, thrust her down on the seat. Instantly the dam gave way and to the accompaniment of humiliating sounds of squirting liquid and blurting gases she let it all flow, oblivious to the presence of her new friends clustered round the still open cubicle door.

When at last the intestinal turbulence had subsided, they hauled her out and stripped her.

There were 'ohs' and 'aahs' at the state of her violently decorated bottom, and the pegs and clamps still fixed so firmly in her swollen teats and bruised looking labia.

53

"God, what a beauty," Renee exclaimed, "feasting her eyes on the purple swollen clit, discoloured and distorted by the cruel grip of the serrated metal jaws.

Eventually she was to thank them for relieving her of the monstrous jaws that bit into her tender nipples and sore vulva but to reach that state of gratitude she had to pass first through the agony of their removal. Their leaving was even worse than their application. She howled unreservedly as the blood ran back into starved tissue, reawakening the numbed nerves which instantly signalled news of what they had endured and she moaned as she accommodated herself to this new and unavoidable torment, while the other women supported and comforted her.

It was messy and humiliating, having to endure this in front of half a dozen women, who were little more than acquaintances, but the relief made everything bearable. Besides, in the last thirty minutes on so, she'd came to think of these women as sisters, not strangers, and to feel one of them. She said as much.

"I think that says it for all of us really," Renee replied, "all sisters under the skin, but you are definitely one stinking mess as well as our sister. Come on, let's get you cleaned up."

Half-naked already, it was only a moment's work to propel her into the shower.

"Here, you're in no state to look after yourself," Renee said, "let me help you."

As she spoke, she pulled her sweater over her head, confirming what the precocious outlines of her teats had already suggested, the absence of a bra and, kicking off her trainers, dropped her jeans, to reveal an equal absence of knickers, not to speak of the clear evidence of a prodigious and very recent caning.

"Trust you to grab first go," Laura laughed, as Renee picked up the soap and began to rub it gently over the lovely, but battered body squeezed into the shower stall close to her.

"Yah! Jealousy will get you nowhere," she retorted, as she slipped her soapy hand between the smooth thighs, which parted unconsciously to give it access. The new sister flinched at the touch on her sore chewed lips, then relaxed and pressed herself against the invading fingers as they found the stiff little wedge of her clitoris.

"It's lovely," Renee crooned, winkling out the darling bud that had drawn her attention earlier, and circling it delicately with gentle knowing fingers, "so big and sensitive. Mmm."

"You'd be sensitive too," came the reply, "if you'd had a clip on it all afternoon." But she made no attempt to evade the soothing caress.

In a moment she began to moan and rock her pelvis at the rising sensation induced, and Renee took her hand away, and began to caress her tight round breasts instead.

"Not now," she murmured, "tonight you have to reserve that for Henry, but another time."

The girl groaned in frustration, her fevered feelings not relieved by Renee's thumbs, which were rotating her turgid nipples, which had erected and engorged instantly under the soapy touch, despite their cruelly bruised state.

"It's all right," Renee laughed, "there'll be plenty of other times in the future when we can play in the shower, or on a bed together. It's only tonight you have to be good."

The panting girl pressed herself against the long naked loveliness in front of her, feeling their bodies touch, their breast rub, their bellies press together, their thighs interlock and on an impulse, she brought her face up and kissed Renee full on the mouth.

"Please! Please!" she begged, "I need it so. There'll be plenty left for Henry, I promise you."

Renee looked at her and saw her need in her eyes.

"Oh well, perhaps just one little one," she conceded, "Henry will never miss it," and returned her artful fingers to the throbbing bud, dark as wine and full as a cherry, now actually standing proud of the fat lips that enclosed it.

"Come for me, baby," she crooned, and felt the spasms beginning in the soft belly pressed against her wrist.

A touch more of this sensuous frotting and the girl was on the edge. The stresses and sufferings of the day, the pleasure in her new-found friends, all conspired to an early ending and soon she was honking out her relief, her head thrown back, mouth open, howling like a she-wolf, then she collapsed for a moment against the knowing woman who had brought her this blessed release of tension.

The other women gathered round the stall cheered and applauded. They stood her under the steaming shower and washed off all the accumulated grime, and much of the soreness in all parts of her body. Their attentions were intimate, as well as intensive, and soapy hands found their way into all her secret cracks and crevices, before the job was done.

When she was dry they sat her down and began to fix her hair and restore her make-up. Someone produced a pair of stockings, her others were a ruin by now, and some quick work with washcloth and tissues served to restore some respectability to her footwear.

"Don't worry about knickers," Laura said, consigning to the trash bin the unsavoury remains of what had once been an exquisite piece of expensive lingerie. "You're expected to stay bare-arsed at a time like this."

"Why's that?" she wanted to know.

"So that the men can inspect the damage of course," Renee said as if it was the most natural thing in the world. Perhaps it was, she thought, and relaxed under their tender ministrations.

Only then did the thought come to her.

"How did you know that I wanted a shit?" she demanded of no one in particular.

They all laughed again and Laura said, "Well, apart from the fact that you were hopping from foot to foot and writhing like a snake, you're not the only one to travel that road. We've all been through it, and the men always seem to like to end it like that. Sort of the ultimate degradation."

"You've all done it?" she asked amazed. "All been on a one-woman treasure hunt?"

"Well, all been initiated in some way," Renee agreed. "Sometimes a treasure hunt like you, but lots of other ways too."

Even at a time like this, feminine curiosity would not be silenced.

"Such as?" she wanted to know.

"Well, in my case," Trudi said. "they persuaded me that Charles belonged to a secret society, like the masons only stricter. Charles couldn't become a senior member unless he could demonstrate he could dominate his woman. I loved him so I went along with it. We went to stay at the 'Master's' house, and I had to accept a caning, two-dozen beauties. I howled like a baby, but I didn't get up. I can feel each one of them now," she said with a shudder of fearful recollection, not unmixed with lust.

"Go on! You're joking. Is that really what happened?"

"I kid you not," Trudi assured her. "After that first flogging I had to go upstairs to bed with them, and take them both. Boy was I ever sore, inside and out. The welts on my bottom were like hot purple ropes, and they'd both buggered me until my bum felt as if it had been reamed out with sandpaper. Just when I thought it was over and I could get some sleep, I was ordered to go down to the study, bend over the whipping bench and wait for someone to come and cane me again."

"And did you?"

"What do you think? Haven't you just allowed everything in the book, rather than let the side down? Yes of course I did, and the Master came and gave me another dozen on my sore bottom, and then they turned me over again, and reamed me some more. Ugh! But it was worth it," she concluded with a sly smile.

"Was it the same for all of you?" Jenny asked looking around the group.

"We all got it as bad, one way or another," Rachel replied, "but always in a different way. The men used their imaginations to dream up fantasy situations that would test us out. They took me out, wrists tied behind my back, and blindfolded. Naked, of course. I didn't know where they were taking me, but I learnt afterwards it was the old barn near the church. I had to stay bent over a table, blindfolded and gagged, until I was told different. They kept me there for two hours, from ten by the church clock to midnight. I'd no idea what would happen to me - just if I was to join the group I had to strip and bend, and not get up whatever happened."

"And what did happen?"

"They came for me, one by one. By the time I was through, I'd been beaten four or five times, buggered by at least six men and fucked from behind more times than I could count. I've no idea to this day just which of those bastards had me, or if some of them came back for second helpings. I know it was all I could do to hang on, and I was never so grateful as when I heard the clock strike twelve and Bill's voice saying, 'Congratulations, slut. You can get up now.' There was a prick up my arse at the time and my buttocks were burning from my last beating, but I was proud and happy to have come through."

"Was everybody treated that roughly?" she asked, incredulous, lying back in the chair and almost purring as Laura continued a sensuous brushing of the luxuriant auburn locks.

"Actually I got it a bit differently," Georgina said, "Chris didn't have to prove anything about my willingness to take a beating. He used to give me my weekly dozen, every Saturday night, before we went out to the club or whatever and any extra punishments on top for what he considered wrong behaviour, so I was pretty hardened, but he knew he could get to me still by humiliating me, especially in public. Still can for that matter..."

By the time Georgina had finished the story of her humiliation and degradation, order had been restored to face and hair, and something close to decency to her clothes... if a knickerless bottom could qualify as decent. Renee asked her how she felt.

"And you don't resent Henry getting you into this?"

"Oh no. Well maybe I'll chew his ear later, but all I want at the moment is for him to take me home and fuck me silly."

"I'm sure that could be arranged, he'll be as raring to go as you. But watch the ear chewing. Once these men get the idea they own you they don't let it go. You may find your tongue will get your bottom into trouble if you're not careful."

"I sincerely hope so," the grinning girl declared, "I've no intention of giving up this life now I've found what I've been missing."

"Hmm. You may be right, but need to wait until you've been a Friday girl for a few months before you can be sure of that," Renee told her.

"A Friday girl? What's that?"

"No time to explain now," Renee said hastily, as if she'd just realised she'd strayed onto dangerous ground, "It's time for you to be presented. If we don't go in soon the men will come through and rape us all in their excitement."

"Chance would be a fine thing," Laura said in mock despair, "they'll only have eyes for little redhead here. We wouldn't get a prick between us."

The cheerful coven quitted the powder room and entered the bar to warm cheers and applause for the new recruit, who found herself the subject of eager male attentions, from burning glances to no nonsense kisses on her mouth, rough

59

but welcoming, and frank tokens of her desirability. She was made to make the rounds of all present, then taken to the low dais at the end of the big room, where a DJ, and occasionally a live group, performed for the frequent dances and discos.

"Come on, darling," Renee urged. "Let them all see you. Here, stand on this chair."

She clambered up onto the hard-back chair and turned to face the audience.

"Not that way," Renee laughed. "Let the dog see the rabbit. Turn your back and lift your dress."

She flushed a deep crimson. Heaven knows she had exhibited herself all afternoon, but this was a different kettle of fish. Still she wasn't going to fall at the last fence and hiked up her dress above her waist, knowing as she did so that her well beaten buttocks, with their peppering of painful red blisters where the pieces of the mat had penetrated, were blatantly on view. While she stood and blushed, the entire gathering filed slowly past, first inspecting her beaten hams, then moving to her front to admire the inflamed and swollen labia of her vulva, the neatly trimmed thicket of russet curls and the darkly bruised grape of her clitoris peeping coyly through its sheltering lips.

"I knew you were the right stuff," Henry said, when he came at last to claim her.

He could hardly manage to spare the time for polite farewells before half dragging her to the car. The short but bumpy ride through the lanes played havoc with her sore bum, but she just leant against him, feeling the warmth of his body as he drove, and went up the stairs with him hand in hand. In seconds they were stripped and in each other's arms. He turned her and started to push her towards the bed, but she fought him off. He paused, uncertain at her resistance.

"Before you have your wicked way with me," she said, "isn't there something missing?"

"And what might that be?"

"I think I'd be a better woman for another six of the best don't you?" she said demurely, "I'd be so nice and warm for you inside, if I'm hot outside."

"Don't go away," he said, and went to get his cane from the hall.

For most of the day after the 'treasure hunt', sore but satisfied she had lazed languidly around the house but by evening, a need to parade her hard won honours took over and she persuaded Henry that she needed to go out, and a visit to the Trident would be just the right tonic. Deeper down she had this sense of triumph, this need to share her stripes and welts with everyone she knew, and strangers too come to that. It was all she could do to desist from stopping passers-by and telling them she was walking round with a dozen livid weals on her buttocks.

Her euphoria subsided gradually, but she was still on a high when she met up with Renee and Laura later in the week to compare notes, and revel in her new-found belonging; a sense shared by the other two women who were fast becoming her close friends.

It was on one of these occasions that she heard another reference to Friday women. They'd taken up their usual stools at one end of the bar. Both the other women had seemed a little uncomfortable, squirming and wriggling on their hard plastic seats. At one point Laura's mini had ridden up and, on the fleshy bulge, where her weight had pressed one tight buttock cheek out over the rounded edge, she could see two things quite clearly. Laura wasn't wearing knickers, and that soft white bottom showed, quite distinctly, the hot ripe tracks of a very recent beating. No wonder she was squirming. Could that be Renee's problem too? Aloud she said:

"You look as if you've been in the wars. And how come no panties?"

"Friday night, Darling," Laura said, as if that was sufficient clarification

"Are you the same?" she wanted to know, looking at Renee, who laughed.

"It's tough being a Friday girl," she said by way of

explanation.

"A Friday girl?"

The two women looked at each other, as if guilty of some indiscretion.

"Errm..." Laura began doubtfully, but Renee interrupted her.

"Oh the cat's out of the bag now," she said, resignedly. "We might as well tell her, since she's bound to guess anyway after we've flaunted our bums so blatantly. We'll have to confess our fault on Friday next, anyway and pay with our bottoms, so we've nothing to lose."

"Tell me what?"

"It's an old custom among Sexton wives," Renee explained. "Friday nights you confess your sins and your man wipes them out for you with a suitable chastisement. Leaves you pained but pardoned. Usually takes place before we go out for the evening, in which case we aren't allowed underwear, as you've already spotted with Laura and," lifting one buttock off her stool, and pulling up her skirt a little, "you can see I've been to confession too."

She blinked a little at the vivid blobs of hot purple bruise visible on Renee's flank. Obviously they ran right across under her. Their partial concealment made it difficult to estimate how many there were, but it was quite obviously a substantial beating.

"What on earth did you do to deserve that?" she cried.

"Oh, nothing in particular," Renee replied, nonchalantly. "Just been getting a little lippy lately, answered back a bit too freely, that sort of thing. Tom thought I'd be better off for being straightened out."

"But didn't it hurt?"

"Of course it did, that's the point of it. It hurt like hell at the time," Renee agreed, "but he was right. I did feel better afterwards, once the first sting had gone off and I'd wiped my eyes."

63

"And what about you?" she asked her new blonde friend. "Did you need straightening out as well?"

"Of course. I did have a couple of actual faults to settle as well, a letter I forgot to post, a scratch on the car, but mainly it was to improve my mood. You have to admit it did," she said with a sunny smile.

She did too. Both her friends had seemed radiant tonight, despite their writhing on their seats or, perhaps, because of them. She recalled her own feelings after her first beating. Her need to show off to someone, her feeling of being especially alive, her pride, that was it, pride, at feeling the stripes under her, and her desire to rip off her clothes and display her 'war medals' to everyone she met.

"Well now the cat's out of the bag, perhaps you should ask Henry to make you a Friday girl as well," Laura interrupted her thoughts with the suggestion.

"Err, I think I'll pass on that one," she said doubtfully, looking at the livid weals where they terminated on her friends' soft thighs, and imagining the thick dark bars that must run across their bottoms, but they were not convinced and exchanged knowing grins across her.

Later, lying happily in Henry's arms in a post-coital glow, his thick seed trickling stickily down the inside of one thigh, she kissed his ear and murmured, "Henry, will you make me a Friday girl?"

He came awake at once.

"Those gossiping witches have been shooting their mouths off again have they?"

"Now don't be angry with them," she pleaded, "they've already said they'll confess all at their next Friday sessions, and clear their consciences if not their bottoms and, anyway, it just slipped out in conversation when I spotted their stripes and their lack of panties."

"And you'd like to sit in the bar on Friday nights, with your bottom bare and burning too?"

64

"Yes please," she said demurely.

"Hmmm. We'll have to see if you're ready for that," he said, doubtfully. "You've hardly been here five minutes. Let's sleep on it," and he pulled her so that her back and especially, her soft warm bottom, fitted tightly into the curve of his body. She smiled secretly to herself as she felt the piston of his flaccid organ begin to stiffen again from the contact. No need to press the matter, she thought to herself, he's already enjoying just thinking of it.

She didn't push it but a few days later, lingering too long beside Renee's pool, a private place where they could economise on swimwear by leaving it safely in the drawer, she had found the delights of her friends' caresses and the surprises their bodies held, had left her stranded, with Henry probably already home and no meal ready.

What had diverted her from her duties as a mate was the unusual configuration of each female body. It had all started as a little affectionate play, some kisses, a little warmer than mere friendship strictly required, some friendly probings of pubes and breasts, the application of hot loving mouths to rigidly erected teats, while their owners moaned and squirmed, the probing of thick fleshy labia by her darting tongue. It had found a sopping gash, as she had expected, but something else; a thick gold ring that pierced the root of each gristly clitoral wedge.

In the heat of these innocent Sapphic salutes, she had not questioned their origin, but continued to explore her friends' open and willing bodies. A hand slipped between the buttock cheeks, at first merely following the tracks of a recent caning down into the deep divide, to explore how the shock of the rod had left impacts well beyond its direct reach, bruising the flesh by making it impact on itself almost as hard as under the actual contact line itself. But the sensitive fingers had found more than the hot spoor of this interior bruising. Where she had stroked along the floor of the groove, expecting to find a slightly depressed dimple where the anus was set, she found a strange protuberance. It was as if the anal dimple had developed a rim, its circular shape compressed by the lightly clenching buttock halves so that it was more like a slot. She was sure it was more than a natural oddity, since both women had the same rubbery extension of the anal ring. Before she could make further enquiries she was called back to reality by Renee reminding her what the time was, and that Henry would be home at any moment.

He'd upbraided her sharply, but fairly, after all it was part of her share of the partnership, now she was no longer going up to the city every day, but she'd found herself reacting to the criticism like a ruffled cat until, at last, she stopped further discussion by blurting out, "Well, if you're so bothered about a little thing like that, you'd better put it on the Friday bill."

He'd looked at her silently for a moment then said quietly, "Yes I'll do that. Now get changed. We're going out to the Bay Tree."

She dressed quickly in a flurry of emotions. Did he really intend to take her up on the question of Friday penance? Probably, she thought, stroking smoky nylon up a succulent thigh and snapping the garter clip onto it, or why was he taking her to the best restaurant that Sexton had to offer?

No more was said at the time, and the evening provided enough distractions to banish the subject. There were several couples there they knew, and one or two diversions to keep her mind from Friday's threat. For a start, when the headwaiter had suggested, "Table for two, Sir?" Henry had nodded to him familiarly and murmured, "Madam will not be requiring a chair, Alexis."

The man had nodded as if it was the most natural thing in the world, and led the way to a table just off the centre of the room, but far from relegated to obscurity. There he had motioned to one of his underlings who had deftly removed chair and place setting, leaving space for one. The waiter had seemed not to notice her presence at the table, drawing out the remaining chair for Henry, who took his seat without looking at her. She was more bewildered than angry, standing there beside him, her breasts moving agitatedly beneath the silver lame of the dress he had chosen for her, a strapless tube that just covered them, and fell straight to her ankles.

"Kneel!" he commanded and, dutifully she went down on both knees beside his chair, conscious that most of those already present were turning with undisguised interest to the scene being played out before them. She was uncertain at first how to hold herself but instinct led her to sit back on her heels and place the palms of her hands flat along her silver covered thighs as she'd seen other women do in this same restaurant.

Ignoring her presence again, Henry took the menu the Headwaiter handed him and began to order.

"Melon, roast Aylesbury duckling, a selection of fresh vegetables."

"And something to drink, Sir?"

"A schooner of dry sherry, and a bottle of number 49, the claret," Henry told him.

The service was good. A pretty waitress arrived within minutes with the sherry balanced on her tray, setting it down without batting an eyelid at the elegantly dressed young woman kneeling submissively at Henry's side. Perhaps she was used to seeing that sort of thing here.

Henry took a sip at the straw-coloured drink then offered it to the woman kneeling at his side. She opened lush red lips and sipped delicately from the rim.

At first she had been angry at his treatment of her but it quickly subsided into excited anticipation. What had he planned for her? What would the others think? She felt a confused mixture of emotions, exposed as she was in this public place, kneeling and at a man's command. That of course was the nub of it, the overt surrender. As the meal progressed she found herself sliding more and more under the spell. There was something primeval and deep in her psyche that this touched. To depend for her very food on what this man chose to let her have, or keep from her, leaving her kneeling empty mouthed, while he ate. She was not physically compelled, she could get up at any moment and go home to a well-stocked larder, but that wasn't the point. She was as tightly controlled as if in chains by just the intensity of the situation and the proximity of all these people, both acquaintances and strangers. As if mesmerised, she stayed obediently on her knees, taking without fuss each titbit as it was offered, even leaning forward to nuzzle his hand with her lips in grateful thanks for his care of her. It may have started out as a form of punishment, a public humiliation, but it had become a privilege, a sacrament almost. Or was it a lesson?

The courses came and went. At first she was too excited to be hungry, though she refused nothing he offered, then, as she got into the swing of things, she ate avidly each piece offered, closing her lips delicately around the morsel on the fork, sipping carefully from the rim of the glass, letting the rich dark wine warm her belly. The pretty waitress went backwards and forwards between table and kitchen, seemingly unaware of the kneeling woman but covertly sending glances in her direction, admiring looks tinged with envy perhaps. When he had placed his order for dessert, Henry rummaged in his pocket and produced a small object wrapped in tissue, and passed it to her.

"Time for you to visit the powder-room," he said, "I want you wearing these when you come back. Oh, and you won't be needing panties. Bring them back in your hand and put them on the table in front of you."

Obediently she rose to her feet and walked across the room to the ladies. Whether by coincidence or design, she strongly suspected the latter in this strange community, their table was about as far as it could be from the entrance to the ladies powder-room and she had to walk past virtually every other table to reach it, encountering the knowing glances of the other guests along the way. Once there she examined the package he had given her. Inside were two small bulldog clips, of the sort used to secure bunches of papers together, tough tin jaws, closed by a steel spring to bite fiercely on anything placed between them.

She had no doubts about where he intended they be placed. The only real choice was labia or teats, and he'd made a very pointed reference to panties. Besides, her teats were fat, well defined cylinders of surprisingly gristly flesh, as he was very well aware, since he loved chewing on the tough little stubs during their nightly play, and it would be difficult to get them in the limited opening of the jaws. Below it had to be. She removed the condemned underwear and pulled out one fleshy love lip, sliding the jaws over it. With grim concentration she let the jaws close slowly on it. It was intolerable! She had braced herself for the bite, but hadn't expected this. The crocodiles on the 'hunt' had been bad, but they were as nothing compared with the grip these steel monsters had. This was going to be a real test of her determination and obedience, as he quite obviously intended it should be. Well, she'd show him she could do it. Biting her lower lip, hissing as the pressure came on, she slowly opened her fingers. For a moment she stood, half crouched, her hands wavering around her groin, as if not able to leave the clip in place, then she shook her head like a diver coming up from deep water and reached for the other clip. It was no easier for knowing how much it was going to hurt her. She hesitated just as long, before she could summon up the courage to set it in place but eventually, with much grunting, hissing of breath, a soft whimper as she absorbed the combined effect of two labia crushed so cruelly, the job was done. She straightened herself and her dress, took up the discarded panties in her hand, and turned to leave the room. Only then did she realise fully, what the effect of these devilish clips would be. On top of the hurt she suffered from just their tigerish presence on her delicate sexflesh, the motion of walking dragged them this way and that, amplifying the pain. All she wanted to do was stand as still as possible and not provoke further agony. From the moment she left the shelter of her stall to endure the speculative looks of the women standing at the basins, observing her red-face shuffle across the room, she was a-flood with shame and pain. And then she had to cross the dining room, her panties in her hand, under the knowing gazes of the men and, especially, the women who were seated there. She did her best, but could not bring herself to close her legs on the beastly biters. No female in the room failed to notice the wide-legged gait and riven face, as she made the crossing.

At the table, she placed the scrap of lace-edged nylon, scented with her body, on the table in front of her place, neatly folded as if ready for her lingerie drawer, and resumed her kneeling position. It was fortunate that the pose she had chosen, and Henry tacitly approved, left her with her thighs slightly parted, easing the pressure of the clamps that bit so painfully into her, and she made a good pretence of being able to ignore them.

Dessert had already arrived, a startling confection of chocolate, ice-cream, cherries and, above all, whipped cream in snowy mountains. As Henry offered generous dollops on an exaggeratedly long spoon, she tried to take them with dignity and finesse, but the sheer height of each creamy pile defeated her. By the time the tall frosted glass was empty, her nose was smeared with chocolate, and a moustache of whipped cream adorned her upper lip. Henry let her blush beside him, as all around admired her besmirched state, including the waitress who smiled knowingly at the panties still lying in front of her. When he had placed his order for

70

coffee and liqueurs, another, smaller, package appeared.

"You're a mess," he told her. "Go and clean up, while we wait for coffee. And while you're about it put this on. You won't have as much trouble this time as you haven't any panties, so don't be long."

Once again the long trek under frankly curious eyes, re-arousing the pain in her groin, forcing her to walk spraddle-legged to try in vain to ease it. This time the packet contained just one item, an electrical clip, just like those she'd worn on the treasure hunt, a tight little crocodile, with serrated jaws and a nasty bite. Well, not quite the same; this had a small silver bell attached, on six inches of chain, which tinkled merrily and audibly as she lifted it out. There was only one so she knew where it must go, though the thought made her cringe.

It was going to hurt whatever she did but she recognised that if she let its full venom engage merely the tip of her sensitive and delicate bud, it could crush, or even tear it. Better to bite the bullet and place it as deeply and firmly as she could. Locked in her stall, feeling like a guilty school-girl, sheltering in the loo for a furtive masturbationary session, she moistened a finger in the seeping gash of her vulva and began the age-old feminine ritual; a gentle circling, not touching the bud yet, closing in until the hood could be stroked back, finally rotating around the bared pink pea until it was hard and throbbing and answering warmth was pulsing in her belly, the first spasms collecting in her womb. Abruptly she checked herself, suddenly realising that she was so aroused that a few seconds more of this erotic frotting would bring her to orgasm. Panting a little she returned to the matter in hand. At least she had attained her object. The little organ was fully inflated with hot throbbing blood, and standing rigid enough so that she could get a good grip at its base, without putting dangerous pressure on the delicate tip. Clamping her teeth shut in a rictus of determination, she let

71

the jaws close over it.

With the lancing pain of the bite her head came back, and she chewed on a gargling howl, never quite letting it escape her. Quickly she adjusted the dress, washed her face and set off back to base. A wave of horror and embarrassment flooded over her as she heard the small silvery tinkle of the bell swinging between her legs, a tiny sound in reality but sounding to her like the liberty bell, or Big Ben himself. This time the journey across the floor seemed really endless, each step an agony, each small tinkle like the clap of doom, each knowing glance from the women a silent accusation. Somehow she made it and took up her station again on Henry's left. He raised an eyebrow at her overt distress, but said nothing merely offering his glass to her bitten lips. The thick, strong syrupy liqueur burnt as it rolled over her tongue, but put new strength into her. Her thanks were full of sincerity, and she leant over to kiss the back of the hand that fed her.

Her gratitude was more mixed later that night when, seated naked on the bed she was allowed to remove the clamps. For some time now the throbbing agony had subsided to a numb ache, though walking still served to fan the flames anew. Now she was given permission to remove them herself, and wished he was doing the job. She was desperate to have them off her tender flesh, but fearful of what she knew would happen as they left it and the circulation was restored. She could never make up her mind whether it hurt more to put them on or to take them off. Freed from the constraints of the public room, she allowed herself the luxury of a heartfelt howl as each metal clamp came away and, for a moment, she writhed in agony clasping her abused vulva. The departure of the clip from her clit produced a display of contortions and vocal pyrotechnics worthy of an opera singer in a gymnast's body. Henry's amusement was as obvious as his erection, and she soon forgot her soreness in his very welcome sexual therapy.

Thinking of it later, she came to a decision. Henry had rebuked her for her fault and she had accepted his rebuke and its consequences, but she still had to make an act of contrition of her own, some gesture to show her formal acceptance of his discipline. Friday night she would offer her confession, and seek formal penance and absolution. It would be the beginning of a new phase in their relationship.

Meanwhile she should give him a little present to make up for the missed meal. When Henry came home the next night he found not only a delicious meal already prepared and a drink poured ready to his hand, but a hostess dressed to his taste as spicily as the food, heels and hose, tiny silk briefs and a pretty bra that exhibited more than it concealed, the very essence of the power of imagination over total revelation.

That evening she served him like a Barbary slavegirl in her master's tent, kneeling to offer each dish, staying when he commanded to take the morsels of food he offered her, drinking from his glass, reliving again all the delights of being owned and fed by a strong man. Afterwards she caught Henry looking at her with undisguised lust.

"Come to bed," he said, holding out both hands to draw her to her feet.

She shook herself free gently.

"No," she said, "I want to do it properly. Sit and have a cigar while I clear away and wash up, as a woman should. You can think about what you want to do to me while I'm at it."

She was standing at the sink, just about finished, when she became aware of the scent of cigar smoke and looked over her shoulder to see him leaning against the door frame looking at her in a contemplative fashion, his gaze aimed somewhere south of her naked waist.

"Your panties are coming down," he said.

She dried her hands quickly and reached for the elastic

73

of the tiny briefs, tugging them tight but feeling no slack.

"No they're not," she answered, feeling slightly foolish at her blushing reaction considering how she had behaved all evening.

Henry grinned widely.

"Oh yes they are," he told her, "I've just decided."

Before she could reply, she found herself bent over the sink she had just been using to wash the dishes, the silken scrap of her panties round her ankles, and something hard and insistent pressing between her bottom cheeks. An arm snaked past her and grabbed the jar of hand-cream she'd had been about to apply, and a cold gobbet laved her shrinking anus and was fingered deep inside.

"Oh, please Henry, not there," she murmured without much conviction and the iron hard prick returned to the creamed dimple and lunged into the tiny crater. She gurgled as it strained her reluctant sphincter but the battle was soon decided and the fleshy rod suddenly sank into her to the balls, his belly slapping against the firm pert rounds of her buttocks. With vigorous and irresistible strokes he commenced an enthusiastic buggery.

The violence of his assault meant it couldn't last. Such a speedy lust-driven attack can only end in one thing, an equally quick consummation. Within seconds, she felt hot gouts of his thick glutinous semen spurting into her entrails. Quickly come, quickly recover. For a minute or two he held her captive over the sink while his penis softened inside her and gently slipped from her anus, followed by a thin sticky trail that ran down into the welt of her stocking top. Another minute and his insatiable member was stirring again and she felt herself swept up in a gorilla-like embrace and flung over his shoulder. It wasn't particularly comfortable, with his hard collarbone pressing into her belly as she watched the floor and then the stairs passing below her eyes, but she didn't care. He flung her down on the bed and, in seconds the scrap of silk was rudely torn from around her ankles, leaving her lying on her back, legs spread, the air cool on a soaked and exposed feminine zone. He was tearing at his own clothes now and in seconds had exposed an impressively restored male organ of handsome proportions that bobbed and swung like a ship's bowsprit as he came to her on the bed.

Foreplay was redundant but too pleasing to be missed. He fastened his mouth on hers and pushed up the silky bra to place a firm hand on each milky mound that it uncovered, taking a turgid teat between the finger and thumb of each hand. As he pressed his mouth even more firmly on her own he squeezed and twisted the gristly nubs until she writhed and moaned beneath him in mingled pain and ecstasy. Without loosing his hold, he took his mouth from hers and slid down to apply it to another mouth, and from there to the little 'nose' above it. Not so little now. She had always had a significant clit, a prominent wedge of sizeable proportions, a fine roman nose which had flourished under the new regime she had entered into and under the stimulation of their erotic dinner, her anal rape, and his searching tongue stood out as big as the top joint of her little finger, pulsing and throbbing so hard he could feel it on his tongue. She squirmed and groaned even more wildly under the combined assault on her teats and tender feminine spot. It couldn't last of course, she was swimming helplessly on the brink, trying desperately to stop plunging over, but he was remorseless and forced her submission as she shrieked and howled in time to the massive waves of her first orgasm of the bout.

He eased off a trifle after she collapsed in sodden surrender, then began again more gently. This time, as she began to respond to his touch he found the quivering entrance to her vagina with the tip of his now iron-hard organ and eased it in an inch. She arched her back to draw him into her but he teased her a little longer, making her wait while he increased the pressure on her nipples back to aching agony

75

again. Once he had her hissing with the pain of his grip, he thrust home in one swift motion, until he was buried to the balls again, his belly slapping on hers this time. As his prick slammed into her pulsing cervix, she screamed again and wrapped her legs around him, drawing him even deeper into herself. In a few frenzied pistoning strokes they reached the peak together and plunged down in mutual spasms, to lie spent and happy in each other's arms.

And then it was Friday night, and one question was foremost in her mind; not what would it be like, being disciplined formally for the first time or, even how she would be able to face them in the Trident, with everyone knowing she had just come from being thrashed but, woman-like, what should she wear for a beating? On the treasure hunt, whipped bare-arsed over the five barred gate, chance had dictated her costume and an inappropriate one at that. In the evening when she'd invited further punishment, she'd been wearing what she always wore to bed, that was a freshly washed skin, smelling of expensive toilet soap and on special occasions, a dab or two of something more exotic in the way of scent. Otherwise bare all over and not, she thought, really up to the formality of the occasion. In the end she settled for some rather superior underwear. It had seemed to attract Henry's attention and approval at their intimate dinners. Might as well build on success and, anyway it would be a good foundation for her outfit when they proceeded to the Trident afterwards; matching bra and suspender belt, with smoky 'thigh-high' nylons, hoisted taut as bow strings almost to her crotch, and leather pumps; sling backs with three and a half inch heels. No panties of course. Friday girls sat bare-arsed on their bar stools, their stripes in direct contact with the hard surface to remind them of their punished and pardoned status.

Of course she'd wear something short and revealing, to

declare her chastised state and she put a satin mini-dress ready on the chair, demure scooped neckline to contrast with the pelmet-like brevity of the lower part. For now though she waited with her apprehensive nakedness barely covered by her undies.

Henry was his usual punctual self, but still she counted every second before he appeared, dropping to her knees when he entered the bedroom, placing her palms on her spread thighs, her chin up, but her eyes turned discreetly down, the very picture of the submissive sinner. It did nothing for her peace of mind or the butterflies in her belly that he left her there while he threw off his clothes and took a shower to wash off the grime of the city before starting to dress. Only when he was clad in the authority of trousers again, did he turn to the business that had brought her there. From the corner of her eye she watched apprehensively as he went to a drawer and extracted a long lean length of straw coloured cane. She hadn't seen this particular instrument before and guessed, correctly as it turned out, that he had purchased a punishment cane especially for these Friday sessions. It seemed he meant business.

"Right then," he observed, giving the rod a preliminary swish through the air, "let's get started. You wouldn't want to be late meeting the rest of the coven would you?"

That beast of a cane was making a distinctly depressing noise as she rose to her feet and went over to the straight-backed chair he indicated. His next words did nothing to dispel the gloom.

"This may be your first time, but I think it would be a mistake not to start as we mean to continue."

As he meant to continue, she thought resentfully then checked herself. After all, it was she who had instigated this new regime and she was honest enough to remember that and also, that she probably needed it.

Henry was still talking.

77

"So we'll have a little confession session, and then you can do penance. What have you to tell me?"

Though she'd realised on one level that this was how it was done, she'd not really thought about her answers. Now she racked her brains rapidly.

"First off there's the thing which started this," she said, "when I didn't have your supper ready. No," she corrected herself, "no, the real offence was not accepting your ticking off contritely. Instead I answered back like a bitch. I deserve a good beating for that."

"Anything else?"

She thought some more.

"Well, I do get into the habit of slagging off men when I'm with the girls. It's so easy when we're just girls together. Seems to come so naturally you know."

"I do know," Henry assured her firmly, "and I'll take that into consideration too."

He thought a moment, looking her half naked and totally desirable body up and down in a mixture of sexual interest and calculation.

"Four or six would suit normally for a livener, or just to remind you that you are a woman but tonight, I think something a little stronger is called for. Would you agree that eight of the very best across that pert bottom of yours would help you to do better and be no more than you deserved?"

She nodded silently.

"Then bend over the chair and grip the seat please. Usual rules apply; take the stroke again if you let go, caned on your palms if you touch yourself behind and start all over from the beginning if you get up before permission. Now hold onto your skin. I'm going to make you feel these."

This was different again. Over the gate was total confusion and bewilderment, while the repeat that evening was a matter of sheer lust; a swift and ruthless fanning of her sexual flame

78

until they were both consumed in white heat. This time it was deliberate, foreseen and fearfully anticipated, a carefully prescribed punishment to help her to be a better loved mate for her man.

He didn't start immediately, but stood gazing lovingly at the peach halves of his girl's cringing buttocks, the resemblance to that delicious fruit not only in the exquisite texture of the succulent flesh, and the neat cleft that divided them but in the delicate in-sink of the wrinkled anus, exactly like the scar where the real fruit parted from its twig.

It was not a big bottom. Covered, clothed, it was neat trim, svelte, undulating languidly with her walk, a motion becoming ever more sensual with her increasing sexual arousal. Bare and bent, it took on another dimension, flaring generously, presenting an ample target for rod or cane, strap or crop. The firm flesh seemed made to absorb whatever cuts he gave it while the flawless alabaster made the perfect parchment on which to write in letters of fire.

How he loved this woman. So brave and intelligent. Her fear was evident in the little fatty quiverings at the tops of her thighs, where they framed the pouting fig of her vulva, the site of so much pleasure for them both with its hot humid sheath fringed with russet hairs. For all her fear she did not leave her position, but waited submissively for what was to come. He would do anything for her, he vowed. With all the power of his shoulder and wrist, he lashed the bitter length of straw-coloured rattan into the quivering cheeks.

It was a ferocious stroke, slamming into the soft flesh just below the absolute centre of the tautened mounds, sending a shock wave through them, visibly lifting the meaty globes. He gave her a ten second interval to fully absorb the disciplinary effect, then delivered another searing cut, equally biting. Each stroke had her gasping and hissing as she clung to the seat for dear life. Fear of earning extra, and a determined pride in her ability to endure, served to keep her in place, although the strokes slicing into her tender taut buttock cheeks at nerve stretching intervals were a whole world harder than anything she had had so far in her brief experience of bare-bottomed caning. For a start this was a proper professional punishment cane, a lean and hungry rod with length, whip and weight to it, an instrument meant to hurt, and wielded by an athletic man who had promised her he would make it do just that.

Each cut raised an immediate finger thick track across her milky white globes, a track that felt as if it were made of fire. When he lashed the fifth of the awful octet into the tender flesh at the top of her legs, just where the 'thigh-high' stocking tops ended, she whimpered and writhed in place. On six he repeated the cut and she bent one leg at the knee, rubbing it against the other with a susurration of nylon threads fretting on each other. He waited until she put the shoe back on the ground and struck again, a little higher mercifully, but also a little overhit, and the tip wrapped itself round her side to bite deeply into her flank. She twisted away from him and clung onto her perch with her hips askew, her left leg pointed down to an extreme as she struggled to stay put. With a growl he ordered her straight and she moved back with obvious reluctance. The last stroke fell full and true across the lower part of the cringing buttock cheeks and she stamped and hissed as she fought to hold on until 'permission' was pronounced.

Finally, after what seemed an age, she heard the blessed word and straightened painfully. Henry held her in his arms for a brief moment, his lips pressed to hers in a forgiving kiss then pushed her from him.

"Get dressed," he said. "Friday girls go on their dates hot bottomed. Besides, those witch friends of yours will be waiting at the Trident to see the damage."

In unquestioning obedience she slipped the mini dress, which was all the covering she was allowed, over her head and followed meekly out to the car.

The beating left her soft and pliant, she found. Not frightened or driven into obedience by terror of another punishment, but dissolved, submissive, malleable. As she entered the car some instinct made her flip up the abbreviated skirt of the mini-dress that was the recognised uniform of a chastised Friday girl, and set her bare welted behind on the cool hard leather. Henry looked across at her and nodded.

"Good girl," he said approvingly. "We'll make a Sexton wife of you yet."

She only smiled and leant against him, not really taking in his words but gripping his thigh in both hands as if in need of an anchor.

As Henry had forecast, no great feat of prophesy under the circumstances, her two closest friends were waiting at the Trident. Their eagle eyes did not fail to note the pride in her carriage, the slight stiffness in her walk, the tightening of her lips as she set her bottom on the stool, that showed as clearly as if she had walked into the room buck naked that beneath the inadequate pelmet of her skirt she was as hot and sore as either of them, and just as bare.

"So Henry granted your wish," Renee said with a grin, watching the pressed lips and agitated manoeuvring as she took her seat on the tall hard stool.

She had the grace to blush, but it was from pride not from her welts.

"And did you two settle for telling tales out of school?" she wanted to know in exchange.

Laura laughed wryly.

"Did I ever. George decided that the only way to curb my tongue was to give me something else to think of. I'm like raw steak down there."

"Me too," Renee said ruefully. "Hamburger steak in my case and as hot as if just off the barbecue."

She was all contrition.

81

"I'm so sorry," she cried, "I didn't mean to get you into trouble."

"You didn't," Laura assured her, "we did it all for ourselves with our runaway tongues. Besides," she added with a sly grin, "it'll all be worth it when George takes me home tonight. Lovely lovely loving. So hot and satisfying. Mmmm," and she licked her lips in anticipation.

"Makes the men as hot as it does us," Renee agreed. "Tom seems to get twice as hard and half as big again, when I come to bed with a flogged bottom. I can't make my mind up whether it's the sight of my roasted rump or the fact that I'm practically ready to rape him that turns him on so. Doesn't matter really, either way we win. It's the end result that counts, and that's pure heaven."

The newest Friday girl pursed her lips in doubt.

"You know," she said, "it doesn't make sense. These beatings are meant to be punishments, to keep us in order, curb our runaway tongues, straighten us out, but here we are literally licking our lips over them. Seems to me they're a waste of time."

"You think so?" Renee queried. "Would you really like another caning just this moment?"

She squirmed in her seat.

"Eh, no," she admitted. "Not just now. I think I'll stay out of trouble a little while longer."

"There you are," Renee said, triumphantly. "It does work. Enough to keep us in check, not enough to cow us, and lovely hot sex all round. What more can a girl ask?"

They all three dissolved into hysterical laughter until warning glances from their men, chatting further along the bar reminded them of the danger of another dose on their hot throbbing bottoms, and they hurriedly suppressed their mirth.

The three pairs of hot welted buttocks pressed their naked swollen flesh against the unyielding mouldings of their barstools, writhing a little as the heartless plastic aggravated the throbbing soreness in their tender girl meat

Three diverse beauties, blonde, brunette and redhead, in heightened states of excitement, though with just discernible traces of puffiness round their eyes to register the severity of their ordeals. They sat together in sociable conversation, squirming collectively on their hard stools their short skirts sliding up with their movements to reveal the tips of the livid marks that ran across their bottoms and just presented themselves on the fleshy buttock masses where the pressure of their seats forced them sideways. It was a fleeting pageant of welted girl that aroused the undisguised pleasure and interest of Charlie the barman, not to speak of several dozen other visitors to the pub.

They had been comparing notes on how many strokes each hot bottom carried; ten for Renee, eight for Laura, just like her own.

"God, they didn't half hurt at the time," she said, "but now. Well, I feel as if I'd had at least three large gins before I even got here. Somehow it's not hurting any more, just exciting."

Laura nodded in agreement.

"Wouldn't it be cunt clenching if we knew we were going to get them all over again, before the evening was over," Renee said in a dreamy voice.

The other two looked at her in amazement.

"You're nuts," Laura said without emotion.

"No, no. Think about it. Going through the evening, having dinner together late, feeling your bottom hot and sore under you and knowing it was going to get another pasting as soon as dinner was over. Wouldn't that make you really feel alive?"

Red and blonde heads shook slowly in silent sadness at her apparent lunacy.

"Oh, all right, have it your own way. Have another drink.

83

It's my round any way. Charlie! Three more Vodka tonics needed here to soothe injured feelings."

"Oh. Thinking of rubbing them on your pretty pink bottoms are you?" the barman asked with a leer.

"Cheeky monkey," Renee replied with no bitterness, "keep your eye on your bar and leave our arses out of it."

With the new drinks the conversation turned to the usual feminine stuff; gossip of all kinds, from who was sleeping with whom to the colour of this season's fashions but when the new dose of potent alcohol had warmed their bellies, Renee went back to where she had left off.

"How about a little dare?" she suggested. "How about we deal the cards to see who's going to repeat their stripes tonight, and who's going to lay them on. Carrot and stick approach."

Laura still looked doubtful, though weakening under her third Vodka; in Sexton the drinks were as generous as the beatings. Her companion was also prey to ambiguous feelings. Of course was out of the question. Bend and bare to be whipped again on her already unbearably sore bottom but, on the other hand... There was this rising warmth somewhere below her navel, and it wasn't all Vodka. Something was stirring in her womb at the though of what might be. She was beginning to see what Renee was after. It was cunt clenching, as the tall brunette had so elegantly put it. She could feel the excitement rising. Somewhere she heard a voice saying, "OK, let's do it."

With a jolt, she recognised it as her own!

She couldn't believe her ears, but it had been her. Laura looked at her with wide eyes then sighed elaborately.

"Oh well," she said, "if you two are going to make idiots of yourselves, I suppose I'm in too."

On the surface it sounded like a reluctant gesture of solidarity with her friends but they were not fooled. Laura was as excited by the prospect as the others.

84

"Got some cards, Charlie?" Renee called and, when he produced a pack, began to shuffle them. The young man seemed intrigued and wanted to know what they were playing for.

"Can I join in?" he asked.

"Strictly female business," Renee told him, "and you wouldn't want it if you won it, though it might do you a power of good," she added.

He went off back down the bar looking very disappointed, leaving Renee to explain the nature of the game.

"First thing is," she told them, "we want to drag it out a bit. Sudden death is no fun. It's watching the cards fall, seeing yourself sliding towards a beating, winding up the fear in your belly that makes it worth while. Like a roller-coaster, where the girls all shriek in fear but wouldn't miss a ride. Here's what we do," she explained, "we deal out the cards and each of us keeps the first card to fall in front of us. We go on dealing and if the same card comes up again in our pile, we keep it. Otherwise it's discarded and we go on dealing. At the end of the pack, if no-one's got four of a kind, we keep what we have but give the rest another shuffle and the next girl takes over the deal. We go on that way until one of us gets the fearsome foursome and she's 'it'. OK?"

The others nodded and Renee began to deal.

Ten for the blonde, knave for the redhead and seven for herself. The dealing continued and the tension mounted.

When they had started, she had been afraid it would turn out to be a mere childish game. She needn't have worried. As the cards fell in front of her she gazed at each as if it had the potential to strike her like a snake, expecting each piece of pasteboard to show another knave, as Renee turned it up. After half a dozen rounds it did, and her belly gave a flip that almost had her off her stool. By the end of the pack Renee and Laura each had only the one, while a pair of smirking jacks lay before her. She gathered the cards and shuffled as if her life depended on the result, then began to lay them out methodically. By the time she had finished the deck Renee had two sevens but she and Laura each looked with butterfly bellies at a trio of knaves and tens respectively.

When Laura began to slide the cards along the bar to each of them she was squirming in her seat, and not just because of the throbbing soreness in her bare buttocks where the hard plastic bit into them. The first to be hit was Renee and now each of them was looking at a threatening trio of cards, but that was it. The deck passed without further score and Renee was shuffling again. As she watched her deft fingers sliding the cards over and into each other, she tried to think what the odds were of getting the one remaining knave in the pack. Once, back in that far off world of business and deals (was it really only a few months since she had voluntarily left it to become one of the Sexton 'coven', as Henry had taken to describing her friends) she would have calculated the odds instinctively and made her investments accordingly, but this was different. Now her arse was on the line, quite literally, but her mind was a mass of other sensations and thoughts than the calculation of risk and she let it go, submerging herself in the womb warming thrill of danger, of putting her buttocks at risk of a new thrashing so soon after the last beating. Suddenly there it was! A grinning knave of clubs leering at her from the bar, as if looking forward to seeing her whipped. Slowly she picked it up.

"Guess I'm it," she said softly.

True to the spirit of the game, they had arranged to carry out execution immediately after dinner when they could adjourn to the ladies' room together without provoking comment. Meanwhile she would suffer/enjoy the excitement and fear of a beating to come on already tenderised flesh. Throughout the evening she intercepted glances from Renee and Laura that showed they too were constantly aware but in their cases with anticipation rather than apprehension. Even

86

Henry's decision to reward her by hand-feeding her as she knelt in semi-public beside his chair, did not totally divert her from contemplating the fate of her already bruised cheeks, soon to writhe anew under the asp-like bite of a cane. Finally the meal was over and Renee swept up the trio by a glance and gesture they could not mistake, and the three of them made off, in invariable feminine ritual, to the powder room to 'freshen up'.

Women were treated well by the Trident and the powder room was large and well appointed with liberal space between the stalls and the vanity units with their bowls and mirrors for 'fixing' female bits.

"Stand back ladies," Renee announced boldly as they entered. "We need room to pay off a little wager. I promise you, you won't be disappointed."

The other women stood back, most with knowing grins, since, from somewhere, Renee had produced a whippy cane, which she swished in an unmistakable gesture. It was not as formidable as Henry's 'discipline' cane, the intended recipient thought, looking at it without enthusiasm but eight on sore buttocks, stiffening now, this far from the first infliction would not be comfortable, to say the least.

Under Renee's direction, she stood towards one end of the long room and bent to clasp her ankles. Renee flipped up the hem of the abbreviated dress to reveal the pale moons beneath, a paleness accentuated by the livid tracks that ran straight and true across it, from centre line to thigh tops.

"Whew!" Renee exclaimed, her eyes opening at the sight of the purple tracks, revealed properly for the first time. "You certainly caught it. You're definitely going to feel these. I'll take the first four, then you can get your breath back before Laura finishes you off."

She could have wished that Renee had chosen some other way of expressing it. Bending there, butt naked in front of not only her friends but a half dozen other acquaintances and a handful of total strangers as well, she felt more vulnerable than on any of the occasions so far. All these women didn't help. Somehow in front of a man, even if she was totally naked, it did not seem quite as shaming as having her bare bottom exposed to other women. Somehow it was natural for a man to see one and impose discipline while with women, it was an artificial concept resulting in degradation and shame.

"Let's see if I can lay it right on Henry's tracks," Renee said cheerfully, and lashed the cane into her cringing bottom cheeks.

She gasped and hissed, as Renee found her mark, laying the slim rod along one of the hot dark weals that ran across her ravaged hinds. Bitch! She thought, but then had no time for more resentment as the rod swept in again and caught her across the thighs, where Henry's penultimate stroke had cut her. She mewled with pain and went up on her toes, knees turning in and knuckles whitening as she struggled not to let go of her ankles. Renee grinned like a she-wolf and struck again, this time a little higher.

It wasn't easy to take but it had to be done. She had accepted the challenge and lost, and now honour and her self-esteem demanded that she endure. With bitten lip she kept down and Renee cut low again, just catching Henry's first thigh stroke. She whimpered at the pain but was still bending when Renee said, "Take five. Then Laura can give you the rest."

She straightened painfully, her hands going behind her, under the minuscule skirt to squeeze and knead her riven haunches. Her head was back as she reached down to the tenderised meat and her mouth hung open. She hung there for a full minute while the women all around her kept up an excited buzz of conversation. Then it was time to resume and the room, crowded now as more and more women finished their meals and came to pretty-up, fell silent again as the poor lacerated bum was put on display once more.

Laura was mercifully swift. The strokes whaled into her sore bottom in regular progression, a compassionate five-second interval between each enabling her to recover enough to take the next without having to swallow each to the bitter dregs. Four grunts and moans later, and she could stand again to let the fire burn itself down to tolerable levels while she kneaded the burning buns in her fists as if trying to wring the pain out of them.

When she could bear to remove her hands from the furrowed flesh of her backside, the other two helped her press a cold cloth to reddened eyes, wipe the sweat from her forehead and make emergency repairs to ravaged make-up. To a standing ovation from the women, sitting ovation in the case of the 'stall holders', they escorted her back to the dining room to rejoin their men.

Nothing was said at the time, it was as if the men were used to these indeterminate absences of women in pairs and trios and didn't give it a thought, but in the car Henry remarked on her puffy eyed appearance in a manner that demanded some explanation. When he had had it he roared with laughter.

"That trio of yours is going to go too far one day. You'll be in real trouble," he commented. "Never mind, a man has ways of coping with that, so you'll come to no harm. Witches you may be, but a man has a couple of wands which, between them can bring even the most potent sorceress to heel."

Nor had it escaped him that, despite her newly whipped condition, she had repeated the ritual of earlier that evening, flipping up her skirt to sit bare-arsed on the leather.

"The way you're dripping on my seats, you'll stain the leather," he remarked, for she was oozing incontinently from her extravagantly engorged vulva. "You can clean it up in the morning. I won't be using it tomorrow, being Saturday," he said, "so you can make a job of it. Warm water and a little

89

washing up liquid will do the job nicely once you've got the worst of the crust off. You can do that with your pretty pink tongue. Stop it from flapping for a minute and give me a rest."

"Yes Henry," was all she said in reply, as she pressed herself against him warmly.

It didn't take her long to be on the bed, waiting hungrily for his embrace. A quick once over with a wipe, to spare him too much make-up on his face and pillow, and an even quicker strip, she was half naked already anyway, and she was lying on her back, knees slightly flexed, inviting his entrance into the hot throbbing sheath of her sex, but Henry had other ideas.

With a vice-like grip he seized her by the hips, lifting her up and turning her over, pulling her up onto her hands and knees. When his rock hard staff started to press against her tight little anus she cried out in protest.

"No, please Henry. You know how small I am there. Besides I need to come."

"You'll come alright, darling, the state you're in," he assured her, "and I'll just have to put up with the tightness until you've been seen to. I'm not wasting a view like this. Your sore arse is a sight for sore eyes, as they say!" and he thrust forward with his hips, driving the turgid shaft deep into her bowel. She howled at the violence of his entry, but then panted with lust at the feeling of being stuffed, crammed, filled to the gills.

He was right of course. In her heightened state of excitement and lust she came as quickly and spent as freely as if he were using a more conventional orifice to penetrate her. In the heat of their passion she quite forgot to ask him what he meant by her being 'seen to'.

PART THREE: TESTED

The 'function room' at the Bull's Head was crowded. Invitation only tonight, no strangers or people from outside the charmed circle of those in the know, but that still provided a packed audience of several score members, male and female. Six of the latter stood on the small stage that on more conventional occasions served to hold a live band or the DJ and his equipment for a disco night.

Tonight the six females were the entertainment. For a start each was a beauty in her own right, and nothing more came between that beauty and the eye of the beholder than a pair of black hold-up stockings and heeled pumps, whose shiny black leather matched the collars fastened round their necks. Otherwise each was naked and her feminine charms available for any of the dozens of pairs of lust-filled eyes to feast on.

It had all started a couple of weeks before. The Friday sessions had become a way of life, as several weeks and many dozens of stripes after Jenny had first experienced the joys of being a Friday girl, she had squirmed on her usual stool, enjoying the company of her friends and the exquisite warm smart of the cuts Henry had applied a little earlier. They had been unbearable when they fell but had matured and tempered with time to a comforting sense of justice done and forgiveness received, not to speak of sexual passion aroused with the promise of hot exciting satisfaction to come.

On that occasion though, the three girls were sitting on their striped Friday bottoms, contemplating their futures with less than their usual enthusiasm. The slightly reserved atmosphere had been occasioned by the news each had had from her partner that evening while they were finishing the minimal dressing permitted to a chastened Friday girl.

She herself had had her head through the rucked up mini-dress when Henry had said quite casually, "We had a challenge from the chaps at the Bull yesterday. I've put you down to represent the Trident. Tom and George are nominating those other two witches you hang about with. Do you all a power of good to exercise a little fortitude on behalf of the Tridents."

Beyond establishing that he was referring to some kind of kind of match between teams of three women from each pub, and that the events would be very physical and probably not only hugely embarrassing but seriously painful too she got little more from him. She got more answers at the Trident.

"What sort of competitions are they?" she had wanted to know, once she had established that each of the others had had the same not particularly welcome intelligence.

"Another local tradition for you," Renee had explained. "From time to time a team from one of the Sexton locals will be pitched against the girls of another. Sort of sports day kind of thing, but rather unique kinds of events."

"After what I've learnt in a few short months round here, I can believe it, but what sort of events? More caning for my poor backside I suppose," she hazarded gloomily, "I'm the first to acknowledge that we women need it regularly and there are compensations too, you know, bedtime and all that," and she even managed a small blush, "but Christ, I'm like raw meat down there already. I don't really fancy getting some more."

"Oh, it doesn't usually come down to rods at dawn," Laura had assured her, "much more interesting things than that, though I have to warn you, at least as painful most of the time."

"So what kind of things?" she repeated.

"Up to the challengers to list three events and the challenged to offer three of their own," Renee obliged.

"You mean we have to think up three particularly nasty things to do, ourselves?"

"Well, not us," Laura had explained, "naturally the girls

don't get any say in this. It's up to our lords and masters to set the rules. We just have to do and die, though we are sometimes given the opportunity to suggest something to the men that they hadn't thought of. Actually they quite encourage it, knowing we are even more likely than them to understand how to get under a woman's skin," she added brightly.

"You're right," Renee had agreed, "Well, we'll show 'em. Let's pick something really punishing and make those Bulls Head bitches wish they were somewhere else before the night is out."

It never seemed to have entered their heads that they might find it too much themselves. Their only thought appeared to be to put these upstart women in their place and show them who was boss round here. She could only shake her head in wonder, but she had gone along with them as they planned their strategy for this Bitches Grand Prix. Even later, when she had had time to consider her apprehension was more than countered by excitement and a determination that their side was going to win.

So here she was, standing naked in front of the packed hall, flanked by her friends and opposite a trio of equally attractive, and equally bare, women representing the home team. Henry was with the other men in privileged front seats by virtue of providing the entertainment. If she had thought to have been spared the coming ordeal by her partner relenting she was disappointed. Henry had grinned from ear to ear each time the coming event was mentioned and promised her a reward if they won, an incentive made even stronger by the promise of the father and mother of a caning if they lost.

As a neutral, Fred, the landlord of the Silent Woman had handed the bar over to an assistant for the night and agreed to act as umpire for the event and now he called the expectant crowd to order by announcing the first event,

"I won't waste your time by making you listen to me any

93

longer than you have to," he began. "You've come to watch bitches do battle so let's get on with this bare-arsed, knock 'em down and drag 'em out, no holds barred cat-fight between the challengers, the Bitches from the Bull, on my right, (Loud cheers) and the Trident Witches, on my left." (Even louder applause). "Round one," he announced. "Individual tit tug o' war. Who's going first for you girls?"

They had worked it out beforehand. She hadn't done this sort of thing before, so Renee, their unofficial captain, would open, Laura would close, and she'd be sandwiched in the middle with a view of the first pair to warn her what to expect, but not carrying the responsibility of last girl in though. However, by the rules they would have to rotate the order as the night progressed, so that all had a fair crack of the whip, as Fred jovially termed it!

The arrangements were simple. Two lengths of cord, passing through a common steel ring, such as might ordinarily carry keys, and bearing on each end one of the ubiquitous clamps she was beginning to both expect and fear. Nasty little toothed devices with a built in toggle mechanism which ensured that the harder the pull on the cord the tighter the jaws would grip. Painful enough from the start when applied to delicate female parts, becoming unbearable as the pull and the pressure increased but ensuring that there was never any possibility of even the slightest relief by slipping, only extra torment to be endured.

Each contestant kicked off her shoes, heels were hardly practical for this event however sexily they shaped their legs, and applied the clamps to her own teats, adjusting them carefully to try and minimise the hurt while ensuring that they were securely on. If they were to come adrift due to improper positioning, the match was forfeit and the discomfort endured would have been all in vain. Once satisfied with her nipple clips each girl then placed her hands behind her back to indicate she was ready and one of the many men eager to assist, placed handcuffs on her wrists to ensure they stayed there.

The contestants were manoeuvred into place either side of a white line painted from front to back of the small stage and the signal to begin was given. At once each girl leant back to take up the slack and apply pressure to the other girl's tender teats. The length of the cords was such that they stood a yard either side of the mark and each tried to exert enough pressure to drag her opponent over the line while enduring the painful grip on her own delicate nubbins. The arrangement of cords ensured that each teat on each girl had to endure the same pull and pressure and it was a matter of who could stand the crushing squeeze on their sore dugs the longest without giving ground to ease the unbearable agony in the tender gristly peaks.

It seemed they were equally matched in strength and endurance. For several minutes the only movement was the stretching of their mammaries as each increased and resisted the pressure. They were evenly matched physically. Renee sported a pair of large firm breasts, with prominent nipples, thick high buttons when at rest, now elongated and flattened by the pitiless pull of the clamps, while her opponent carried equally formidable globes and appurtenances in comparable crushed condition. As the minutes passed each girl began to groan under the strain of the agony in their breasts and beads of sweat stood out on their naked bodies. Renee was moving her head from side to side slowly, making little animal grunts; her opponent had her mouth open and a small thin keening came from her tightened throat.

So far neither had gained an inch, despite the shouts of encouragement from their supporters and calls to heave the bitch over or tear the tits off her. The girl from the Bull was first to try and break the deadlock. With an audible intake of breath to prepare herself, she threw her weight back, dragging a scream from her own lips, and an answering cry from Renee, who gave ground, her stockinged feet now six inches from the line. But she held it and the attacker became the attacked as she ran out of steam to sustain the self-imposed torture of her stressed tits. She relaxed her effort, seeking to stabilise the situation and consolidate her territorial advantage but Renee was having none of it. As soon as she felt the other girl relax the remorseless pressure on their suffering mammaries, she threw herself backwards, forcing a shriek from her opponent to match the shrill scream with which she had launched the new attack, and carrying her forward. This time there was no relief. Caught off balance by the unexpectedly quick counter-attack, the other girl was still screaming as Renee hauled her across the line and collapsed to her knees from the effort.

Watching Renee in action, the number two of the Trident team felt her belly crawl, and her nipples harden at the sight. The butterflies in her stomach were hardly quietened by Renee's moans as the clips were prised from her tit meat, or the sight of the terrible tooth marks that had all but bitten through those tender points. Now it was her own turn to taste their bite and she went forward with a weakness in her knees, fighting a desire to cover her nipples with her hands to protect them from the same fate. Actually she was proud of her breasts, and with good reason; nice tight cones of succulent flesh crowned with very prominent teats of a dark pink; appetising morsels for a man's mouth, or a girl's come to that. No, she would have walked proudly, throwing them out deliberately if it was just a matter of exposing them to public gaze, but those teeth! Ah that was something different and instinctively she shielded them with trembling fingers until the last moment.

When she finally could cover them no longer and had to offer her pert gristly nubbins to the hungry steel jaws, she found the clips were all that she had feared, and more. She rolled her left dug carefully between the fingers of one hand, holding the hated clip in the other, until her nipple erected and she could place the jaws close to its base where it met the slightly darker circle of the areola. She pulled firmly on it to ensure maximum extension, both to ease the pain to come, Renee had advised her that it was tenderest on the tip, and to make sure it did not disqualify her by slipping off during the contest.

Try as she might to set them in place without causing herself unbearable pain, she was panting and gasping even before the contest proper began. Although they were designed to maintain their hold by increasing their grip in proportion to the pull on them, the clips also carried a venomous initial bite which was enough to have her flinch as she let the jaws close on each tender nipple, shaking her head, and biting her lip to keep herself from ripping them from her delicate points and fleeing the stage.

Finally it was done, and she put her hands behind her for the cuffs and the feeling of helplessness they brought. A woman with her hands fastened behind her is peculiarly vulnerable and she was very conscious of her position. Only then did she have time to consider her opponent. Somehow she was unprepared for the look of pain on the girl's face, but she had been too much distracted by her own aching tits to fully realise that the other girl was hurting just as much.

The MC called them to take up the strain and she winced anew. If the initial bite was tough, even the slightest extra pull on the cords sent shock waves of pain through her tender teats and into the stretched meat of her breasts. She tried to brace herself against the pain to come. As the MC gave the command to pull she sent her weight backwards and fairly howled at the agony it produced. She set her teeth and, moaning and hissing, tried to resist the inexorable pressure, her tortured nipples crying out for relief, praying for even just a second's relaxation. Instinctively she moved her feet forward half a step towards the line. There were cheers from

97

the Bull's supporters, and groans from her own, as she teetered on the edge of defeat. With a despairing cry she set her feet firmly and tried to off-balance her opponent by throwing her weight back suddenly but the damage to her own aching breasts was too much. The strain of the pull was drawing them out into unflattering stretched cones, the pretty buds of her teats flattened out of recognition. As she tried to hold her ground the girl from the Bull counter-attacked and, with both girls screaming hoarsely, dragged her onto her toes and, keeping up the assault, over-balanced her so that she had to step forward to avoid falling. Fred, the MC held up his hand and it was all over. Well not quite all. As she wept in mortification at her defeat, Renee released the cuffs from her wrists and loosed the clips from her throbbing dugs. She whimpered in pain as the blood ran back into the tortured flesh of the crushed points.

Laura went next, repeating Renee's success, using much the same tactics, resisting the initial attack by her opponent, then counter-attacking fiercely until the girl caved in and let herself be dragged forward by her racked and anguished nipples.

Fred announced the score; two bouts to the Tridents, one to the Bulls, 8 points against 4.

"Well that's a pretty good start," Renee observed. "Let's hope the other events go as well."

Laura had been facing the other way, looking over Renee's shoulder while she was speaking. Now her face screwed up in disgust.

"I don't know about that," she said, without enthusiasm. "Look what they've brought on."

Her teammates turned to see two of the men wheeling on a metal rack, such as is used in the rag trade to transport clothes or display them in a store. This one, however, didn't come with a row of fashion garments on hangers, but, instead, it carried half-a-dozen bulging red rubber enema bags, their menacing tubes clamped off and, dangling down below, black plastic nozzles, as big as a man's prick, with just a drop or two of pearly liquid on their tips to prove that the contents were thick and potent. Beyond them they saw the Bull's team grinning in triumph.

Laura groaned.

"The rotten bitches," she moaned. "God how I hate enemas. It's just gross, and in front of everybody too. Oh yuck!"

Nobody else was looking very pleased on the Trident team, but the Bull bitches were smirking smugly, as if hugging some secret to themselves.

Fred explained the rules. They all started square, getting their unwelcome bellyfuls together, then they had to stand in a ring marked on the floor. On the very front of the stage a row of buckets had been placed and, as each girl left the ring to get to a bucket and void her aching gut, she had to do so in full view of the mocking audience. The winner was the last in the ring, with others placed in the order in which they left it.

It was humiliating right from the start as a pot of Vaseline was passed round and each girl had to lubricate her own anus to accept the man-sized nozzles. Jenny would have tried to do without but the others persuaded her it might be a bad idea to risk tearing her rectal lining. Those black penises would try any girl's back passage, even with the lubricant. Dry, it was a risk not worth taking. They were going to be humiliated enough in the near future, nothing was more certain, so she might as well avoid adding injury to insult. Blushing with shame she crouched and thumbed a generous portion of the pale greasy jelly into her apprehensive orifice, conscious that she was being watched by scores of mocking eyes.

They were made to line up on all fours, three each side of the rack of dripping enemas, their bare buttocks, with their lubricated anal openings, turned towards the rack. Willing volunteers from the audience came up and worked the nozzles deep between their buttocks until they almost disappeared; responding to Fred's injunction to, "Put them right up. We don't want them to miss any."

As far as she was concerned the more she missed the better. The girl from the audience who claimed the right to insert her nozzle did not believe in half measures. She stood over her back, a nyloned calf either side of her bare waist, trapping her body securely, and probed with a sharp nailed forefinger for the shrinking anus. Her mark located, she placed the blunt nose of the nozzle against the sunken dimple and without the slightest introduction or preliminaries, thrust it forcefully home right up to the base where the rubber tubing joined it. She bucked at the impalement, letting out a small shocked cry.

"Save your breath," her remorseless impaler advised. "You're going to need all you've got once they open the clips and let the enema fill your belly. I hear it's a mixture of glycerine and castor oil, and it's been warmed too. Your guts are going to turn themselves inside out once they've swallowed that dose. Those bags take a litre and a half if they're well-filled and these are positively bulging."

It was bad enough waiting with a fearsomely dimensioned dildo stretching her anus and filling her rectum. In some sense her crouched position protected her from public gaze, but its implications and her butt-up posture were humiliating in the extreme; and she had hardly started yet! Fred called to the assistants and, as one, the clips on the feed pipes were loosed and the noxious mixture began to flow under the pressure of the elevated bags. She could feel it squirting into her belly

Hot castor oil, with glycerine topping! It was a powerful brew and her belly reacted at once. Even while she was still crouching the first spasms began to hit. Her guts cramped and her anus ached to expel the lethal cocktail but there was no chance of that. The butt plug was large and inflexible and it had been inserted so far that her sphincter had closed over it and was holding it immobile. After several minutes had passed Fred went along the line checking the bags to see if they had been fully emptied. He found a couple where there seemed to have been sufficient resistance from the connected colon that there was some residue, and these he had the minder press by hand until the last drop had been forced into the reluctant bowel beneath. Finally, satisfied that all had swallowed their dose he ordered the nozzles extracted.

"And keep those bums closed tight," he warned. "Any leaks and you're out."

She found it almost as hard to bear as the abrupt insertion, as the girl in charge of her whipped it from her cringing bottom hole as ruthlessly as she had thrust it in; worse perhaps; as she feared she might lose control as it parted and discharge onto the stage, losing the contest before it had fairly begun and disgracing herself in public into the bargain. She whimpered in her panic as the cramps in her belly increased past bearing. Now they were ordered to their feet, the Trident girls huddling together for comfort with no agreed plan of action to carry them through the contest.

It was obvious that the girls from the Bull were infinitely better prepared; indeed they had probably been in training for just this event. For a start they looked far less affected by the noxious brew, whose strength and effectiveness had taken the Trident girls completely by surprise. And while the latter were still trying to come to terms with their cramps and spasms, the difficulty of keeping their protesting sphincters closed, hopping from foot to foot, bent half double with their arms across their heaving stomachs, the girls from the Bull converged on them, picking them off one by one, digging a sharp elbow in a straining belly here, thrusting a bone hard knee between shaking thighs from behind there, generally

101

buffeting and hustling the competition.

Jenny found herself swept willy-nilly from the circle and the MC declared her 'out'. She made the best of a bad job waddling, spasming and leaking, to the front of the stage. Some sadistic genius had arranged the buckets on the very edge, so that a girl had to turn her back and display her spouting butt as she squatted over her bucket; all thoughts of modesty and restraint abandoned in her urgent need. Flatulent blurts and watery eruptions accompanied her noisy evacuations as waves of embarrassment and humiliation swept over her in her public degradation. Renee crouched over the bucket beside her and it would have been a complete whitewash, with the Bulls registering maximum points, if one of them had not tackled Laura with more enthusiasm than sense and, misjudging her aim, bounced off the blonde's ample buttocks to spin out of the circle herself, seconds before Laura crossed the line. The Tridents crouched in misery on their line of brimming buckets as Fred declared the Bulls the winners by 14 points to 7.

She was trying to wipe her soiled bottom, and get her belly to stop cramping, when the announcement was made.

"How do they work that out?" she asked Renee, who was conducting a similar hygiene exercise alongside.

"You add up the placings, and that's the other side's score," Renee explained, "We were 3, 5 and 6. Thank God Laura managed to hang in there or it would have been 15 - 6, and we'd have been really up the creek."

As it was, the score stood at 18 - 15 to the Bull Bitches, and they would have to work hard to overcome the deficit.

There was a short interval while the residue of the enema contest was cleared away, then they were called out for round three. This time the equipment was pretty basic; just a large bucket, a broomstick and... those damned clips again!

She groaned at the sight of them and was not cheered when Fred explained the nature of the contest. They were back to individual trials of strength again, a girl at each end of the stick, the bucket secured by its handle in a groove exactly half way along. At each end a pair of the deadly toggle clips was fastened to either end of a short cord going through a metal eye screwed into the end of the rod. With a clip on each labia, the girls could lift the bucket off the floor by straightening their legs, the weight of the bucket, and its contents, being shared equally between them.

The contents were the killer. The weight of the bucket, she found, only evoked a bearable pain in her fleshy lips, despite the high initial tension of the built in springs but, with each round, a smaller container of water was emptied into the big bucket, and the weight soon became considerable.

After each lift, they were allowed to crouch; their wrists cuffed behind them, and let the bucket rest on the floor, while another couple of litres was poured in. Then, on command, each had to straighten her legs, and lift the bucket clear, taking its weight on her sore stretched labia, which soon began to look like flaps of raw meat as they reddened and swelled around the fearsome bite of the serrated jaws.

She was suffering badly after the fourth fill, and could feel the sweat running down her back from the effort and the pain, but she felt she could cope. This was just pain, and a woman should be able to take that, especially in her genitals. She was made for that by nature, and she would live up to it. Besides, she had not contributed much to the team effort so far, and she had to make amends if it killed her. As the command to take the load came again, she bit her lip, and straightened her knees, feeling the agony in her stressed vulva, the whole genital area now inflamed and protesting violently at the abuse to which it was being subjected. She risked a glance up at her opponent and was gratified to see that she too was covered in a film of sweat and that her face was screwed up in a mask of pain to match her own. The bitch was vulnerable after all. Next round she would get her.

Fred let them relax after the mandatory ten second hold, then called to a helper to add another measure. By now there were eight quarts, twenty pounds of water in the bucket, and each pair of wrenched labia would have to lift ten pounds weight. It wasn't just the direct weight either. That weight got translated into pressure from those devilish serrated jaws, steel teeth that threatened to bit right through the tender flaps that enclosed her female parts. Whining through her nose, her lower lip caught between her even white teeth she forced her legs to straighten, ignoring the pain it created in her suffering cunt, driving herself remorselessly upwards, taking her end of the pole and her share of the weight with her. She could feel her opponent respond as the pole levelled but before Fred had counted three it began to dip again. She opened her eyes and looked up from the view of her own stressed fork to see the other girl slowly sinking as her knees buckled under her. She held on until the other's knees touched the ground, then folded gratefully herself, oblivious to the fresh anguish that always accompanied the relaxation of the horrible jaws, and the restoration of circulation in flesh that had had the blood crushed out of it. Her sex may have been ruined but her honour was restored, she felt.

She had moved to take the first bout, and Laura followed. At first she seemed to be doing well. Her opponent, another blonde, seemed to be extra sensitive about the genitals, and flinched from the clips from the beginning, even making a false start on one occasion, spilling a little water from the bucket as she more or less staggered to her feet, rather than lift her end of the pole smoothly. Two lifts later and she seemed to be in some distress, whimpering and writhing as she tried to maintain her load for the necessary ten seconds, but then disaster struck. As she straightened her legs for what must surely have been the final lift, for the blonde was surely in too much pain to go on now, Laura must have moved her feet slightly, to get a better stance for the increased weight, and slipped on the spilt water. One leg flew sideways, and she came down heavily on her cunt, the wooden pole she had been lifting between her legs now catching her in the genitals. She screamed in fright and pain and fell on her back and was ruled out.

That left Renee to try and salvage something from the wreck. She was up against the anchor of the Bull's team, a big brown girl, whose beautiful features suggested she or her family had come from some East African country on the Nile, though the paleness of her colouring also suggested that a more recent ancestor was European. Whatever her origins, she was a formidable opponent, big, strong and brave, and had already scored well for her side. Renee went up against her with a determined look.

It was ding-dong all the way. Neither gave an inch, each lifting cleanly each time the bucket was added to, each suppressing her suffering to grunts and hisses, though they could not disguise the sweat of agony that streaked their naked bodies, or the hapless state of their genitals where the labia stretched like rubber and the teeth bit deep. The bucket was nearly full now and Fred looked at it doubtfully, trying to assess if there was any risk of damage to these battling beauties.

"Fill it up," he ordered. "Right to the brim. Let's finish this thing."

The helpers poured in water carefully, until it lapped the rim of the bucket, and the MC gave the word. Slowly, painfully, both girls responded, forcing their knees down to lift the hideous burden from the floor. Inch by painful inch it rose to grunts and whimpers from the two contestants. Their bellies strained and twitched as they held their positions. Snot ran from their nostrils as they snorted down their noses, shaking their heads as if to try and clear them. Fred counted steadily on.

"...five...six," surely something, or someone would have

to give, but no, the two straining figures held their agonised ground, "...nine...TEN! I declare a draw," Fred concluded, and both whimpering girls collapsed to the floor, the bucket falling with a crash, water flooding the stage.

Four points each, and the Tridents still trailing 19 - 22 at the halfway mark. Time was running out to make a comeback.

The next event was another Bull choice, and Laura groaned as the rules were explained.

"What's with those Bull men?" she complained. "They're so anal!"

"More like plain sadistic," Renee suggested. "This is going to hurt."

She was right of course. The equipment was simplicity itself, another broom handle but with its ends capped with smooth plastic balls, nearly two inches across. The Vaseline pot was passed round again, to provide lubrication and a minimum of protection to delicate anuses already tender from the enema exercise, and the girls paired off again, on hands and knees, butt to swelling butt. A helper thrust one ball end up against a shrinking fundament and worked it in, to the accompaniment of assorted groans and grunts from the unwilling recipient. The girl gave a shocked gasp as it finally forced her straining sphincter and sank suddenly deep into her reluctant rectum.

With one end lodged deep in a protesting gut, the helper turned her attention to the other end and coaxed the opposition into crawling back and pressing her wrinkled dimple tight against the second ball end. With all possible slack taken up, the helper was able to thrust this end home as deeply as the first, leaving both girls panting and gasping like fish out of water, joined together by the arse, with a yard of pole separating them.

They had been positioned in the same circle where they had stood to try and hold their enemas, each facing outwards, pressing back against the padded pole in her guts. Fred called,

"Shove," and they thrust as one, trying to push the other out of the ring. The effect took Laura, who had opened for the Tridents, by surprise and she screamed at the sudden pain in her belly, so much more sharp and rending than she had expected. She gave ground, but managed to stay in the ring by moving sideways and the conjoined pair began to rotate like some maniac's toy, spinning slowly round. It couldn't last and, as her opponent gave a series of short sharp jerks of her hips, Laura screamed again, and threw herself forward onto her belly, relieving the pressure in her entrails, but hitting the ground outside the ring with her dangling bare breasts.

Laura out, and now it was Jenny's turn. She'd drawn the brown girl, who took the pole end first and she was startled to see that the anus she offered to the intruding ball was as strangely rimmed as her two friends. Actually, come to think of it, the previous girl had displayed the same raised rubbery ring around what in other women was a depressed dimple. Before she could think more about what it might imply Fred was ordering her to take her position behind the bent brown buttocks and ease herself back onto the pole.

It felt enormous. Surely it couldn't penetrate her delicately furled orifice without splitting her? Henry had buggered her often enough, indeed he didn't seem able to have enough of her warm humid rectal tube but, magnificent as his erection was in full lust for her lascivious loins, its girth could not compare with this unyielding plastic butt plugger. She bit her lip and tried to hold steady as the helper shoved it none too gently into the reluctant ring of anal retaining muscle. Just as she thought it must tear, and her mouth was opening to let out a scream to protest the agony it was arousing by its anal rape, it forced the pass and sank suddenly deep into her guts. She jerked forward to relieve the pain of it hitting the wall of her bowel, first indication of the anguish she would be subjected to when the brown beauty really began to thrust.

There was a pause of a second or two, as they were

marshalled into the centre of the ring. Then Fred called and they were off.

It was every bit as bad as she had feared, a numbing sort of pain in her gut that seemed to spread throughout her belly. She only hoped the men had got it right and that the ball ends would be sufficient protection against internal damage. For the moment the impalement felt more like a sword in her entrails than a smooth plastic sphere... a bayonet not a billiard ball. She screamed as her tawny opponent began a series of short sharp jabs with her hips, apparently impervious to the pain herself, and she scrambled sideways to try and get away without crossing the line. Once again she sensed that these bitches from the Bull had had prior notice of what their men were cooking up for the match, and had been able to practice tactics, rather than meet the monstrous pain quite unprepared, like the Tridents. In despair she tried to make some sort of riposte, jerking back her hips and being rewarded by a short cry of agony from behind, echoing her own, but it was too little, too late. In return she caught a blast that had her rolling sideways, her shackled hands helpless to support her, her head and shoulders out of the ring.

If it wasn't for Renee's sheer gut courage against the softer blonde from the Bull, they would have been destroyed. As it was Renee sweated it out with the golden haired Bull bitch, shove for shove, scream for scream until, by sheer guts and will-power she wore the other down. Inch by inch she drove her to the edge and when, with a final despairing shriek, the blonde flopped onto her big soft dugs, her face on the floor inches outside the ring, she had to be helped away, crouched over her aching belly. And the score line didn't help their morale any. 8 - 4 against them and the deficit widened to seven points. They would have to take both the last two events to make that up and in their present battered condition, it seemed an almost hopeless task.

All six girls were in a distressed condition, the abuse of

their guts having taken its toll, and a time-out was called while they cleaned up their soiled buttocks and tried to freshen their tear stained faces.

"I don't want to go through that again," Renee said bitterly, "I think that was the worst thing I've ever endured. I'll take a flogging to the blood any day, rather than have those things up my bum again. Let's hope our men put in something more civilised for the next event."

What the menfolk from the Trident had provided for them was a towel-rail, the sort connected to the central heating to keep the Terry towelling warm and fluffy, but adapted for something more fleshy than bath sheets and face cloths. It was mounted on a solid wooden base and connected to somewhere back stage by a set of hoses. Fred came front stage again.

"The Trident men have provided us with a novelty tonight. The hoses you see are connected to a shower head," he explained, "which gives us complete control over the temperature of the water flowing through the rack and, particularly, the top rail. The little ladies sit astride the rail, facing each other, and the last one to leave is the winner."

"Jeeeze! They're going to scald the cunts off us," Renee muttered. "It's all Tom's doing, I know. He's been banging away out in his workshop all week. And he's been making silly little jokes about how I'll have a hot cunt by Saturday night. I'll give him hot cunt."

"Cheer up," Laura urged. "It's going to be equally hot at the bitches' end, and they haven't had prior notice of this one. Bite your lip and think of England. We're just as tough as them. It's only bad luck, and a bit of quiet cheating on their part that's got us so far behind. We can do it."

She was as good as her word. When the time same, she swung her leg over the rail, and parted her fleshy labia carefully, until they clung either side of it, then put her hands behind her for the inevitable cuffs. The other blonde faced her, equally divided by the chrome tube in the slice between her thighs, and Fred called for the blocks they had used for mounting to be removed. Now they carried all their weight on their split vulvas, their most intimate flesh pressed tight against the pipe, still chill from the cold water that filled it.

Fred signalled to the assistant in charge of the showerhead. For half a minute nothing happened but then, first one then the other of the naked beauties mounted on the rail began to squirm and shift as the heat began to get to them. As the flow increased, they could be seen to rock backwards and forwards, trying to spread the heat over as much of their feminine folds as they could, relieving one extremity of their vulval slot when it could take no more, only to rock back again as the other end had had enough. In any case they couldn't free the whole length and the temperature was still rising. The Bull blonde was sweating now, and whimpering quietly, while Laura managed to maintain a psychological advantage by appearing not to be suffering, although her twitchy belly and strained thighs gave her away. The shower control had been on maximum for some minutes now, and both girls were red-faced and perspiration ran freely between their shoulder blades to disappear into the cracks of their bottoms, while their legs were making frantic pumping motions in time with the helpless but futile rocking of their bodies. Suddenly the girl from the Bull had had enough. She shrieked aloud and swung one leg over the rail, to be caught as she fell by one of the assistants. Thankfully Laura followed her example.

Renee went up next, onto a rail now chill as before, feeling its cold on her clit as she settled into place. She had drawn the short straw this time and was up against Dana, the beautiful African. The girl seemed immortal and unstoppable, sitting stony faced as the temperature rose, only the slightest movement of her body giving away the fact that the rail pressed into her fork was now hot enough to scald. She seemed unwilling to lean forward, but otherwise seemed little affected. Renee stuck it out bravely but could not match her. After five minutes of sweating struggle, punctuated by small moans of pain and futile rocking, she had had enough and called out in a strangled voice, asking to be got down.

With Renee and Laura gone, and only one win between them, it was Jenny's turn, and she just had to stick it out and score, or they were lost. With grim determination she walked up to the rail and mounted. Standing on the blocks, she carefully parted her thick red lips, then bent her knees and let the tender tissues of her cunt come down on the chill metal of the tube. She gave a small involuntary shudder, partly from the cold, partly from the thought of how that rail was going to feel in a minute, when the hot water was flowing freely through it. None of the girls who had gone before her had looked in the least happy with the scalding hot kisses on her pubes and she wasn't looking forward to it much herself. She put her hands behind her and felt the now familiar hardness of cuffs, and the feeling of helplessness and commitment that their embrace always induced. She let her weight fall fully on the rail, as Fred called for the blocks to be removed, and waited apprehensively for the water to flow between her legs.

At first nothing happened. The hoses were full of cold water from the cooling after the last pair had dismounted, and it took time for the hot water to reach them. Besides, the audience wanted a show and the temperature would be raised gradually to prolong their hot-crotched ride, leaving the watchers to scan their faces for the first signs of discomfort and speculate on which girl would cry 'enough' first as her vulva cooked on the slowly heating rail.

To begin with it was cold rather than heat that made them squirm. The water seemed almost chilled and she even wondered if the men, with their fiendish ingenuity and twisted sense of humour, had connected the flow through the cooling

111

equipment in the pub cellar. It certainly felt as if iced lager was flowing across her tender vaginal opening. The chill had begun to numb her before she sensed even the slightest rise in temperature and, when it came, her labia and the sensitive skin of her perineum were so frozen the warmth set up aches and tingles, like fingers frozen in the snow and then put under a hot tap. It didn't last long and her fear rose with the temperature between her legs. As she felt it rising she couldn't help remembering the agonised expressions on the other girls' faces, and their whimpers and moans as the temperature rose to scalding and they tried desperately, but in vain, to ease the torture in their cunts.

Now it was happening to her. The water had reached a quite respectable heat now, and she was beginning to feel it enough to want to try and lift herself off it. Without a foothold, and with her hands cuffed helplessly behind her back, all she could do was lean her weight forward to try and take the heat out of her perineum, and ease the weight on her coccyx. It hardly helped. Her weight and the steadily increasing heat were still on her vulva, scorching the delicate tissues round the meatus, touching the tip of her clit in this forward position. She moaned and rocked back again but found no comfort in applying the already scalded parts around her anus to the hot pipe that formed her seat. She tried to clench her thighs around the thin tube to help take some of her weight, but it was no more successful. With a pipe that small, she could get no significant grip and all she did was touch the scalding hot metal with the delicate skin of her inner thighs, nerve endings that had not been readied by contact with the tube as its temperature rose steadily, and which reacted in outrage at having it applied with no preparation. She flinched and hissed in pain.

The heat was really biting now. She moaned and shifted yet again. She could feel the sweat running down her back, and a trickle between her breasts. Her nose ran and her eyes

112

watered with the pain. She stole a glance at her opponent seated equally uncomfortably in front of her.

Good, the bitch was suffering too. She could see the clenching of her thighs, the rocking on her cunt, beads of perspiration standing out all over her strained body. I'll see you damned before I give in, she vowed, determined that this time she would do all she could and more to keep up her end.

She did it the traditional way, one step at a time. She bit her lip and counted to ten, as slowly as she could bear, then rocked slightly and began the count again. Die, bitch, die, she screamed in her mind. Aloud she whined shrilly, a hurt animal sound. She didn't hear the other girl's answering cries but suddenly she wasn't there. She was alone on the horrid bar, her mind almost too dazed to take it in and then the pipe turned cold between her thighs and she was being lifted off by strong male arms and set on the ground, the hurt in her groin subsiding into mere throbbing soreness.

Another time out, with drinks and ice cold cloths for sore pudenda, although the cold itself made breath come hissing in on first application. The Trident girls huddled together as if for protection, and contemplated the task ahead. 8 - 4 to them that round, so they went into the last 31 - 34 down. They'd have to make a supreme effort if they were going to overhaul that tally in one game, whatever it was.

Fred came to the front of the stage again to give the details. Clit poker, he called it, and once again produced the hated toggle clamps, but a different twist this time. Gone were the rather wide flat jaws that had crushed their teats and labia until they had screamed. They had been replaced with longer, narrower versions, more like the crocodile clips she had worn on the hunt of blessed memory, but those had not featured toggles to tighten the grip in proportion to the load hanging on them. She accepted the pair offered her with justifiable apprehension, after all, every time they had had clips on

113

before it had hurt atrociously, and her fear was soon justified.

For a start a clitoris, even on a sexually heightened female like herself, is not so large that reasonable sized jaws cannot be got around it. She did her best to get it to engorge, stroking a finger round the tip, and up and down its fluted spine; to have put the jaws on the tip itself was unthinkable and she worked hard to increase the size of the rapidly swelling little organ, so that she could place the jaws on its root. At last, panting and red-faced from her public masturbation, she felt she could find room for the jaws along the underside of the sloping wedge and coaxed them into place, grimacing in pain as she eased the pressure on the handles, letting the weight of the springs fall on the jaws, driving the teeth into her most feminine flesh. Their men had no intention of damaging them, or their sexual apparatus, so the teeth were not sharpened but they still indented the tender tissues deeply, with corresponding agony. At last it was done and she could straighten stiffly, the short chain attached to the clip, with its small hook, dangling between her bare thighs as she took her place in the circle of similarly equipped girls.

Glancing round the ring, she was struck by the beauty and variety of the clits on parade. They all seemed to be above average but her guess was that it was more nurture than nature. She was very aware that her own prized possession had grown significantly since she had entered the sensual world of Sexton Hinds, and she strongly suspected that the others were the same.

All but Dana. That magnificent specimen must surely be her birthright rather than some artificial creation, her clit was large and proud, a pink tip protruding from a substantial knurled brown roll lying along the slit between her fleshy lips. Actually she seemed to be having some difficulty adjusting to the clip which held the fat little cylinder atrociously tightly and she had been the last to offer her hands for the inevitable cuffs and take her place in the circle. Jenny

114

couldn't find the words to describe this beauty Dana wore between her fat brown labia. A bizarre lipstick laid in the furrow of the plump lips, the pink end set in its fat brown case? An asparagus tip, stained red and wrapped in brown bread, laid out on a plate? Perhaps. At any rate it looked good enough to eat and she felt a surge of lust ripple through her belly, diverting her thoughts from the contest to come.

But not for long. Fred was arranging his equipment on a small stool in the centre of the ring; a weight pan, with a ring to engage to hooks on their chains, and a box of gleaming brass weights.

"It's a simple game," he explained. "You each step forward and bend your knees so that I can engage the hook on your chain in the ring on the pan, then you straighten your legs and lift it cleanly. If it's a good lift, you go back in the line, and the next girl takes her turn."

"Is that all?" someone wanted to know.

"Oh how silly of me," Fred replied in mock dismay. "Did I forget to mention that each girl can call for as many weights as she likes to be added before she attempts to lift the pan and, of course, if she manages it, the girls that follow have to lift the additional weight too. Think of it as clit poker."

Standing between Renee and Laura, Jenny looked at the heavy pieces of polished brass and shuddered.

"At least," she said glumly, "our tits have got off lightly. The men seem to be intent of making us one throbbing ache from arse to cunt. It's practically all been below the belt."

There wasn't time for any more chat. They stood while the inevitable cuffs rendered them helpless again, and the round began. First off was the blonde from the Bull. Without hesitation she asked for one weight and bent her knees to allow Fred to hook her to the pan. He had come equipped to do justice to the occasion with the white cotton gloves and formal manner of a referee at a snooker championship, setting the weight in the exact centre of the pan as if replacing the

115

black then setting the hook in place and standing back to allow unfettered view to the audience. The fair-haired girl straightened with care. That was a solid piece of brass Fred had put in place and, together with the pan and the initial grip of the clip, it was enough to make the girl grunt softly as she took up the strain and straightened her long shapely legs, the pan and its burden swinging gently between them.

"Good lift," Fred declared and she bent her knees and let the stool take the weight again quickly. Her slightly twisted lip told of the bite on her clit even at this early stage. Laura followed, without raising, as did the second girl from the Bull. When her own turn came she deemed it was time to step up the pace if they were to have any chance to make up the deficit. She called for another weight to be added, and bit down hard on her lower lip, as Fred slipped her hook into the ring. As steadily as she could manage she began to straighten. As the weight came on she began to regret she hadn't played it safe like the others and taken the minimum weight to start with, to get herself acclimatised. But she calculated they couldn't afford that luxury and had to go for broke. It cost her dear in sweat and strain, and her eyes were watering by the time Fred called out his approval and she lowered the pan back on the stool, grateful to be rid of it, at least for now.

Dana had come to the stand and, as Fred hooked her on, she thought she saw a small shadow of fear pass over the big brown girl's finely sculptured face. As the coffee coloured columns of her legs straightened, taking the weight, the girl seemed to wince. Was she showing weakness at last, after the apparently unstoppable performance so far? Watching closely every move, the redhead resolved to find out, following the brown girl's reactions until the point where she completed her lift and was able to set the brazen load back on its stool.

Renee seemed unperturbed for the moment though she

didn't raise the stakes, and made a clean lift with only a sour twist to her mouth, and a grunt to show it had got to her where it hurt.

The Bull's blonde lead didn't seem to like two weights any more than Dana, but managed to overcome the pain in her sexual centre enough to make a valid lift, though she gasped and moaned all the way. Laura and the next of the bitches were also content to leave the weights where they were and, even so, could only just make it. Laura's legs, in particular, seemed like rubber as she took the pan off its stand, and Fred had to hover round her for several seconds before he was satisfied and gave it the all clear. When she stood up from setting the pan back on its stand there were tears streaming down her cheeks, and the corners of her mouth were turned down in doleful commas of distress.

Once more it seemed to be up to Jenny to crank up the pace. With a quaking belly she asked Fred for another weight, three now, and not an easy dinner to digest. Very carefully she straightened, taking the weight on her clamped clit, the jaws gouging in under the extra load. She whined noisily, she just couldn't help it. The pain was atrocious, but she fought through it and, through a mist of pain, heard Fred call, "Clean lift."

Words more beautiful than a Shakespeare sonnet she thought hysterically as she sank down and let the stool take the strain.

She was still hurting when she looked across at Dana, but the ache melted away in hope as she saw the fear in the big girl's eyes. This was it, the moment of truth. Had she guessed right? Forgetting her own troubles with her chewed clit throbbing between her legs, she held her breath in excitement as Dana attempted the lift. She nearly managed it. She got it in the air and, for a moment, Jenny thought she had miscalculated but then the coffee coloured columns of the lovely legs folded like broken straws and Dana gave a howl of defeat as she sank back down again. That fat and luscious clit had proved a weakness after all... the female equivalent of an Achilles heel. One down and two to go.

But it was a Trident who bit the dust next. Laura had reached her limit. She tried bravely to get it up, but collapsed in tears like Dana before her. The strain was telling on them all now,

Nobody seemed keen to raise now, and the pan came back to Renee still with three weights. She looked across at the two bitches still standing and called for a fourth weight. With a grim face she started to lift. Half way up, and she seemed to have lost it. She hesitated, as if unable to go on then, throwing her head back in a long howl like a she wolf on heat, she gathered up her strength and went the last inch that had Fred calling another clean lift.

It was too much for the blonde. Ashen faced she made as if to try, got the chain taut, the pan rocking as if about to achieve lift-off, then dropped it back, wailing disconsolately at her own perceived weakness.

The second bitch was tougher. Small and wiry, she seemed able to bear this peculiar pain better than most. It cost her some, but she managed it, lifting a few inches at a time, giving a short shriek at each thrust of her legs, as if cheering herself on. When she set the pan down she too was crying openly.

Well, Jenny thought, no point in raising now, I'd only be attacking Renee and she's got enough to cope with. Besides, who says I can lift this lot anyway.

Once more she committed herself to the hideous bite of those sharp teeth on her most sensitive part, squeezing the life out of the nerve-rich stem, dragging painfully on it until it felt as if it would be torn out of her flesh. She had to let vent to her feelings as she struggled with the monster, shrieking disjointedly all the way up, but she managed it and stood back, hurt but relieved.

Renee made the only move possible and called for weight number five. As the audience oohed and aahed with anticipation, Fred did his referee turn again, centring the weight with mathematical precision, connecting the hook with a dramatic flourish, and Renee made her desperate last throw. It was hopeless but a brave effort. She screamed as she jerked the pan off the stool but fell back immediately onto her knees, her head bowed and her shoulders shaking with her sobs. Fred took the extra weight off and gestured the remaining bitch to come forward.

The girl seemed torn between leaving things as they were, and hoping she could outlast her one remaining opponent, or make an all out attack. She played for safety, and made a clean lift of the four, though it cost her dearly in tears and howls.

Then it was Jenny's turn again and she faced the same dilemma as the girl from the Bull, now on her knees, bent over her tortured groin. To stick or to raise? Finally she chose the latter, and Fred put back the weight that had been Renee's downfall. She prayed it wouldn't be her own.

Even after four rounds the slight tug on her sore clit, as Fred dropped the hook into the ring on the weight pan, sent a shudder through her. She was intensely aware of how much this was going to hurt and the tiny vibration through the connecting chain gave notice that that hurt was now immediate and inevitable. Trying her best not to let her knees tremble, she straightened slowly until she could feel the weight come on her throbbing female stem, then slowly, but steadily, increased the pressure. She had tried jerking the weight off the stool earlier, when it wasn't so heavy and decided it was a mistake. She would be best gritting her teeth and putting in a smooth seamless pull, taking the rising agony as it mounted and hoping that she could make it all the way, and that Fred wouldn't keep her hanging on the peak. She had got the weight of all the brass cylinders now and it was killing her. She mewled and grunted through clenched teeth as the toggle drove the teeth deeper into her tender flesh. It wasn't just that it hurt; it was the manner of the hurting. The teeth didn't actually penetrate her skin, but they indented it deeply, pressing on the root of her clitoris, where it lay at an angle above the rest of her vulva. The most sensitive nerve ends may have been in its tip, and thus spared the direct effect of the clamp along the base of the tapered ridge but, inside the crushed stem, the root was a mass of nerve bundles too, and the teeth bit into them remorselessly. It was like being connected to a live electric cable, at the same time as someone applied a hot iron to her flesh. She couldn't imagine anything more difficult for a woman to sustain, however tough. Her whole body cried out in revulsion and tears spurted from her eyes.

But she was winning her private battle with pain and supersensation. Her knees locked, she threw her head back and howled, Fred was merciful and the call came instantly. She collapsed to her knees, the pan catching the edge of the stool and spilling the weights which fell with an ominous thud to the floor.

While she knelt and wept, her whole body shaking with her sobs, Fred restored the weights to order and called the Bull's champion to the stand. She advanced firmly enough and, at first, it seemed she was going to try for it then, at the last moment, she shook her head and turned away.

Fred turned to the audience.

"Last girl retires," he announced, "12 - 9 to the Tridents, and the match tied at 43 all. I declare it a draw."

But before the girls could relax and hope that the rest of the evening would be a pleasant matter of some compensatory drinks and a little sex to make them better, there were interruptions from the floor where someone was calling for a tiebreaker.

"Yes! Yes!" agreed an excited female voice. "A tiebreaker.

Don't let them get away without a result."

Fred looked disconcerted for a moment, then bowed to the pressure and consulted with the men who owned the contestants, seated in privileged positions close to the stage. Some whispered conversation and he was up again to announce that a tiebreaker it would be, and a suitable event to serve as a decider had been agreed.

Jenny was squatting, thighs wide to allow Renee to apply a cold wet cloth to her aching clit and being congratulated on saving the match, when Fred made his announcement. It seemed it was a Pyrrhic victory after all. Now they were going to have to wind themselves up again to face an unknown tiebreaker, where all that was certain was that they weren't going to like it one bit. Renee tried to put a brave face on it.

"It can't be worse than what we've done already," she encouraged, "and you can bet those Bull's Head bitches are at least as sore as us. Besides, we came from behind and nailed them. They can't be too happy about that."

"You won't be quite so cheerful when you see what they're bringing out now," Laura observed darkly. "It's the tit breaker."

"Oh shit!" Renee said with emphasis. "I could have done without that."

The third member paused from bathing her inflamed and swollen clit.

"You mean tiebreaker, don't you," she said, still looking down at the puffy inflamed morsel of feminine flesh between her legs, so swollen it wouldn't even lie back between the fleshy lips of her labia.

"That too," Renee observed glumly, turning her head to see what was happening on stage, "I hoped the men would have had enough and settled for a draw but it seems we're really for it tonight."

"Can't be worse than what we've just been through," came

121

the reply, emphasised by a small hissing sound as she touched her misshapen erotic appendage too incautiously and sucked her breath in through clenched teeth. "Blast! I don't think I'm going to enjoy sex with this thing ever again."

"I'll ask you again in the morning, when Henry has waved his magic wand over it," Renee replied, "but right now I'm more worried about that tit breaker they've just wheeled out. We're none of us going to enjoy this very much I'm afraid but I, for one, am not going to let those cheating bitches take the match, not after all we've done to claw our way back. And especially after you damn near wrecked that pretty pink clit of yours, darling. They're not going to take that away from us."

Jenny looked up from her restorative work on her mangled sex bud to see what all the fuss was about. Nothing much at first glance, just a simple wooden stand, about breast high to a kneeling woman, for whose knees a shelf was provided a couple of inches above the floor, a smooth flat top about eighteen inches by twelve, with a shaped ridge along one long edge. A thin but menacing cane hung on a hook on the side together with a bundle of pieces of cord. It was difficult to see why it should arouse such consternation in her companions. They soon disillusioned her.

"It may look nothing," Laura explained. "But it's broken better girls than us. See that edge with the two curves scooped out of it? You have to kneel and let your tits lie in the cutouts, resting on the top of the table, and stay there while one of the other team cuts them with that cane. It may not look very heavy but on a girl's breasts it's hell," and she shuddered again at the thought of it.

"Those men of ours are total bastards," Renee observed grimly. "They didn't have to agree to a tiebreaker, they could have settled for a draw and even so, it needn't have been the tit breaker. I'm going to give that Tom hell in his bed for a week for this."

"No you're not," Laura told her. "You know perfectly well they're entirely within their rights to do so. We all gave them that right when we submitted to them and anyway it's part of the thrill that it's always just that little bit worse than we expect."

"Guess you're right," Renee agreed. "I'll settle with Tom at the Friday session for questioning him."

So now here they were lined up naked in front of an eager audience again, preparing to do battle for the honour of the Trident, and the pleasure of their men. Fred handed each of them a length of cord.

Jenny looked at it, puzzled.

"What do I do with this?" she asked.

"Wrap it round your tits, until they swell up tight," Laura told her, starting to attend to her own firm pair.

"But I can't wrap anything round mine," she complained. "They're sort of, you know, conical. I wouldn't be able to make it stick in place. Besides, why should I want to make them swell up? It's going to be bad enough as it is, having them lashed with that beastly cane, without blowing them up as well."

"That's what you think," she was corrected. "In the first place, any girl with any tits at all can tie them. Just lift one in your hand and start wrapping the cord round the base. As soon as you get a turn around it you'll find it begins to swell and you can make another, tighter turn. By the time you've wrapped it round three or four times, and pulled the knot tight, you'll find it well bedded in and your tits are tight and round as balloons."

"As to why you should do that to yourself, believe me it's for the best," Renee assured her. "For a start you've got to be sure they sit on the top there and don't slide away. If they're not well on display and ready for the other girl to cane them you'll be disqualified before you start but aside from that, you'll be better off anyway. If you let them flop on the top,

123

the cane will crush them against the hard wood and, believe me, you wouldn't want that. Tied up tight like this," she jiggled her own firm globes, now turning red and as round as beach balls, "the cane sort of bounces off. I won't try and kid you it doesn't hurt like hell but at least the bruising isn't as bad as if they were trapped against the table."

Jenny didn't argue; these two had been here before and she respected their advice. It proved to be easier than she had thought, her firm cones rapidly transforming themselves into hard red balls, her teats, always an outstanding pair of decorations on the milky globes now, not just engorged, but thrusting out as if propelled from within, huge as a goat's dugs. The sensation was odd and unsettling, her tight globes bouncing on her chest as she moved, as if with a life of their own. She felt top heavy; all tit.

The arrangements were simple. Each girl in turn knelt on the ledge at the front of the stand, pressing her chest against the top edge, and arranged her swollen breasts in scooped cutouts, so that they lay entirely on the tabletop. Once she had got them positioned correctly, she had to take her hands away and clasp them behind her neck, then tilt her chin up so as to allow direct access from above to the two tempting targets.

A girl of the opposite team stood on each side and, once the position was judged correct, lashed the cane down on the offered mammaries in turn. To qualify, the victim had to maintain her pose throughout. Since this was a tiebreaker there would be no concessions and any refusal to offer one's breasts, and failure to position them correctly, any involuntary grasping of wounded dugs before permission to rise was given, would lead to instant disqualification. Fred spelt it all out for them so that there would be no misunderstanding, then stood to one side and called the first girl forward.

Linda, the Bull's blonde member went first, and was understandably reluctant about it, but did enough to comply with the rules laid down for this demanding sport. She knelt, leant forward against the whipping stand, her trussed breasts cupped in her hands, and laid them in place. She adjusted the elastic globes carefully to fit them to the scoops, and drew her hands out from under them in a forward direction, to ensure they lay fully on the tabletop. She seemed far from keen to leave them there, so totally exposed and vulnerable but, eventually, took her hands away, clasped them behind her neck and tilted back her head until she was staring at the ceiling. Renee and Laura moved into position and Laura lifted the slim cane. At a nod from the MC, she brought it ripping down to strike across the darkly red meaty targets.

Linda screamed as the thin rod whipped into her turgid twins and an even darker line sprang up on the ruddy surface of their tops. She dropped her head on her chest as Laura handed over the stick, but straightened at once when Fred checked her. Renee lashed in a wicked stroke from the opposite side and drew another scream, the track of her cut paralleling Laura's, a half inch nearer the nipple. Linda was allowed to rise and Laura took her place. In moments a second pair of inflated breasts, darkly pink and with tumid teats thrusting fiercely, were set out for the torture of the rod. This time it was the girls from the Bull who were dishing it out and they didn't hold back. Laura screamed in her turn as the cane bit into the tender tit meat, across the swelling tops both sides. She screamed even louder at the second stroke from Dana's sinewy wrist. The tall brown girl could dish it out as well as take it.

Tina, the pocket Venus with the tautly muscled figure, laid her neat paps in the positioning grooves next. Her normally pert cones had become almost sausage shaped in the swollen elongation the harsh constriction of the cords around their base induced. Though they were small, the tight bondage made them easy targets. Laura, whose sore breasts might have hampered her stroke, handed the rod to the third

125

member of the team and the two Tridents hewed into Tina's soft vulnerable dugs.

Under other circumstances women might be expected to be somewhat inhibited in wounding another woman in that place, breasts having almost mystical properties for the female sex, but this was war and they had to hurt and be hurt if they were to survive. Each drove the searing rattan remorselessly, sending their target away tearful and shaking.

Now Jenny had to face up to this untried horror herself. Suddenly she felt terribly exposed and vulnerable, as if only just aware, for the first time, of the nudity she had worn all evening. Somehow she felt these swollen flushed caricatures of her usual smoothly curved hemispheres made her twice as conspicuous, their jutting finger-sized teats, hard and red, waving in mockery at the audience to remind them of her shameful exposure. Instinctively she wrapped her arms around them protectively as she walked to the front of the block.

"No good trying to shield them," Dana said, as she hesitated before the whipping stand, "I'm going to cut those turgid teats right off your chest."

She tried to ignore the ugly threat coming from those beautiful lips and dropped to her knees in front of the stand. She pressed her chest against the unfeeling wood, slick now with the perspiration from the sweating girls who had already taken their cuts, warm from the touch of their inflamed breasts, and lifted her inflated red globes onto the top. The shoulders of the cutout dug into their tender under-sides, and she squeezed them together a little to make them fit better. Her hands were trembling as she stroked them along the under-sides of the heavy orbs, settling them on the tabletop, sacrificial offerings on a temple altar, about to be immolated to appease some jealous Goddess. She put her hands behind her; her left palm cupped in her right, and tilted back her head, closing her eyes tight. She didn't want to see what was coming to her. Feeling it when it arrived would be quite enough without stretching out the agony by watching the girls prepare to thrash her tender breasts.

Linda held the rod first, bringing it down like a flashing sword. She might have avoided seeing its arrival, but there was no way she could shut out the ripping echo of its passage as the young blonde drove it into her, putting all the pain and shame of her own earlier breast whipping into it, as if that might somehow relieve the agony still infecting her own trussed and welted mammaries.

Now she knew why all the others had screamed. The pain when the cane bit into her swollen breasts, laid helplessly on the hardness of the tabletop was unlike any other, and quite unendurable. All she could do was let her mouth fall open and the bubbling cry issue forth, taking some of her wounded feelings with it. She shook her head, trying to clear it, urgently willing herself not to move, not to wrench herself away from the stand or remove her flaming dugs from further torture.

Her head had fallen forward in her struggles and she panted from the shock of the fearful cut, her hair loose and spilling over the livid track across the tops of the swelling mounds.

"Chin up, Darling," Dana said, sweetly. "If you thought that stung just wait until you feel what I've got for you."

With a small mewl of fear she forced her head to go back and leave the tortured breasts to Dana's untender mercy. It seems the brown girl had none on offer just then for her cut was vicious, hard and true, right across both straining heaps of girl flesh and it extracted its due of scream and sweat. Her victim rose to her feet still sniffling. Just two strokes! She could hardly believe it. She felt as thoroughly thrashed as if she had taken at least a butcher's dozen across her buttocks, and that from a penal. This tit breaker was a demanding sport alright.

Now it was the brown girl's own turn to lay out her goods

for processing. With seeming nonchalance she let her large tawny melons drape across the tabletop, as if challenging them to do their worst. Laura and Renee did the honours while the latest victim licked her wounds, each lashing down a searing cut. Dana gave a strangled grunt at each, but held back the screams that could just be detected choking in the back of her throat. Glum faced at their apparent failure to make any significant impression on the Junoesque Dana, Renee set her own tender tits on the stand, and contributed a couple of stricken screams of her own, as Dana and Linda, the former apparently quite unfazed by her own breast whipping, cut viciously into them, writing throbbing red lines across their delicate uplands.

One round completed, and Linda to go in again. She didn't seem keen on the idea but eventually got herself correctly placed. Laura sent in a sizzler which had her screaming again, her face falling forward, her shoulders shaking with her sobs. Fred had to give her a warning to get her to position herself again. Renee raised the whippy rod and drove it powerfully down to impact just above the nipples. It was too much for the blonde and, as a fresh scream rang round the room, her hands left her neck to wrap protectively round her wounded breasts. First blood to the Tridents.

Their jubilation did not last. Laura had to offer her bound teats for caning next. She approached the ordeal with a set face, positioned herself carefully, as if trying to spin out time before that fiendish stick would bite into the tops of her bound and swollen dugs. She took the first stroke well enough under the circumstances and with a great struggle she held her pose, all the while sobbing and choking from the agony of a full blooded cut into her tender flesh but like Linda before her, was too weakened by the pain and fear to take the second. Almost before Dana's ripping rod had fallen away, revealing another dark track on the reddened surfaces, she was covering them with her hands and rocking helplessly backwards and

128

forwards over her wounded treasures.

Fred checked out the strained and sweating girls, with their inflamed and welted breasts looking as if they had been laid on the bars of a barbecue, and called a three-minute time out.

The two survivors of the Trident team huddled together for support.

"We'll never break that Dana. She seems to be made of iron. We might as well give up now," she wailed into Renee's ear.

"We don't have to," Renee told her. "All we have to do is make sure we get Tina to rights, before they get us. Work it out for yourself. Linda went first, so we're one point up. So long as we can get second and third it doesn't matter that Dana is the individual winner. We get the team prize, and that's all that matters. One thing though," she went on. "When we have Dana on the block, don't bother with trying to hurt her breasts, or cut her nipples. Just make sure the rod goes into her armpit. If we can make her a bit sore there we might just slow her enough so we can take another round. I'm pretty sure Tina is about all in."

"And you don't think we are?" Jenny asked.

"Course not!" Renee assured her confidently. "You can go another round and that will be enough. You're made of the right stuff, I know."

The three minutes seemed to be over in a flash and they were back on stage, ready to continue with this savage breast-beating. Tina looked grim as she settled her small swollen tits on the frame and Renee brought the rod slicing down to extract a shriek of agony from her, her tears starting afresh. Renee passed the cane to her remaining teammate who laid it into Tina's lividly striped globes, grunting herself with the effort. Tina shrieked again and seemed to waver. With rising hope her opponents watched, thinking they saw salvation, but the pocket Venus held out, her elbows going back behind her shoulders and Fred indicated it was a fair stroke.

Up until now Jenny had been concentrating on trying to break Tina and had almost banished the thought of submitting to another onslaught on her own breasts, but now it came home to her like a blast of icy water that she was going to have to put them up on the sacrificial altar to suffer all that Tina and, especially, Dana could do to them. If she had felt vulnerably naked the first time she had approached the block, now she felt as if she had doffed her skin with her clothes. Her breath rasped in her throat as she lifted her sore and throbbing breasts in her hands and laid them in the grooves provided. She felt an almost overwhelming urge to place her hands on top of the tortured mounds to protect them but forced herself to clasp them behind her neck and set her elbows well clear of the trajectory that the rod would follow on its way to cut them.

She was past any pretence of holding back her cries. The moment was gone when she might salvage any dignity by appearing to be unmoved when it was obvious to anyone there that she was suffering excruciating agony as the cane bit deep into the tops of her bulging breasts, raising an instant welt as heavy as the pair that already adorned them. It was Dana who struck the first blow, to give Tina the maximum time to recover, and she could only hope that the small bitch from the Bull would be weakened enough that her stroke would be a fraction less devastating than the brown girl's murderous blow. She writhed and sobbed over her hurt mammaries as the rod changed hands, but finally managed to get herself into position to accept Tina's contribution to her agony. She howled in pain as it cut her just above the nipples, and rocked forward violently time and again, almost thrashing her head on the table top as she bent over her mangled beauties, but her hands never left her neck and as she regained a small measure of control Fred gave the all clear. She staggered to her feet, cradling her wounded dugs in her arms.

Dana, indeed, seemed unbeatable, mocking them as she slapped her great tiger striped globes on the line, as if challenging them to make any impression on her. For all her brave show, though, her lip was swollen and bitten as she set herself to take the cuts which her two opponents delivered with the strength of desperation. Renee went first, again to spare the most recently whipped girl as long as possible, and drove the rod across the very top of the bare brown mounds, narrowly missing the loops of hard cord tightly bound around their bases, hitting 'long' so that the cane wrapped around her side, biting into the tender flesh of her armpit, the tendons under the arm exposed by it being raised up high. Dana grunted loudly, obviously hurt, and dipped over the wounded part, but held her pose. Ten seconds later she gasped again, a second cut biting into the ligaments of her whipping arm. They could only hope they had done enough.

Renee took her place, her mouth a grim pained line. Like her teammate, she made no attempt to hide her pain, howling at each hideous cut she received, writhing like a cut-worm after each, but surviving, she knew not how. Fred called another two-minute break.

"It's got to be now or never," Renee told her companion. "Give it all you've got."

"Do you think it's safe to aim for her nipples? They're big and fat at the best of times, and now they're like a nanny goat in milk."

"You'll just have to see how you feel about hitting them true," Renee said doubtfully, "I think it might finish her, but you'd better not risk it if you've any doubts."

With the break Renee felt recovered enough to take first go again. As they stood either side of the block, Tina approached, her face white, her lip trembling. She knelt in front of the whipping stand and gingerly took her breasts in her hands, cupping them gently, flinching from the soreness just touching them created. Very carefully she laid them on the tabletop, leaning forward so that they lay fully on it, small round red lambs to the slaughter. She was already sobbing as she put her hands behind her head to offer them for their whipping. Renee obliged, driving the rod with all her remaining strength into the fullness of their upper sides, aiming for the seared tracks of the earlier strokes. Tina screamed and rocked her whole body, her elbows coming forward over her tortured tits. For ten seconds she wailed and writhed, then by some superhuman effort drove herself back upright.

Looking on, the cane Renee had passed her gripped nervously in her hand, Jenny willed the stricken girl to give up, then felt an emptiness in her own belly as she realised that the girl had survived the blow and, if she didn't finish it now, she herself would have to try and go another round, and she despaired of being able to take it. This tit breaker was punishing stuff, and no woman could be expected to keep going indefinitely. It was going to have to be all or nothing, the nipple shot or defeat. She looked at Tina's swollen mounds, where they lay on the hard polished surface of the wood, a surface now swimming in female tears and sweat. They were not all that large but, as she'd observed to Renee, the teats, always a magnificent pair of thumb-like projections, would now not disgrace a goat suckling its kid; ripe red juts of tight flesh, the elastic tubes inflated by the pressure generated in the martyred breasts by the tight constriction of the cords wrapped firmly round them close up to the girl's chest. If she could hit them true she was pretty sure she could split at least one and it was unreasonable to expect a woman to go on with a ruptured teat. Short of bursting her clitoris she could not imagine anything harder for a female to bear. With a cry of desperation, fear and anger all mixed up together, she lashed the cane down as hard as she knew just on the base of the pneumatic jut of the ripe and turgid teats.

132

Tina shrieked in anguish at the outrage to her tender points and dropped back on her heels, cradling her injured breasts in her arms, her head bowed over them, her whole body racked by sobs.

They had won, and she threw herself into Renee's waiting arms. Dana looked at them without understanding.

"It's not finished yet," she said with emphasis. "You've still got me to deal with, and you'll never break me."

"We believe you, Dana, darling," Jenny delivered the winning stroke, and the knowledge that she would not have to face any more of this hideous tit-breaker had restored her spirits miraculously, "and you've earned your victory. We resign but look at the score. 2, 3, and 5 makes 10, so even though you get to be first the team prize goes to us."

Later, in the ladies, licking their wounds, they made it up with the bitches and there were kisses all round. She even dipped quickly to her knees to kiss Dana's amazing clit.

"Darling it's lovely, I could eat it," she murmured.

Dana grinned with satisfaction.

"That could be arranged," the brown girl told her, smiling.

Later still, safely back in their bed together, Henry turned to her to give comfort in the best way possible for a healthy sensual young woman who has just had her bare breasts cruelly whipped.

"Turn over, darling," he whispered, "those poor sweet tits I love so much aren't going to want my touch tonight."

"No Henry, please. I want to feel your arms around me, and your mouth on mine. I don't care about sore tits any more. They'll love the feel of your hairy chest. I don't want to be treated gently at times like these. What I need now is a man who'll grab me and have me and make me better."

Henry made sure she got what she needed.

PART FOUR: TRAINED

Even more than after her 'triumph' in the treasure hunt, the successful battle with the bitches had made Jenny feel 'one of them', a true Sexton wife. She confided as much to her two friends

As was usually the case when they exchanged confidences and gossip, it was one of those occasions when Friday bottoms squirmed striped and hot on hard unsympathetic stools. Their blood was quickened by their burning buttocks and the emotions roused by their recent castigations at the hands of their conscientious and attentive men, and the added influence of short drinks and even shorter skirts led to that loosening of tongues so dangerous to the feminine gender.

"Can't be a Sexton wife 'til you're ringed and rimmed," Laura told her.

"You have to graduate before you're a real Swive," Renee added equally enigmatically.

"Ringed? Rimmed? Graduate? Come on girls," Jenny pleaded. "Give us a break. What's it all about?"

It took a while to penetrate their lust-and-alcohol softened brains, but it got there in the end.

"Oh no," Renee said emphatically. "We got it in the tail badly enough when we blabbed on to you about Friday girls. Tom'll skin my arse like raw liver if we tell tales out of school again."

"Yeah," Laura agreed, "George promised me a beating for breakfast every day for a fortnight if I didn't learn to control my tongue better. I don't think I'd fancy that. Mind you, a small livener occasionally, while the sheets are still warm, before he leaves for work, reassures a girl her man still cares for her but every day for two weeks! A woman could be seriously sore at the end of that."

Jenny let it drop. One didn't knowingly let one's friends in for a beating; well, not unless it was a bit of a lark. Still, she couldn't help wondering. Every time she seemed to be lifting the veil and coming closer to being a full initiate of this mysterious group the curtain seemed to move a little further away. Would it ever fully lift for her, she wondered.

She got her answer about a month later. She was sitting at breakfast with Henry, a warm comfortable feeling suffusing her belly, her teats still erect, her thighs still hot from last night's particularly satisfying bout of sexual exercise, when he remarked quite casually that Laura and Renee would be calling for her later that morning and she was to be ready to go with them for a little trip.

"What sort of trip?"

"What you've always wanted. To become a Sexton wife," came the calm and astonishing reply.

"How did you know about that?" she wanted to know.

"Oh come on!" he protested. "You don't think those two witches you hang out with could keep your girlish confidences to themselves do you? Besides," he added, as if stating an immutable law of nature, "they're fully fledged Sexton wives and know their duty. They each confessed to some slight indiscretion in the matter and will be taking their rewards with them on the flight. From what Tom and George told me, hot cross buns might be a fair description."

"I bet they will. Steaming hot and striped like tigers no doubt, in the generous way you men have," she replied, acidly, "but what's all this about flights?"

"Oh didn't I explain? We, more specifically Richard - but he makes it free to any of the men round here - have a very convenient villa in Marindorra, up in the mountains. Being an independent Principality the authorities don't interfere in private activities. In fact their laws are still based on women as property which suits us very well."

"I bet it does," she remarked. "That's all we are to you, aren't we?"

"Of course," he admitted, "but you are all very precious

135

property, and cherished much more highly than mere nagging wives could ever be or, heaven forefend, so called 'free' women. When you're not letting your hackles rise at phrases like women as property you might like to consider just how much love and care you receive as a mere chattel."

Mollified to some extent, her curiosity got the better of her again. She went to kneel beside him and place her hands on his knee.

"How long will I be away?"

"A month is usually sufficient to complete the initiation," he told her.

"A month! Oh my goodness. I'd better get packing now."

She jumped up and started for the door.

"Come back and finish your breakfast," Henry advised. "You're not going to need anything where you're going. You'll probably spend the whole month naked and, if there is anything you do need, the girls will provide it."

Gradually some inkling of what might be in store began to dawn on her.

"This is going to be tough, isn't it?" she said quietly, resuming her place by his knee.

"Mmm," Henry agreed, stroking her hair with loving gentleness. "Most girls do come back a bit chastened for a while, but no-one has actually come to any harm and they're all transformed in the end."

"What's going to happen to me, Henry?" she asked, in the same small voice.

"I don't know the details, that's strictly woman's business," was Henry's rather unhelpful reply. "I'm not familiar with the means employed, only with the results. A woman trained to give maximum sexual pleasure, and some interesting body modifications to go with her new status."

"What sort of modifications?"

"Haven't you noticed any little differences in your friends and the other women round here?" he asked in return. "You hussies go around in such a state of near nudity most of the time that you can't have missed them. Anyway," he cautioned, "don't you think you're asking a few too many questions for an obedient and submissive woman?"

She made a pout of distaste at the suggestion but was wise enough to refrain from pressing him further on what to expect in Marindorra but there was another question coming to the forefront of her mind which she couldn't prevent herself asking.

"If we three are going to be away for a month, you and Tom and George are going to get a bit lonely, aren't you?" she suggested.

"Eh, well, I expect it will be a case of share and share alike," Henry answered, somewhat evasively. "Plenty of guys round here will be willing to help out by lending a woman for a night or too. Besides," and she was rewarded by the rare sight of Henry looking a touch sheepish, "Greg is going to be away himself most of the month and suggested that I might like to try out Dana while he was away. Keep her up to the mark and so on," he added hastily, seeing the look in her eye. "Women can get so out of hand if you neglect them too long, and she has her needs."

She thumped him on the chest with both balled fists in only half pretended anger.

"You bastard!" she yelled. "You beast. I haven't even had her myself yet and I've earned her the hard way. I don't expect she cost you more than a few drinks at the bar and you didn't have to lay your tits on the line like I did and get them hacked with a beastly whippy cane. Ugh! They still ache a little, even now."

He held her hands gently but firmly and she quietened under his touch.

"Mm, I can see a month may be barely enough," he said. "Still you're ready and you want to go, and Laura and Renee will take no nonsense so you'll do well enough."

"What do you mean, I want to go? Nobody asked me," she came back indignantly.

"You mean to say you haven't made it clear to all and sundry that you want to be a true Sexton wife, whatever that might be?" he reproved her. "As to asking, a woman's the last person to give an opinion as to her treatment, and quite rightly so. No, I talked it over with Tom and George and we were all agreed you were ready for it, so off you go."

Evening found all three of them climbing a mountain pass in the big hired car, nearly two hours out from the airport.

"Nearly there, darling," Renee told her. "I think it's time you got your kit off. Girls go into the villa as naked as they leave it. Sets the right kind of atmosphere for what we're here for."

What exactly 'that' was, she had been unable to get from them so far. Renee had pointedly lifted her bum off the seat to show her a set of livid ridges that covered every inch of what was visible, which was considerable, given that her skirt barely reached her thighs when standing and, sitting, left nothing to even the most fevered imagination.

"Tom promised he'd have my back flogged if this wasn't enough to keep me quiet," she informed her, "and I'm not going to risk that. Bottom beatings are bad enough but at least there's something part way sensual about them that warms a girl's belly, but a bare-back flogging... That does nothing for a girl but hurt her, believe me."

So Jenny held her peace and did as she was told, pulling her blouse over her head and unclipping her bra to let her breasts fall free. Naked to the waist, she kicked off her shoes, and lifted her modest skirt to unclip a stocking and roll it down an ivory thigh and off her pinkly painted toes. When its fellow had joined it she lifted her bottom off the seat to pull down her panties and add them to the little heap of clothing that Laura was stuffing in a plastic bag she had produced for the occasion. With another wriggle of her svelte hips the skirt joined the rest and she sat on the cool leather of the rear seat as naked as the day she was born.

"Your rings please," Laura requested, "and I'll have your watch and your handbag as well. Nothing like being stripped of every last thing to put a girl in a receptive mood."

While she had been stripping, the car had debouched from the tight winding road of the pass onto the level floor of a rock-walled crater several miles across. Smooth green pastures and leafy hedgerows were interrupted here and there by the roofs of several large buildings. Renee guided the car to the gate that guarded one of these and spoke briefly into the intercom. The heavy iron gates slowly opened to let them in and they pulled up on the wide gravel sweep in front of the villa.

"This is where you leave us for a while," Renee informed her. "Just walk in the front door and you'll be taken care of. When we meet again it will be as your instructors and you will treat us accordingly. Now come here, darling," she turned in her seat and reached for the naked woman in the back and kissed her long and passionately. "That's the last until we're finished. Make the most of it. From now on all you'll get from Laura and me are tears and welts but, always remember, however much we hurt you, we do it for love and to make you one of us."

The door opened and she was thrust out onto the chill gravel of the driveway, small sharp stones hurt her bare feet as she stumbled across ten yards of it before she could reach the comfort of the steps leading up to the imposing front door. Even then she wasn't quite free of them, a handful of the sharpest and most tenacious digging into her soft feet and clinging on as she ascended the steps. She stopped and sat down to remove them, flinching at the feel of the cold stone on her bare bottom, very conscious of her nudity in a strange place. She was quite alone now for the car had pulled round the corner of the house, presumably towards a stable block or wherever vehicles were kept. Nothing for it, naked and alone she would have to enter this strange house and face whoever or whatever she met inside. She pushed open the heavy oaken leaf and stepped in. Marble slabs felt cold under her feet.

Helpless and hesitant she stood, having no other instructions and waited for someone to come. After a minute a tall gaunt woman appeared, probably a housekeeper from her dress, and gestured her to follow. Whether the woman was dumb or just did not care to speak Jenny never discovered. She followed the daunting figure down a hallway, into a narrow passage and down even chillier stone steps into what she assumed was a cellar. When the thick wooden door swung open though, she saw it was more of the nature of a dungeon, fitted with rings and frames on its grim stone walls, and a row of small barred cells, little more than cages, along one side. The housekeeper swung open the grille door of the nearest and invited her in. She had to crouch to enter; the roof was so low that there was no possibility of standing. With a clang the door closed behind her and the gaunt servitor turned a massive iron key to secure it before leaving by the iron-studded door by which they had entered, leaving her quite alone, naked and helpless.

At least there was light enough to see her surroundings. The cell, or rather, cage, was too small to stand up in and she had had to bend double to enter. It was obvious she couldn't remain like that indefinitely and she dropped to her knees while she investigated her new quarters. Along one side planks, raised a few inches off the floor, indicated a sleeping platform while, in the far corner, an ominous bucket with a lid suggested that toilet arrangements might be equally primitive. She squatted on her plank bed, which she decided was marginally preferable to the stone tiles of the floor itself, and awaited developments.

She was becoming stiff from having to squat, rather than stand, the height of the cage not permitting it, when there were footsteps outside and the door swung open to admit the jailor/housekeeper, bearing a stoneware jug and a wooden board with a hunk of coarse country bread. She pushed them through a small opening at the base of the barred door, and left again, still not having uttered a word. The purpose of her mission was pretty obvious though and she had had nothing to eat or drink since the plane had landed several hours ago. She tried the jug, and finding it contained clean water made a simple supper, breaking the loaf in her hands and drinking from the lip of the jug. Scarcely had she finished when the hidden overhead source of light snapped out and she composed herself as best she could for sleep on the hard planks, without benefit of blanket or pillow. At first she wondered if she would ever get to sleep, given the hardness of her bed, but it had been a long day and fearful but exciting things lay ahead for her. She was young and healthy, the cell, despite its oppressive stone construction, warm and dry, and in ten minutes she was fast asleep.

Without a watch time meant nothing but when she blinked awake to the returning light, to see the housekeeper at her door, unlocking her cage, it felt like no more than dawn. She crept out on all fours when invited by a gesture to leave her cell and found herself leashed like a bitch going 'walkies', with a wide leather collar around her neck and a long leather lead attached to it, the far end held in the woman's determined grip. Her only other adornment consisted of steel cuffs holding her wrists behind her back. A sharp yank left her with no option but to follow and she found herself out in a chilly dawn-lit yard between high stone walls. Still tethered like a bitch, she was led to a corner where she was invited to squat and make use of a sandbox. Although the woman still had not spoken, there was no mistaking her intention.

At first she felt like rebelling, unwilling to degrade herself

141

in this manner, but checked herself as she recalled why she was here. To be trained in obedience amongst other unspecified things and this was clearly part of the process. She wasn't going to fall at the very first fence. Blushing over every inch of her bare pink body she crouched over the heap of sand and emptied her bursting bladder and straining bowels, under the watchful eye of her silent jailor. Averting her eyes from the shaming steaming evidence of her morning motions, and denied any means of cleansing herself, she scrambled to her feet again in response to a commanding tug on her leash and was led across the yard into a circular stone enclosure, about twenty feet across, with a vertical steel post at its centre. The post carried a coiled rubber hose with a brass nozzle, and a horizontal arm reaching nearly to the perimeter wall.

Still without speaking the housekeeper uncuffed her wrists and fastened them to the end of the rotating arm at the level of her head. For a few moments she stood there, uncertain what to expect, while the wordless wardress made some sort of adjustment behind her. Suddenly she shrieked in shocked surprise. A jet of ice cold water, like a chilled steel bar, struck her between the shoulders, propelling her forward. Constrained by the rotating arm she began to run round the outer edge of the circular chamber, pursued all the time by the merciless jet. It struck into the divide of her buttocks, attacking her tender anus, it found her vulva through the gap of her thighs and pulverised it, leaving her gasping as it chilled her hot clit. As she twisted away from the force of the watery blast on her back and buttocks, her tormentor directed the pressure hose at her flopping breasts, driving the air from her lungs, then moved down to hit her in her rounded belly, knocking the remaining breath out of her. She doubled up with the blow but her arms, fastened above her head, held her up and the jet switched to her face, driving her head back and bringing her upright again, turning away from the hissing hose to present her backside for more treatment as the irresistible jet drove her round the curving wall, and returned her to her starting point. There was no way she could stand against the force of the freezing water, directed by the experienced hand of the gaunt housekeeper. If she had had time to think about it she would have speculated on how many naked girls had run helplessly round this hideous circle, bruised and battered by the jet. As it was she could spare no thought at all for anything but her own battle for breath and her pleas and prayers for it to stop.

It was a brutal bathing, five minutes of agony as the powerful jet thrashed her bare flesh, front and back, hurting like a whip and leaving her gasping and shivering when it was finally over, her naked body blotched with the cold and the bruising. If this was to be her morning routine she was in for an even worse time than her fertile imagination had surmised. At last it was over and, her wrists unlocked, she was given a surprisingly luxurious bath towel, warm and fluffy, to dry herself with. The unexpected luxury shocked her almost as much as the freezing jet. Still bemused, and with her hands once more cuffed behind her, she answered another tug on her lead to follow her captor into the house.

There she found Renee and Laura, seated at breakfast. Each was clad in a 'uniform' of crisp white shirt with collar, straight navy skirt, dark stockings and sensible leather shoes though, a small feminine touch to soften their severity a trifle, they sported medium heels to flatter the calf muscles without interfering with activity. Each had plaited her hair and wore it in a firmly pinned crown above a face decorated with a minimum of make-up. Altogether a demonstration of no-nonsense business-like and purposeful intent, reinforced by the short whip that each wore clipped to her waist like a badge of office.

"She's been properly purged and cleansed, I hope?" Renee enquired of the silent servitor, who nodded in confirmation.

143

"Thank you. You may leave her with us now," Renee went on. "We'll take over from here."

She was made to kneel, as she had been accustomed to at Henry's side, and was given food from their plates, which she had no doubt would be all the breakfast she could look forward to in her totally subservient condition. She accepted gratefully all she was given. A pounding with an icy jet in the chill of dawn does wonders for a naked girl's appetite.

While they fed her they told her something of what she might expect during the coming month in Marindorra. She was to be trained to be a perfect sexual companion.

"Yes, I know darling, you love Henry," Renee conceded, when she protested she already tried to serve him as best she could. "We all love our men and try to be as pleasing for them as we know how but the fact is we know nothing. No one trains girls for their futures. Oh yes, we spend years in college, absorbing knowledge like sponges, learning every skill known to man, everything that is, but the one thing we need for our primary biological purpose, to be satisfactory and satisfied mates."

"It would be interesting to hear what the Women's Studies Department of our old alma mater would make of that," Laura suggested with a grin.

"What we need is fewer women's studies courses and more woman study courses," Renee assured her. "Somewhere we can learn to be female, to make love like angels or devils as required, pleasure men in a thousand different ways and keep our bodies in prime working order to bring about the greatest possible happiness in the men we love. Incidentally, and quite by the way of course, we would get the benefit of it ourselves. There's nothing inspires either love or lust quite so much as the reciprocal pleasure of one's partner. Orgasms shared are orgasms doubled."

"Your training proper will start tomorrow," Renee vouchsafed as she offered the last of her coffee cup to the kneeling postulant. "Today you'll be sent over to the medical clinic attached to the local house of correction for women. Greta's the doctor in charge and don't give her any trouble or you'll regret it."

"May I speak please?"

"Fire away."

"Why do I have to go to a clinic?"

"To be ringed and rimmed, of course," Renee replied. "To be fitted with these," and she pulled up her skirt to reveal that her uniform did not extend to knickers. Nestling in the dark curls of her abundant bush, was the glint of gold from the rings which Jenny had observed many times before in Sexton, during lazy days at the pool or, more especially, those torrid nights when the girls had shamelessly caressed each other's bodies in sensual embraces.

"And your pretty teats, too," Laura threw in for good measure.

"And what about the rimming?"

"Oh, that," Renee said with a smile. "Don't tell me you haven't noticed how Laura and I are shaped in our bottoms. You've dabbled your greedy fingers in our bumholes often enough to know we're different."

"I know that, but what's it for, and how's it done?" the kneeling girl wanted to know.

"Greta will explain it all," Renee assured her, "so no more questions."

A press on a bell-push brought the silent servant back and Renee handed over her charge.

"Take her over to the doctor please," she directed. "She is expected."

Once more she found herself on the end of a leash, walking naked in the open. The path through the pinewoods to the neighbouring property, the dark bulk of the female correctional establishment, was strewn with pebbles of various sizes and sharpness, besides hard twigs and tight fir

145

cones. She stumbled many times as she followed her wardress along more than half a mile of broken ground until they came to the side entrance of a low annex to the frowning pile of the prison. The housekeeper dropped the end of the leash over a hook in the wall, rang the bell and, without waiting for an answer, turned and moved silently away, back to the villa.

For what seemed like an age she stood obediently at the end of her leash, feeling a light breeze on her skin to remind her of her naked condition as she waited for the bell to be answered. Finally the door opened and a woman, wearing a doctor's white coat, stood looking her up and down. From her appearance she was a Northern European of some kind, stocky, blonde, with a face that was nearly beautiful but carried a hint of hardness around the mouth and eyes suggestive of a streak of cruelty that made her remember Renee's warning. This must be Greta.

"Hmm," the doctor murmured to herself. "You'll do. They weren't exaggerating. You'll wear rings and rims perfectly. You could be made for it. Come on, let's go take a proper look at you," and she tugged on the leash, drawing her 'patient' into the house and to a large, well-appointed treatment room, complete with gynaecological examination table.

But there were other humiliating preparations to be made before she would mount what she was certain would be her ultimate destination; the gleaming chrome steel and shiny plastic surface of the examination table with its stirrups and restraints for fastening a woman securely open for inspection and treatment of her most intimate parts.

Without bothering to remove the manacles that secured her 'patient's' wrists behind her, Greta ordered her to her knees and then made her bend forward until her forehead touched the tiled floor. It was a degrading and undignified posture, exposing her vulva and anus between the bent

146

stretched halves of her naked bottom cheeks, a humiliation made a hundred times worse by the touch of a greased nozzle to her shrinking anal rose.

"This'll flush you out nicely," the blonde doctor informed her. "Nothing like a good hot enema to ease the bowels in the morning."

"But, please, I've already been," she protested, blushing anew at the recollection of her degrading performance on the sandbox.

"Another good flush won't do you any harm," Greta assured her, pumping on an inflator bulb to seal the nozzle inescapably in her rectum, "I don't want any accidents when we get to the rimming," and the contents of the bulging enema bag burst into her cringing bowels like an oily Niagara.

She writhed and panted as the quart of hot oil spread into her guts, provoking immediate reactions from the walls of her rectum and the coils of her entrails. When a second dose was forced in to join the first, her belly hung between her knees like the udder of a cow ready for the milking parlour. Cramps were tearing at her and she could hardly breathe for the pressure on her diaphragm. She felt stuffed to the gills and perspiration trickled down her back and under her arms, where the cuffs held them to her sides. When at last Greta helped her to mount the handy toilet, and unscrewed the valve that kept the sealing bulb inflated, she was panting and straining from the pressure in her belly, scarcely able to walk. With a whoosh the nozzle was ejected and a humiliating series of watery noises, interspersed by gaseous explosions, announced that the overloaded bowels were expelling their contents as fast as the dilating sphincter would permit.

It seemed to the crouching girl to go on forever, returning in a new paroxysm of flatulent energy just when she thought calm might be restored. When the last violent convulsions of her belly failed to discharge even a drop of degrading effluent, Greta finally relented and released her wrists, so that she could use the paper roll provided to restore some decency to her person. It was a very subdued and chastened young woman who finally rose, when ordered, and made her way to climb onto the chilly plastic surface of the examination table. No doubt Greta had had in mind the possibility of an involuntary discharge during her coming operations on the girl's tender body but she was also experienced enough to know that the girl would be made much more malleable by the administration of such a gross purge and the humiliation involved in discharging it. Her redheaded charge was the picture of docility as she climbed onto the table and lifted her legs to part them widely and place them in the stirrups provided. She was equally obedient when ordered to place her arms on the shaped horizontal shelves arranged for them and it was only a matter of moments to pull tight straps at knees and elbows, neck and waist, that secured the girl rigidly in place, unable to move any part of her body that might interfere with Greta's work.

First a very thorough medical examination, complete with blood pressure check and an anal temperature reading. As Greta's hands moved over her, it occurred to the girl trapped helplessly on the table, that the doctor had more than professional feelings for the young women that came into her hands. There was a certain indefinable but definite, sensuousness in her touch, particularly on nipples and clitoris, that owed as much to lust as to medicine though, she was equally certain, that lust was as much sadistic as amorous. Despite herself she found her body responding to the fingering.

"My, but you're a sensitive one," Greta purred admiringly, as a nipple hardened under her touch, "I do enjoy a responsive girl. Wait until we ring this," and she stroked a probing digit over the rapidly engorging wedge of her clitoris, "I can't wait to see you writhing as the needle goes through."

She had known all along that she would be pierced for

148

the rings that denoted the true Sexton wife, but had not let thoughts of the details of that ringing penetrate too deep into her imagination, but now she could not avoid them. She shivered as she visualised Greta forcing a sharp instrument through her most delicate flesh. Her thoughts were interrupted by the feel of cold metal at the entrance to her vagina, where Greta was preparing to insert a speculum. She gasped as the chilly instrument, its curved blades closed, penetrated between the delicate lips that guarded her sex sheath and slide firmly home. Even if Greta hadn't liberally coated it with lubricant jelly, her own secretions were flowing so shamefully freely it would have had no difficulty entering her to the hilt. Greta worked the screws to open up the leaves of the instrument, top and bottom, until her vagina was stretched open from labia to cervix, all its pink lining exposed, as the feel of cool air on mucus membranes rapidly informed her.

"Fine healthy cunt," Greta assured her. "Nothing wrong in that department. Well serviced from the look of it; should shape up well in training. Now let's look at the other end."

She withdrew and cleaned the instrument, then tilted back the table, until Jenny's head was well below her fork, the cut-out edge of the table giving free access to the puckered anal whorl, where it nestled at the bottom of the deep divide of the buttocks. She felt a frisson of chill as a thumbful of cold grease was applied and thrust deep into the tight closure, then the metal nose of the speculum was presented again. This time the battle was fiercer, the resistance more sustained but Greta had forced a hundred sphincters on this table and was not deterred, even if her patient could not believe that the seemingly huge blunt instrument could penetrate her delicate anal bud without tearing it irreparably. Accompanied by a grunt from Greta, and gasps and whimpers from the recipient of the steel intruder, the blunt nose forced the barrier and suddenly sank in its full length. Jenny gave a shocked

149

cry as it entered her, seeming to fill her guts. She whimpered even more painfully as Greta opened up the instrument, top and bottom, until the rectal tube was revealed, its glistening pink surface strained and stretched by the operation.

"This one's healthy too," she assured the panting owner of the tender passage. "We'll start your rimming today."

With brutal efficiency, and a fine disregard for her patient's comfort, she collapsed the jaws and whipped the shining monster out of its fleshy bed in a single movement, drawing yet another shocked cry of outrage.

When she'd cleared away the instruments used in the inspection, and restored the table to its starting position, Greta returned to her examination of the turgid teats that sprouted so exuberantly from the firm mounds of the shapely breasts.

"We'll start with your tits. Nothing to it. Just a nice clean puncture with this," she held up an instrument like a leather punch, with a curved section of fairly large bore hypodermic needle fixed to one jaw, a small plate with a matching hole, to the other.

Preparation consisted of swabbing the straining teats, and their surrounding areola, with some sort of spirit. The shock of the chill and the slight sting on the most tender parts of the surfaces did nothing to drive them down, seeming if anything to increase their engorgement. Greta gripped a straining nipple between finger and thumb, stretching it painfully, then presented the point of the needle carefully to the very base of the extended teat, aiming to place the piercing as close as possible to the base of the gristly stem. Slowly she closed the jaws until the girl could feel the first prick of the sharp point.

"Now, we don't want to rush this," she observed. "Wouldn't do to have your rings lying crooked on your chest. Better a little discomfort now to ensure a nice neat job, don't you think?"

She didn't know what to think. Certainly she didn't expect

Greta to take any notice of her opinion. One thing she was sure of. If this flinty operator said there might be a little extra discomfort, she meant, 'this is going to hurt like hell, so hang onto your socks'.

She braced herself as the jaws continued their inexorable closure, the needle pressing deeper and deeper into the teat, without actually penetrating the skin. Her nipples were large in proportion to her breasts, forming when engorged, as they most certainly were by then, twin cylinders of dark red flesh, slightly dimpled all over like ripe strawberries. Greta was putting on the pressure and the beleaguered teat could not last much longer. She was squirming and hissing and still the pressure increased. Then suddenly it was over. The point penetrated the skin and disappeared, fetching up in the hole in the anvil on the other jaw. The partially flattened nipple sprang back into its usual neat cylinder as she gave another shocked gasp of pain. Actually it wasn't so much the sharp stabbing bite, which had come almost as a relief after the persistent crushing of Greta's careful approach. No it was the feel of the flesh giving way. The tissues of her teats were nubbly, almost gristly in their toughness, which was why Greta had been at such pains to ensure that the needle did not wander as it went through. Although this meant they resisted the needle up to a certain point. Once penetrated, they gave way with unexpected suddenness and an almost audible plop of rending flesh, which sickened her stomach.

As she recovered from this belly churning shock she became conscious of a new discomfort. Greta was feeding an open gold ring into the perforation left by the withdrawn needle and the riven tissues within the wound were objecting vigorously. She was whimpering and gasping anew by the time the ring was in place and its ends closed. One done. Now all she had to do was lie back in her bonds and wait for the second tender peak to be perforated and plugged with its own gold ring like that already lying on the soft curve of her

151

right breast.

"Well that's the easy bit done," Greta announced cheerfully, when she had completed the twin operations. "The next bits may be a little uncomfortable."

Her patient sighed deeply at the news but otherwise made no comment. In her helpless condition it would have made no difference anyway if she had objected, besides which she was here at her own desire to become a fully fledged Swive, as her friends called their status, and she wasn't about to cry 'uncle' at this stage.

Greta moved down to her crotch, tilting the table back a touch and adjusting the stirrups to widen the already spread thighs. A sudden stinging in her genitals announced that the doctor was using a spirit-based cleansing fluid to swab the pouting pinkness of her vulva prior to commencing operations. She clenched her teeth against the sharp pain and hissed loudly. Greta laughed.

"Caught you on the raw, did I? Just you wait. That's nothing to what comes later, but first we'll attend to these fat lips of yours."

She could feel the jaws of the piercing tool closing on her right cuntlip, first a pricking sensation, then more serious pain. The lip was fat and fleshy and Greta took her time going through it. This time she didn't even have the excuse of wanting to maintain a level opening for the ring to lie in. It hurt considerably and there was the same belly curdling shock as the thick tissues finally parted and the needle went through with a rush. Placing the ring wasn't any picnic either and she was panting and sweating by the time a neat gold circle adorned each plump nether lip.

"Now this is the interesting bit," Greta announced, swabbing stinging alcohol onto a shrinking clitoris, extracting an even more pained intake of breath from the prostrate girl, "Your Mr Maltravers sent a note along with your friends asking for some special treatment. Usually the men who send

152

you girls here just leave it to us to fit you out in the conventional way for Sexton women, but your Henry has asked for a Christina. Don't often get asked for that, so I'm going to enjoy this session. Can't promise the same for you, I'm afraid," she added, almost as an afterthought, "but in the end you'll thank him for it. It's a very neat arrangement."

Cursing herself for even asking, her patient enquired what a Christina implied, half of her mind desperately curious to know, the other half equally anxious not to. As usual female curiosity had won the day.

"A Christina?" Greta replied. "Oh, it's a special form of clitoral piercing. Mostly we do triangles; that's what you've seen on your friends, a ring set underneath the head of the clit, where it lies in the furrow between the labia. It doesn't actually go through the nerve stem of the clit itself, just passes under it. The Christina, on the other hand," she went on, "travels quite the other way. It goes in at the same level as the triangle but runs along the length of the stem. Lying where you are now, the stem of your clit is lying more or less horizontally between your lips, and I'm going to push the needle through in a slightly upwards direction. That way it starts below the tip, crosses the stem at an angle along its whole length and comes out at the base of your belly, just above where your labia join. Can't put a ring in a straight hole that long, of course. I'll fit you with a ball-ended bar. All you will see of it will be a neat gold ball where it comes out at the top and, for your more intimate friends, another just under the tip of your clit."

She hated herself for having asked, she really wished she didn't know now, but then couldn't resist enquiring further.

"So I won't get a ring in my clit, like the others?" she said.

"Oh, yes. Can't have you missing out," Greta assured her. "Can't give you a triangle, the two piercings might clash, so I'll put it through the tip of your clit instead. Might make

153

you jump a bit, but it will look fine. Actually, you've got a pretty big clit, so there'll be plenty of room to work in. May be rather more sensitive from now on, but that's no bad thing in a girl. There's never any harm in a girl being kept aware of her sexuality and it will give your lovers a useful means to both control and arouse you."

From the slight thickening of the doctor's tone, and the gleam in her eye, it was obvious she would like to add herself to the list of those privileged to do so.

For the next, longitudinal, perforation - the 'Christina' - Greta was using a long hollow needle set in a holder for better control. She parted the labia with the finger and thumb of her left hand, exposing the wedge-shaped clitoris, where it lay between them and she set the point where she had described, under the tip, at the base of the furrow. This time she had real reason not to hurry, as she guided the needle through the sensitive stem, keeping it carefully on track to emerge at her aiming point in the fold of flesh above where the labia joined. It was a long slow progress through nerve-packed tissue, the heart of her feminine sexuality, provoking extraordinary feelings of pain and passion, feelings so strong they lost their identity and became pure unbearable sensation, filling her belly with nausea. She writhed and spasmed as much as her tight restraints would allow, which was precious little, and made curious gargling sounds in her throat. Again it left her exhausted, gasping like a landed fish, her face running with beads of sweat.

"Prefect," Greta announced, "though no thanks to you, my girl. You were squirming like a cut worm. Do try and hold still for the next part."

Abashed by the unfeeling doctor's reprimand, she composed herself as best she could and felt the piercing tool used for the previous rings in her teats and labia, gently gripping her throbbing clit, inflamed and erected now as a result of the over-stimulation it had received from the traverse of the long needle, and the insertion of the gold bar with its gleaming ball ends. As the pressure on the tool increased, so did the urgency of her hissing protest, then it was through, with the usual sickening suddenness and she squealed in mingled shock and relief that it was, at last, all over bar the insert of the last ring.

"Well, that's a good morning's work," Greta said with satisfaction, a moment later. "Five rings and a Christina, all nicely placed though I say so myself. You'll be grateful to me, once you can see the result," she promised. "That Christina sets off your fat clit perfectly."

She swabbed the area of her operations with more stinging alcohol and cleared away her tools.

"Time for lunch, I think. We'll carry on with the rimming this afternoon."

'Lunch', for her patient at least, consisted of a large bottle fitted with a baby's rubber teat and suspended on a spring from a stand above the examination table. Apparently she was to stay where she was while Greta went to seek her own refreshment.

"I want every last drop sucked up," Greta ordered, settling the teat in her patient's mouth, "or else!"

She didn't specify what else, but then she didn't have to. The menace in her tone was quite sufficient for a naked girl trussed helplessly at her complete disposal, her genitals opened, and with an unknown but frightening afternoon session to come.

The contents of the bottle were disgusting, thick and glutinous, what little flavour it had was salty and unpleasant. She gagged and had to force herself to swallow it but Greta's threats, and her own vulnerability ensured she kept the degrading teat in her mouth, like a baby in its pram, and sucked and swallowed conscientiously until she had downed the whole nauseous concoction.

When Greta returned after a prolonged interval, she

examined the bottle and pronounced herself satisfied.

"Enjoyed your lunch, I see," she observed.

Strengthened by the rest and the nutriment, however unpalatable she had found it, her patient found the spirit to reply.

"Not much. It was disgusting," she said. "Whatever was it?"

"You should know semen by now, even taken cold," the doctor replied with a malicious grin, "full of protein and excellent nutriment for sexually active girls. Set you up no end for your exercises at the villa. Now let's see what we have here."

'Here' was her upturned anus, lifted by the tilting table until it was presented at a convenient height for examination. Greta stroked her fingers over the dimpled bud and positively cooed.

"How sweet," she said. "Quite delicious. And I love your fuzz. So soft and curly."

She twisted a tendril of the stray russet fringe that sat sparsely around the whorl of the clenched sphincter.

"It's lovely, but it'll have to go. Can't have it getting in the way of your rimming. Of course I could shave it but the tweezers would be so much more fun, don't you think?"

Jenny thought nothing of the sort but wisely kept her mouth shut. There was no way that Greta was going to take account of her wishes, and she would probably only make things worse for herself.

In the event it was difficult to see just how that might have come about. Greta took each curled ginger hair individually in the tweezers and slowly pulled on it. As the pressure increased, her victim writhed and hissed, praying it would give way and allow itself to be extracted, but Greta was enjoying herself too much to hurry it and kept her suspended in a refinement of torment that sapped her strength of mind. Tears streamed down her face and she was sobbing with pain and frustration. As hair after hair was pulled with excruciating slowness she began to dread the feel of the steel jaws against her skin, the tension building as the hair was lifted and teased. She would have settled for the worst beating of her life, and she knew exactly what a severe caning was like, if she could only have them whipped out quickly and without fuss. But Greta was having too much fun to let that happen and she delayed consummation until the very bitter end, smiling evilly as she watched the tiny cone of flesh extend around each pulled hair, judging expertly just how far she could go without actually extracting it, licking her lips at the inviting twitch of the tortured flesh, as the hair was finally plucked and added to the little pile of russet fur on the kidney dish beside her.

All good things have to come to an end however, even the tormenting of a lovely naked girl strapped helplessly into a gynaecological stand, her genitals and anus presented for whatever delights the operator's twisted mind could dream up. Though prominent in their ginger glory, the russet hairs around the shyly sunken anus were not as numerous as Greta could have wished and soon she was all business again, her brief diversion over. With busy fingers she stuffed a generous portion of greasy lubricant into the now denuded anus, thrusting it deep into the rectal tube with rubber covered fingers.

"Time to rim you," she announced.

Once again curiosity got the better of her fear of knowing what might be coming.

"What are you going to do to me?" she wanted to know.

"Make you perfect for a man," Greta replied, "and, in the process, mark you as a Sexton wife."

"Yes, but how?"

"It's all to do with buggery," Greta explained. "It's the most positive way a man can have a woman. There's no question of it having anything to do with procreation, so she

157

can't hide behind any such disguise for her actions and it goes against all the deepest taboos she's been taught since childhood. By handing over control and use of her anus she really does give herself."

"I can see that," the potential 'rimmee' replied, "but exactly what are you going to do, and why?"

"The point is," Greta told her, "that a healthy young woman like yourself has a very powerful sphincter muscle, and all her training ensures that even when she tries hard to relax, it will still close with considerable force on anything that penetrates it. That includes a man's penis, and that's not the most exciting sensation for him. The man likes to be gripped and 'milked' along the whole length of his prick, not just at the root. What we are going to do is stretch the outer part of your sphincter muscle permanently, so that the grip is more evenly distributed along the length of a prick put up your rectum. Once we've done that, your exercises at the villa will ensure that you learn to grip properly all the way along your rectal tube and give any man who has you that way the maximum of pleasure, your destiny as a true woman."

She slapped the stretched pale buttock cheek nearest to her as if to signal the conversation was at an end, at least for now, and took up her tools. Gleaming chrome glistened with oily lubricant on a shorter version of the speculum she had used earlier to inspect the vagina, as she presented it to the grease-packed opening of the furled anus. The flesh seemed to shrink from it as she pressed it home, the wrinkled tissues turning inwards and opening under the wedging action of the pointed nose. Inexorably she increased the pressure, setting her victim to puffing and blowing as she felt herself forced and violated in her most secret place by unfeeling steel. Soon the sphincter had been forced enough that the bulk of the instrument could follow, and it sank deeply into the opened passage. A strangled grunt greeted its reception.

"Now we can start the stretching process," Greta announced with satisfaction.

"But I'm stretched to bursting already," the impaled girl protested. "You can't make it any bigger. You'll split me open."

"Nonsense girl," the sadistic doctor replied, "we haven't even started yet," and her helpless victim lay back with a small wail of despair.

The instrument differed from a conventional speculum in having more than just a pair of jaws. In fact there were six in the set, and their upper parts were enclosed in a flexible rubber jacket, now firmly embedded in the plundered sphincter. Adjustments to the screws that controlled the steel jaws expanded the ring, stretching the anal sphincter further and further to low moans and incipient rebellion from the patient.

"Stop being so silly," Greta commanded, emphasising her words with a heavy slap on a bottom cheek already carrying the outline of her handprint in red. "A girl can be stretched way beyond this. You're young and elastic and can easily take much more. You will too before your month is up, but we'll pause here for now."

The relentless extension of her overwrought anus certainly paused but her processing was far from over. A sharp prick announced the presence of a needle at her anal ring, now stretched out of all recognition from the tiny winking rose that had adorned the deep divide of her trim buttocks only minutes before. She winced as it was plunged into the stressed tissue, then opened her mouth in a 'yah' of protest as she felt something injected into the muscle, something that stung like a hornet.

"Relax," Greta counselled her. "Nobody's going to kill you. It's just a muscle relaxant. If the sphincter is treated while it's fully stretched it doesn't go back to its former shape when the plug is removed. This injection I invented myself.

It partially dissolves the fibres, so that they can't restore their former strength entirely."

"But it hurts," her patient protested. "It feels like I've been stung in the bum by a hornet."

"Hmm. I expect so," Greta admitted. "Actually it isn't surprising, seeing that it's prepared from the sting of an Amazonian insect. It paralyses its prey by weakening its muscles. Don't worry though; it's been thoroughly tested over the years. You don't see your friends in any trouble, do you?"

She had to admit that Renee and Laura had come through unscathed and took what comfort she could from that, although her present state was far from comfortable. Greta was completing a ring of six equally spaced injections around the whole circuit of her drum tight anal ring and she was in agony.

"Don't worry," Greta said cheerfully as she put away her syringe and bottles. "It'll pass and you'll be as right as rain. Mind you," she added, to her victim's dismay, "you have to come back for a repeat dose every other day for the next fortnight if the job's to be done properly. By then you'll find your rectal tube can still close as tightly as before but the outer part of your sphincter can't fully contract and it'll stand out in a rim, like your friends' and the other Swives from Sexton."

"It doesn't feel as if it'll ever close again," the girl complained bitterly.

"Oh nonsense. In a month you'll be as good as new. Well," she admitted, "there could be some slight difficulty if you go in for too much drink and rich food but a panty liner should take care of the occasional seepage, and just think how much more pleasure you'll be able to give your Henry."

As the stinging smart died to a mere burning sensation, Greta seemed to think she had accomplished enough for one day. She removed the external levers from the stretcher and placed a plastic cap to seal the opened anal aperture. She undid the restraints, one by one, and allowed the girl to clamber painfully off the table, stiff and sore, and stand on unsteady feet while she fastened a leather belt around her waist and connected light chains, fixed to it front and back, to hold the anal plug firmly in place. Satisfied, she replaced the collar and lead and fastened the cuffs behind her back once more. Reminding her that she would be seeing her again in two days and with some advice on the care of the wounds in her nipples and labia, not to speak of the tormented clitoris, she led her to the door by which she had entered and left her with her leash hooked on the wall, just as she had been when she had first arrived. Some twenty minutes later the housekeeper appeared to walk her home.

Until that time she had given no thought as to how she might manage with her newly applied decorations and the monstrous plug in her anus but as they set out to walk the half mile of rough track back to the villa, she was made acutely aware of their presence. Her nipples presented no problem, indeed, diverted as she was by the protests of other parts of her abused anatomy, she was able to ignore them, but the motion of her walking disturbed the swollen clitoris and, pierced both lengthwise and crosswise, it made itself felt in a mixture of throbbing soreness and unwelcome sexual stimulation. As for the plug in her anus! Every swing of her thigh rocked the unyielding metal intruder in her sore stretched sphincter, rubbing on the inflamed inner cheeks of her bottom, straining at the tender lining of her rectum, playing havoc in her bottom. She found she was waddling with the humiliating gait of an egg-bound duck, her body bent, her bottom thrust up into the air behind her. The walk over that morning seemed a carefree amble in the country compared with the agony and shame of her return. At least she had no time to think of the spectacle she presented, a bound naked girl led like a dog on a lead.

That evening she was given her usual bread and water

161

diet for supper and returned to her cage early, to sleep off the excitement of the day.

But the next morning there was no respite from the stark regime to which she was now subject. Dawn brought the housekeeper, and another humiliating visit to the sand-pile, the only difference now being that the woman removed the cap from her stretcher to allow her to empty her bowels, and did not replace it until after the bruising shower, when she took particular care to direct the freezing jet into the open rectum, causing the girl to shriek out in shocked protest as the icy torrent entered the very core of her being.

Breakfast came as a relief, with titbits from her trainers to supplement the adequate, but deadly dull, diet of bread and water and the revolting 'high protein' liquid lunch she had had to suckle in Greta's domain.

"Well you've got the medals," Renee observed, after a close inspection of her charge's rings, and the monstrous plug in her bottom, "so it's time you did something to earn them. Let's go and see the Marindorra donkey."

Not wishing to credit the horrendous possibilities the suggestion opened - for she could believe anything could happen here - she followed her trainers into a large room, whose forbidding furnishings seemed expressly designed to make the most alarming impact on a bare and helpless girl. For a start the walls were lined with every instrument of correction known to man, and restraints to match. The floor carried what could only be a whipping post, with its black iron rings set into a gnarled and greasy upright baulk of timber. Several other pieces looked like frames for holding a girl to be caned or birched and overhead bars and ropes threatened the possibility of suspension.

She thought at first she had solved the mystery of the Marindorra donkey, when she spotted a large trestle-like structure, with a crosspiece of triangular timber, the sharp edge upwards. There had been hints of riding the wooden pony from several of her friends in Sexton, when drink had loosened female lips and rendered female bottoms liable to corrective silencing, and she cringed from the thought of being put up on it with her clit and labia still so sore from their recent piercing.

But it was to something quite different that Laura led her. The machine with which she was confronted was low on the ground, a black box from which a short squat arm projected, and which carried several dials and buttons to control it. In front it extended to form a long narrow platform adorned with a variety of rings and straps. At the far end of the platform a short vertical arm carried another dial or counter and a pair of indicator lights. There seemed to be some sort of mechanism to adjust the relative angles and positions of box and platform.

"Meet your new friend... the Marindorra donkey," Renee said, with a grin. "He's a girl's best friend, always ready and willing, a neat fit for every vagina and back passage, the most tireless and accommodating lover you will ever find. Neddy here will never go off prematurely, or fail to come up to scratch. Give him a nice kiss."

She was horrified.

"You mean I'm to be raped by a mechanical monster?" she protested.

"Now, now! Where're your manners," Renee cautioned her. "I didn't hear you ask to speak. Well, I'll overlook it this time but if it happens again...!" and she let her hand fall significantly onto the short plaited whip she wore on her belt.

"I'm sorry... Ma'am," the girl said apologetically, "but, please, what's it all about?"

"Training. That training to be a woman we were speaking about," Renee told her. "Here you will learn to use your mouth and cunt to give the absolute maximum of pleasure to any man to whom you are given, in other words, to be the perfect sexual woman. Once Greta's done her work, you can include your arse in that as well."

"But having that thing rape me won't achieve that," she protested again "Besides, everyone tells me I'm very enthusiastic in bed. All the men I've had, sorry, that have had me, seemed to go away satisfied."

"That's because they're too polite, even too grateful, to say differently," Renee reproved her. "Nearly all men, even the strong ones like the men who own us, are brought up not to insult women and, in the most recent generations, in an atmosphere where women's satisfaction and pleasure is put first, second and third. Nobody seems to give a damn if the man is satisfied. What Neddy is going to help you achieve is the perfect working cunt, the most elegant mouth, the best educated anus. We'll start with the basics today, so we'll just select a nice fat prick for your greedy cunt and show you the ropes."

She opened a locker under the black box and removed a tray of very life-like replicas of erect penises of all shapes and sizes.

"Here, take your pick. Which do you think is most like Henry's?"

She hesitated a moment at the unusual request then said, "The thick one, third from the left on the bottom row, I think."

"Then he's not far off Tom's, I'd say," Renee replied, lifting out the named member and offering it to the end of the stumpy arm projecting from the box.

When Laura had released her from the cuffs that had held her arms behind her up to now, she was directed to lave the prick with her mouth, letting her saliva wet it thoroughly.

"Make a good job of it girl," Renee advised, "it's the only lubricant it gets before it goes up you."

Obediently she complied, letting her tongue coat the soft plastic moulding with her saliva but, privately, she could feel the warmth rising in her belly as she imagined this dead phallus was her beloved Henry's loving bone, and she knew that lubrication would soon be superfluous. It was three nights now since she had had the benefit of a hot prick in her belly, and a girl has her needs.

Her task completed to Renee's satisfaction, she was directed to turn around and place herself on her hands and knees on the platform, where cuffs around her wrists, and straps tightened over her calves, held her securely in place. A hum of motors and she found herself moved back and her height adjusted until the tip of the prepared phallus just nosed the opening of her slightly gaping vagina, now becoming engorged and moist as she continued to think of Henry and sex. It seemed her reaction to possible danger or distress was to moisten, rather than freeze up. Well, she thought, I'm not the first to react that way in Sexton.

More adjustments to the platform, aided by her own wriggles and squirms as the cold replica teased her rapidly warming cunt, and she found herself impaled by four inches of man-sized plastic lying in her sopping love tunnel.

"You're ready to start work," Renee told her, "here's how it goes. The arm that dildo up your belly is attached to has very sensitive sensors. It can measure the force required to push it into you, and the force to drag it out of your greedy quim. It does this whether you are passive and it is raping you, as you so elegantly put it, although I doubt if anyone watching you juice right now would call it rape, or if it is stationary and you are working on it with your bottom sliding back and forth."

There was a click and the prick slid all the way into her, its ten inches filling her belly and making her gasp, then it pulled out until only the nose rested just within the vestibule to her vagina.

"You see how it goes," Renee said, stopping the machine again, "straight in and out. We can vary the speed and the rhythm of the strokes to replicate any masculine mood from violent passion to contemplative relaxation, and it's up to you to fall in with his mood and pump him gently or suck on him like a vacuum cleaner, as appropriate. Now you see those little indicator lights in front of you?"

She did.

"When the green light comes on, you've gripped the prong just right and the man will be happy and satisfied. A red light, and you've boobed. Gripped him when he wanted to be allowed to go on quietly soaking, without provoking ejaculation, left him slack when he wanted his neck wrung; timed it wrong, so that you interrupted his rhythm, or some other sin."

"But how will I know which it is?" the crouching student wanted to know.

"The same way you would if you were in bed with a man; feminine intuition," Laura explained. "It'll be up to you to try and gauge where you went wrong, and try and correct it on the next stroke."

"And just to help your mental processes, you'll be judged on your performance at the end of the session and, just like old time schools, you'll have the lesson written on your bottom with this," and she indicated her dangling badge of office. "That counter you see in front of you registers your valid strokes. It goes up for every green light you get but," she added warningly, "it goes down for every red. Be warned. It's up to you how long the session lasts, so make sure those green lights keep coming. For starters we'll set your target at 100, just to let you get the feel of it."

There was the click of levers and whirr of motors behind her and the rod in her belly stirred into life. It thrust deep into her, moving slowly to touch her cervix, then equally slowly, slide backwards in the slick passage until only the nose was lodged in her female tract. The green light blinked approvingly on the inward thrust but was immediately cancelled by a flash of red as the monster phallus completed its withdrawal.

She'd forgotten what she was there for as she tried to master the strange sensation of being ridden by an inert machine, but a slash from Laura's quirt brought her sharply back to reality. She'd done nothing as the plastic prick had penetrated her, and had got a green light but equal inattention on the way out had cost her a red and a rapidly thickening purple welt across her bent bare buttocks. With this slow rhythm to the simulated copulation it didn't take a genius to work out that her virtual sexual partner, who existed only in the ingenious machine's built-in computer, was looking for a nice comfortable session, with an easy slide into her hot depths, but a firm milking grip on the way out. Still mindful of the sting in her bottom from Laura's sharp reminder, she set herself to relax her belly on the next in stroke, then call on the muscles of her vaginal wall to bear down on the intruder all through the out stroke, as if she couldn't bear to let it go.

She was rewarded with a green light on each passage of the prick in and out of her urgently contracting cunt, and the counter in front of her clicked up 1.

"You see, you can do it if you try," Renee congratulated her, "now all you have to do is keep it going for 99 more."

It didn't prove too difficult, once she got her mind round the pattern, 'lean back and relax', 'lean forward and squeeze'. Soon it was coming quite naturally and there were only three more red lights to spoil her record by the time the counter had clicked over to 100, each rewarded with a cut of the whip from one or other of her personal trainers.

"You did all right," Renee conceded, "but that was about as simple as they come. Now for something a little harder. Concentrate carefully this time, or you'll be seriously sore before Neddy's satisfied."

There were more clicks and mechanical noises and this time, when the cock sprang into life, its movements were far more vigorous. It plunged into her with more of rape than dalliance in the thrust, shaking her belly with its violence, then drawing back quite slowly, only to drive home again with the same force. As she tried to gather herself under the battering, the red light flashed and winked in derision. Gasping, she steadied herself and tried to make sense of it. The same pattern as before didn't help, so she tried reversing it, resisting the penetration, but relaxing as it left her body but, again, she failed to score. She seemed to be getting greens for her resistance to its inrush, but her slack vagina on exit seemed to infuriate the computerised Casanova and it winked a baleful red eye at her for her efforts. In desperation she closed up and clenched tight constantly, but even this didn't win the prize, or check the steady thrashing she was getting from the whips.

As Renee had forecast, she was getting seriously sore and something had to be done. She tried to imagine what might be in a man's mind at a time like this or, rather, what kind of a man Renee had conjured up for her. He was being brutal to her, thrusting without feeling, hurling his loins against her. If it had been a flesh and blood man behind her his belly would have been battering her buttocks for sure. It was the action of an angry man, a man determined to punish her for some fault. How would he want her to react? Not resist him, that was for sure, but neither would he want to plunge into an inanimate lump of flesh. No he would want to feel her submit to his battering but be unable to take the violence of his strokes against her cervix so that he would feel her involuntary clenching as his prick approached its deepest penetration of her womb. And on the way out? Total submission, for sure. She changed her tack, letting the prick move forward inside her, clenching down tight on it as it reached its full depth, then relaxing the grip as soon as it had moved an inch or so backwards. Two green lights! She had cracked it. Now all she had to do was to keep up the unnatural rhythm until she had clocked up the 300 that she had been set.

It wasn't easy, but she set her mind on it, to the exclusion of the whip cuts that still fell from time to time and eventually they slackened, then ceased altogether, as the red lights became less frequent, then virtually disappeared altogether. By the end of something approaching ten minutes sweat and strain, to say nothing of blazing buttocks, she had forced the counter over the 300 mark and the machine fell into merciful stillness.

"Not bad at all, for a beginner," Renee admitted. "Did you just find that rhythm by chance or had you worked out that that was an angry man who was determined to take it out in your cunt and reduce you to a snivelling heap?"

"I guessed what might be happening," the panting trainee got out between gasps, trying to toss the sweat soaked strands of hair out of her eyes. "He certainly didn't fuck like a lover, so some sort of disciplinary action seemed the likely answer."

"Well that was a tough one deliberately, to test you. Now we'll get down to the real work," and she turned back to the controls to set the next exercise.

For an hour every morning, sometimes two, and a similar session each afternoon, the training went on. Sometimes the prick was set to ravish her under its own power, sometimes it sat still and relaxed, while she rode it, teasing out its mood, adjusting her speed and pattern to meet its wishes, always strengthening her control over the muscles of her vagina until she had developed them into the perfect instrument for male pleasure.

And not only her vagina. Her mouth received a similar education, sometimes entertaining a passive prick, sometimes laving and sucking on an active rod as it worked its way backwards and forwards between her caressing lips and deep into her throat. At first she gagged, it was set to penetrate so deep but, gradually, she learnt to let her throat relax and accept

169

the solid gristle, taking its length far past the point where, when she started, her instincts told her it would choke her.

After the first fortnight there were more muscles to exercise. On alternate days she had returned to Greta's lair where the plug in her anus had been cleaned and adjusted, increasing the degree of stretch to the inflamed anus, until she was convinced she would tear and be permanently damaged. Into the distended tissues Greta injected her stinging muscle weakening fluid, its effect as painful as ever each time the needle went in. And there was always 'lunch'. Now that she knew what the glutinous and noisesome fluid was she had to suckle on, her stomach revolted even more strongly, but Greta would brook no refusal. Under threat of the whip and other, unspecified torments, she sucked on her loathsome bottle, drawing in the nauseous substance that was, Greta maintained, the finest protein for a sexually active girl that Mother Nature could provide. Two weeks on, and Greta declared the rimming process complete, the anal ring's elasticity so degraded that it could no longer contract enough to contribute to the defence of the rectal tube from invasion. Instead, it protruded where before it had sunk shyly in the humid trench between the fleshy buttock halves, a raised ridge, the celebrated 'rim' that marked the true Sexton wife or Swive.

Now that she was declared fit for service in all orifices, she had to present her newly modified anus to 'Neddy' and repeat the programme of exercises she had undergone to train her cunt to an educated and intelligent organ. Her hours working with Neddy extended every day, his ingenious micro-brain constantly coming up with new combinations to test her. Any time not spent copulating with the mechanical sex maniac, she had to devote to strenuous exercises, to firm her belly and strengthen her pelvic floor, improve her pectorals and thereby throw her not inconsiderable breasts into even greater prominence, their firm mounds thrusting out the thick teats that seemed to be permanently engorged these days. From her icy douche each morning, until she dropped exhausted on the hard planks of her bed, where she slept as if they were the softest down, her every minute was taken up.

Her appetite grew to match her exertions. Although she was not starved, her rations were carefully monitored to ensure her bread and water diet was just sufficient for her needs, without adding an ounce of superfluous fat to her frame, the starkness of the diet relieved only by the rewards that Renee and Laura condescended to offer her. Sometimes she was so hungry she felt she might almost welcome the nauseous 'bottles' that Greta had provided; almost but not quite.

And she missed Henry. It was not as if she was not getting sexual stimulation. Neddy was programmed to replicate a man's varying moods as intercourse progressed, from animal capture of a mate, to sensuous pleasure in riding her, to the crescendo that led ultimately to explosive ejaculation. The plastic cock was even fitted with a device to inject repeated gouts of hot creamy semen substitute into her mouth, her vagina, her butt. A healthy sexual animal like herself could not help but respond to this stimulation, indeed, her mentors insisted that she surrender to it, letting her body heat with gathering arousal, timing her orgasmic spasms, when they burst, to coincide with the hot jets of spunk hitting her cervix, her rectum, her gaping throat.

But Neddy didn't taste of Henry, didn't smell like him, lacked the wiry feel of the hair on his chest, the hardness of his muscles as he gripped her during their lovemaking. She yearned for his embrace, for the chance to show him how much she could pleasure him now she was aware of herself as a woman. In a month she had learnt more of how to make use of her body for a man's benefit than a professional whore after a life-time career between the sheets, and she was desperate to demonstrate it to the man she loved. She suspected that Renee and Laura were feeling the loss of their men as badly, but they could take some comfort in each other's warm human bodies. She was stuck with a metal mule and she hungered for human flesh.

The reunion took place, as did most social events in Sexton, in the bar of the Trident. As the three vibrant young women entered the long low room there was a pause in the general buzz of conversation as all heads turned to see them, then a spontaneous outbreak of applause. Walking proudly between her sponsors, a fully fledged Swive at last, Jenny moved directly to Henry and dropped to her knees before him. She wasn't left there long. Henry snatched her up in a bear hug and pressed his mouth to hers in a long kiss that left them both panting, she with nipples that threatened to burst through her blouse, and a hot wetness between her legs, he with an iron hard poker tenting out his pants. Politeness dictated that they should stay and let her greet all her acquaintances, but their need was obvious and no one could have been surprised when they slipped away to find each other again in the privacy of their bedroom.

At first Henry teased her, keeping her at arm's length, while he explored and approved her rings and the neat rod that pierced her clit from end to end, turning her, and making her bend, while he admired the delicate architecture of her remodelled anus. She was panting with her need and begged to be allowed to serve him, to show him just what she could do.

"Please, please, Henry," she pleaded between her parted legs as she hung head down looking at him where he stood behind her gloating over her lovely bottom, and the gleam of gold in the gap, "I can't wait. Don't be so cruel. Let me rape you right now."

He laughed and threw himself back on the bed, his penis pointing skyward like a flagstaff.

172

"Permission granted," he replied, and was overwhelmed by an avalanche of hot pulsing femininity.

PART FIVE: DISPLAYED

"I reckon we'll be the dream team this year," Renee said, as she sipped her Martini. "One Blonde, one brunette and a redhead. Now that you've become one of us and qualify for the festival, the set's complete."

"What are we going to have to do, anyway?" Jenny wanted to know. "All Henry would tell me was that I'm elected and to report to Lady Hartington up at the manor for training."

"All you need to know, as an obedient Swive. Men aren't obliged to tell us anything they don't want, or can't be bothered to," Laura reminded her.

"I know that, but I can't help wondering."

"Then we'll put you out of your misery," Renee laughed. "There's no law against it."

"Shouldn't be too sure of that," Laura put in, "it's sure to come under being mouthy or some such but, hell, we can sort that out on Friday night."

"As per usual," Renee agreed. "Anyway, Friday bottom or not, it's an annual affair, a left over from a very ancient fertility rite they say, even before the Romans came this way. At one time virgins were deflowered in the fields to help the crops along but there seems to be a shortage of such these days, virgins that is, so more experienced women, to whit Swives, appear in public with just a token nod to decency, but little else on, and ride on decorated floats from village to village. All the pubs in the valley enter a float, usually with something relevant to their name as the theme. Being the Trident, we usually have something to do with the sea."

"So what's it to be this year?" the latest recruit wanted to know.

"Ah, that's a secret," Laura said, "Tom and George and some others lock themselves away in the big shed behind the pub every evening. Besides consuming a fair amount of beer, they bang away on their little secret and won't tell us a

174

thing."

"We'll find out soon enough," Renee assured her, "and, knowing our men, I have no doubt we can look forward to being both very uncomfortable and very embarrassed."

Lady Hartington was a well-preserved woman somewhere in her mid fifties, just possibly a year or two older, her grey hair but upright carriage making estimates difficult. The girls were disinclined to ask her since besides a totally commanding manner, she also sported a very vicious crop which, she made clear from the start, she had every authority and intention to use on their tender behinds should discipline be infringed, or duty shirked.

The purpose of their twice-weekly visits to the manor, where Lady Hartington lived, was twofold. In the first place they were to construct the costumes that they were to wear on the float and, in the second place, they were to undergo periods of special exercises to acclimatise certain vital parts of their anatomy for the occasion. Mostly they were able to combine the two.

The costumes consisted of fishtails, made from a specially moulded plastic material with the texture of giant fish scales, which wrapped around their closed legs, leaving them with the appearance of mermaids. The material had to be measured, cut, sewn, fitted with eyelets for laces along the back, and attached to a pair of flippers that would take their feet below. It was obvious that the maritime motif was to be maintained. It seemed to the most recently joined that the costume might be a little less than adequate for an English rural scene, seeing that the fish scales came scarcely up to her mons, and there were, as yet, no signs of any covering for her not insignificant breasts. She was discouraged from curiosity in the matter though after Lady H had dismissed her questions as irrelevant and emphasised the point with three stinging cuts of her ubiquitous crop to a pair of tautened buttock tops.

The cuts were delivered vertically from above on two swelling hams overlapping an inadequately seated stool, an immensely painful way in which to be hewn by a length of leather covered whalebone. Moreover, the cuts had to be taken with perfect immovability not only because it would have been considered insubordination to wriggle while whipped, but because the stool was equipped with a very substantial vertical phallus, and that phallus was lodged firmly and deeply in her protesting rectum. The pole sitting was part of the preparatory exercises prescribed for these nubile float riders and they were made to mount these punitive pegs whenever the nature of their work allowed it. It did not bode well for their comfort on the day of the festival; since it did not take much imagination to deduce in what manner they would be seated on the float.

Their leg casings completed to Lady Hartington's satisfaction, at some considerable cost in female yelps and writhing from her favourite crop, they were given a mass of imitation plastic seaweed, from which they were invited to cut suitable pieces to just cover their nipples and surrounding areolae. Too much modesty was punished in the usual way, certain backsides becoming seriously sore and, the minimal coverings being deemed acceptable, they had to fit them with some nasty looking spring loaded clamps, whose sickle blades and sharp teeth promised more misery on the ride. Finally, their anuses well-exercised, their costumes complete, the day of the festival dawned bright and clear, and they were introduced for the first time to the vehicle they were to adorn with their near-naked nubility.

The float carried an enormous fibreglass head of the sea god Neptune, with beard dripping seaweed, and a hand grasping a huge trident, rising from a sea of rolling waves, each forming a seat for a mermaid attendant, dolphins emerging to cover the front of the pick-up truck that formed the basis and motive power of the exhibit, blue tinted glass slots enabling Tom, who was to drive it, to see out.

One mermaid sat either side of the head, and one in front. Each had her feet and legs encased in a tight 'fishtail' of moulded silver latex, which just came onto her buttocks behind and wrapped around her hips to finish along the creases at the tops of her thighs in front, just about covering her mons and leaving her belly and navel quite bare. The rest of each female body was just as bare, save for bunches of seaweed strategically placed to barely cover the nipples and their pink areolae. The green sea-wrack seemed to be without visible means of support though it was, in fact, securely fastened to their dugs, and only the girls knew the true cost of this inadequate concession to 'decency', and how much pain they were suffering from the cruel clamps that chewed unmercifully on the gristly stems of their teats.

The girls appeared to sit quite freely on their moulded seats, their arms able to wave at the crowd and throw small blossoms from the baskets in their laps. In fact they were as much prisoners as butterflies pinned to a board. The 'tails', which bound their legs so cruelly they ached from the moment they were donned, tight laced behind to ensure absolute rigidity from ankle to hip, were secured to the deck at their feet and, moreover, were split behind, under their bottoms. Here was the ultimate cruelty, for the small bucket seats, that supported them, letting their partially scale covered buttocks flare out over the edges, carried two prongs, seven inch cylinders, one tapering from a root over an inch and a half across to a one inch neck, above which a knob like the male glans swelled, and a very well endowed male at that. The other phallus was an inch and a half all along its length, crowned with a two-inch ball. Once the shafts were inserted, and locked by wing nuts below the seats, there was no way the girl could extricate herself. She had to stay on her impalement, feeling it thrust deeper against her womb and guts with every jolt of the float. Luckily for them, the

177

procession moved at a slow pace, but the village street was pitted and uneven and, even at a walking pace, there was many a gasp, and a smile momentarily wiped out by a grunt of pain. When the wheels from time to time, encountered a more well defined obstruction, they clung to the float as best they could, Laura gripping the shaft of the trident, where it rose beside her, Renee throwing her arm around his maritime Majesty's moulded neck, the third member of the nubile trio leaning back against his beard, and holding on as best she could.

Their problems had not begun though with their public appearance. The mounting had been agonisingly slow and difficult. For a start, each girl had been responsible for greasing her own dildos. The process brought her face to face with the rampant prongs she would have to accept into her body, and they needed no encouragement to daub them liberally with Vaseline and, for good measure, thrust solid wads of the same semi-solid lubricant deep into their own threatened sphincters and vaginas. Squatting, naked, beside the float, each dipped her fingers deep into the jar, then worked the greasy gunge past her anal ring, rotating her fingers to distribute it evenly to try and ensure the least painful entry she could contrive, though accepting these brutal, insensitive intrusions in their rectal regions would never be a picnic. There was less urgency about their vaginas. As healthy and well-serviced young women, they were never actually dry between the plump labia that graced the fork of their shapely thighs, but a little extra on the edges of the lips themselves was a wise precaution against them becoming trapped, and drawn painfully into the vaginal entrance when the bald alloy knob sank inexorably home under their own weight.

The anal plug was fixed in unyielding verticality, though inclining forward slightly, the better to enter a seated female bowel. Its tapering stem was a daunting inch and a half at the base, the size of it causing sphincters to cringe before ever making contact. A bulging glans, even more monstrously gross, crowned the seven-inch horror, and the future rider's fear.

The vaginal visitor was a simpler, if rather larger, affair, a two inch ball set on a one and a half inch stem, but it was adjustable, lying to one side before use, and a cause of much less fear, each girl knowing that a ball that size would present no real difficulty for a vaginal canal designed to accept the head of a babe, and already well exercised by the male member. Its stem passed through a slot in the seat, and would be locked in place by a nut beneath, when it had been located correctly to bear internally against the rigid anal distender, and make her prisoner by the infernal pincer movement on the walls of vagina and rectum.

Laura was mounted first but, before she could gain the top of the float, there was an interruption, and she was recalled to the ground.

George had come to supervise the mounting and give them final instructions and inspection. Now he stood before the three naked women, lined up with their backs to the float, while he addressed them. Their attention was assured; if they had not already learnt to dwell on his every word, by the lean and hungry length of yellow cane he flexed in a straining arc between his capable hands.

"The Trident has always turned out a dazzling float," he told them, "we have been renowned for it for generations. Do not let us down this year. We are expecting you to win when the judging takes place."

He looked them over searchingly. "Yes, you are all beautiful," he assured them, "but you are not tranquil. Your nerves are on edge, your knees tremble, there is apprehension in your faces. You must not show it to the people in the streets and, particularly, not in front of the judges. You are sea nymphs, riding proudly with your lord on his watery chariot,

179

proud and confident. You need something to calm you."

He gestured with the wicked wand of pain in his hand.

"Turn around Laura, and lean yourself over the front of the float." he commanded.

While the other two still faced unswervingly to the front, Laura turned and moved behind them. George moved out of their sight in her wake, and there was a short pause, filled with small sounds of naked flesh being laid on the float, a slight creaking as the suspension adjusted. The silence that followed stretched their nerves, for they had no illusions how this 'calming' was to be achieved, only how big their tally was to be. Then came the familiar heart-stopping whirr of the rod parting the air on its way to wreak havoc in tender buttock meat. The loud report of its landing was accompanied by a gasp from the bent girl, then a pained intake of breath as the fearful cut into her bent nates flowered into its true agony. The waiting girls could not see the execution but could hear every nuance, counting the strokes in mounting fear, knowing they would have to endure the like themselves, before they came to mount their float for the parade. They were horribly conscious that they would have to ride their painful mounts with the additional distraction of fresh searing welts under them, on the hard seats. Two, three, four, five, the count mounted, and the women trembled. Laura's gasp on the sixth stroke was almost a cry, experienced though she was at this exercise, and there were shudders of mingled fear and relief when it proved to be the last of her count.

Now it was Renee's turn to bend over the rounded prow of the float, while Laura took her aching backside to stand with the remaining naked nymph facing away from the scene, but hearing each cut as it fell. The hard plastic moulding dug into Renee's belly as she stretched herself over it, parting her legs without instruction. She had taken this position too many times now to need directions, and dropped her waist to cant up her pelvis to the rear, offering the under-side of

180

her buttocks, where the rod would bite deepest and the welts would be placed on that part of her that would bear her weight on the long afternoon pilgrimage through the villages

Her skin shrank from the flogging to come. She hated the cane; oh how she hated it. The strap stung and burned, the paddle's slap sent sheets of flame through bruised buttocks but the cane was the worst of all, combining all that was hardest to bear of each. Moreover, its effects lasted longer, ached and throbbed when others had died to mere warmth, awoke to sore remembrance on sitting days after. Now she would have to sit on these flaming brands, as well as her other hurts to come. She would not flinch from it, she steeled herself not to disgrace herself, but it would be hard, so very hard.

George was cutting deep today, the first stroke nearly undoing her as it burrowed into her flesh below. God, she had forgotten already how such a rod was twice as potent in the hands of a male, than even in Lady Hartington's rigorous grip. It seemed to slice her in two, and her breath was driven from her in a grunt of pain as the fire burst across her haunches, then she was sucking it in again as she fought the flooding tide of the returning blood and the agony it brought with it. The rod returned, she bunched her fists and beat on the float as she fought to bear what was almost unbearable. If George could bring her to the edge of disgrace in two strokes only, and he had tested her severely, how was she to endure four more of the same? Of the same! The next seemed not of the same but infinitely worse, as he wrapped the limber stick around the base of her buttocks, catching the crease of her thighs.

It was a horror of a cane, long whippy and full of weight, especially the last few inches, which seemed denser than the rest and drove deep into her flank. She sucked in air as the flame burst in her tender under flesh, her head back, eyes staring blindly at the sky, as she fought to control her

181

rebellious body. The pain rose and rose. Just as she prayed it would get no worse, for she despaired of enduring it, the cane returned.

Again to the same place, and the last two only millimetres higher. She was barred heavily right under her 'seat' when she was finally allowed to rise and yield her place to the third victim. Her eyes were wet with tears, the sweat of agony was in her armpits, her lips were puffy from the pressure of her sharp teeth from her desperate efforts to stay down for the cruel flogging.

Another two minutes, filled with the flash of the cane and the redheaded nymph's answering gasps and hisses of pain, and it was done. George dismissed them to Lady Hartington's attentions and went off to join with the rest of the group gathered on the green in front of the pub. It had been cruel, certainly, but not wantonly so. As she stood there, her buttocks still aching, the throbbing agony scarcely subsided yet; she knew he had been right. They had all three been subject to a rising excitement, bordering on hysteria, as they had faced the ordeal of self-immolation and their public exposure, near naked and impaled front and back. Now they were sore but calm. She began to understand a little more how the men knew them better than they did themselves.

Once again, Laura went to mount first, climbing up, quite naked, to stand on a small ledge just in front of and below her appointed seat. Lady Hartington stood on a pair of steps alongside, ready to assist.

The girl picked up her 'fish-tail' costume, lying waiting for her and stepped into it carefully, one foot at a time, drawing it up tightly until the back just reached the edge of her buttocks behind, wincing as it came in contact with the fresh flaming brands across the base of her bottom. With Lady Hartington's help, the lacing was tensioned and tied off, until her legs were bound tightly together along their entire length, ankles, calves, knees and thighs, until she was

182

no longer a biped but a single-limbed marine creature.

Next she tugged up the front edge, straining until it just reached her shaven mons, and took the side flaps round her hips to join the clasp, just above her coccyx.

Her buttocks were now covered, at least any part of them that overhung the bucket seat when she lowered herself into it, but the fish tail gaped behind, between thigh tops and her anal cleft.

She reached behind and inserted her fingers in the divide of her buttocks, pulling the cheeks apart to reveal the small thick-rimmed crater of her anus glistening thickly with its anointing of petroleum jelly.

Very thoughtfully, her underlip caught between her sharp white teeth, her forehead creased in a frown of concentration, she bent from the knees and sought the waiting, Vaseline slick apex of the phallus with her quivering anal opening. A couple of false starts and she had it located, the tip lodged. Slowly, oh so slowly, she eased her weight down, the snake head of the dildo depressing the whorled anus to start with, then gaining a little purchase between the raised ridges of the rimming, and wedging the sphincter open. Her frown deepened, her lip paled as she bit harder with the effort of will she was making and she let more of her weight come on the solid moulded stake. It responded by stretching her anal muscle further still and burrowing deeper. Sweating now, she kept up the effort and slowly, painfully slowly, reached the widest point, the utmost stretching of her muscular ring and then, suddenly, thankfully, she was past the greatest distension and contracting gratefully onto the lesser rod below.

She let go of her nether cheeks, the impalement was automatic and inevitable from now on, and began to sink slowly towards the seat.

As she did so, Lady Hartington manipulated the ball headed monster into her vaginal entrance and ensured both impalements proceeded together.

With the widest parts passed, and her weight less and less supported by the thrust necessary to achieve penetration, the motion accelerated suddenly and she groaned as her impalements almost shot home the last few inches. As she reached the root of the rear intruder the flared base began to stretch her anal ring again, but there was no stopping it now. This far down, and at the angle in which she was crouched, she would never be able to get her weight off the rod and would have to endure as best she might as her cheeks flattened on the hard shaped seat and her anus renewed its protest.

It was not the only protester. The pole was seven inches up in her gut, filling her, feeling as if it was in her throat, and bruising her entrails. As she panted and groaned, trying to accommodate the distension, Lady Hartington adjusted the vaginal plug until the ball end pressed firmly through the wall of her sheath against the glans of the anal shaft, and locked it tight. Now, even with assistance, she could not vacate her seat until the fixing was relaxed.

Lady Hartington closed the access hatch below the seat, through which she had worked the front prong, and locked it, then took hold of the fins at the end of the tail. Laura straightened her bound legs, letting the last remaining weight come off her finny feet onto her seat, and the two impaling rods, and Lady Hartington threaded the strap sewn under the tail fin through a hole in the float and secured it underneath. The attachment gave her stability and she would not fall from her perch under any circumstances, though she had no illusions that her ride might be comfortable in any way, or that she night not suffer severely in the process of maintaining her position.

Decency was preserved below, but only just, with the scales of the costume barely covering her vulval slot, leaving the polished dome of her pubic mound bare, as the minimal costume curved away to wrap her buttocks down to the edge of her seat. Decency, of a sort below but, above, her breasts were bare. Lady Hartington handed up the rest of the costume that she had worked on so hard during the weeks of preparation. It consisted of two pieces of artificial seaweed, each large enough to cover about two thirds of a generous breast and they were artfully irregular in shape but, in the centre of each, was concealed a cunning and diabolical clip. Its two sickle shaped halves were spring loaded, and she must open them and then let the clips close around the base of each nipple. Her cherries were already a little erect, but not entirely so. The long hard struggle to achieve impalement with minimal agony and without injury had dampened her natural arousal at being naked and about to be publicly exposed. She had to manipulate her dugs to get them sufficiently engorged and erect so that the clips could grip them securely at their base, where they would remain securely, rather than at the bulb or, worse, the tip, when there would be a risk that the barely adequate protection might fall or the nipple be injured.

At last she was satisfied the blood filled nubbin stood out sufficiently for safety and pressed one hard teat into the wide held jaws. She knew what came next; they had practised this manoeuvre too during those long sessions on the training poles. Gritting her teeth, she released the spring and the sharply pointed serrations on the inside of the jaws bit deep into her tenderest flesh.

She hissed through clenched teeth until the first wave of stabbing pain passed, then subjected the other nipple to the same abuse.

Only now was she ready. She smiled wanly at Lady Hartington and nodded to show she had completed her preparations. The tweedy Lady of the Manor moved off to set up the next female sufferer.

One down, and two to go. The next in line had watched Laura's desperate efforts to impale herself with mounting misgivings. When the girl gasped, as the anal dildo sank home, Jenny's own russet fringed sphincter had flinched in sympathy. She had already shaved her pubis, powdered her legs carefully to receive the scaly leg casing, and anointed the twin dildos of her own seat liberally, together with her anus and vaginal opening. Seeing Laura's struggles, she took up the pot again and stuffed another generous dollop of greasy lubricant into and around her wrinkle rimmed rear crater. Better safe than sorry! Now Lady Hartington was coming towards her and the frantic butterflies in her belly went into overdrive.

At Lady Hartington's command, she clambered up to her allotted seat and stood on the ledge below it, taking up the fishtail costume.

It felt cold and heavy, the thick latex sheath, with its moulded scales, clammy against her skin. She inserted one foot into the split fin of the tail without too much difficulty, but had to push hard, and wriggle her toes, to get the other in. The thick latex clamped her ankles together tightly and she pulled the rest of the tail up her legs to her thighs, shivering at its rubbery coldness on her bare flesh. Even with the rear lacing slack, it pressed her calves, knees and thighs together tightly. She wriggled her hips and worked it up to the under-hang of her buttocks, where they formed a slight crease at the tops of her thighs, a spot still marked and sore from her most recent beating.

Lady Hartington gripped the laces and pulled them tight, working from ankles up, and buttocks down, until her legs were fused into a solid mass, the mythical mermaid without thighs or crotch.

Now she took over her own encasement again, worked the upper part, setting the topmost row of scales to touch the hairless pout of her waxed pubis, fitting neatly into the creases of her thighs, where they formed a vee directed downwards towards her vulva. With the crucial slit just covered, the gold ball of her 'Christina' piercing gleamed brightly against her pale hairless skin. She tugged on the sides and held them behind her for Lady Hartington to grip.

Grim-faced, the horsy aristocrat seized the ends and yanked hard, almost knocking the girl off her precarious perch, but making the clasps on the ends meet at the base of her spine with a very positive click, the final link in the rubber bonds that encased her from ankle to hip.

The only interruption was the gaping slit giving access to her anus and vagina. She reached behind and put her fingers in the gap, plumbing the depth of her crack, then puling the cheeks apart.

Now was the moment she had been dreading, when she must approach the twin dildos awaiting her, one springing rampant from the centre moulding of the seat, craning forward at a slight angle, the better to penetrate her, the other allowed to fall away for the moment, but the great ball end full of greasy menace, nevertheless, as it lurked in readiness to fill her vagina.

Still holding her cheeks open, she bent her knees, lowering her buttocks and seeking out the thrusting conical nose of the rampant dildo behind her. Too high! The nose touched the bottom of her anal cleft above the cringing sphincter's insink and she raised her hips slightly to slide it down the crack towards its target. She could feel it creeping inexorably along the Vaseline coated groove and then it was pressing insistently at her portal, and would not be denied. She took a deep breath and let her weight fall harder on it. The point responded by depressing the delicate brown whorl that closed the space inside the raised rim that marked her for a Sexton wife. More pressure and it forced the pass, starting to open the bud and stretching the sphincter that controlled it.

She steeled herself for the inevitable discomfort, and pressed even harder and the unfeeling wedge responded by driving in deeper and widening the opening. She was

187

approaching the widest part now, over an inch and a half across, and it was becoming distinctly uncomfortable. She hesitated a second, arresting the painful progress, and Lady Hartington growled at her to continue, emphasising her point with a solid smack of a work hardened hand on the portion of buttock still exposed above the low cut costume.

Desperately, she shoved her bottom backwards and downwards, and her sphincter closed with relief over the bulging knob, grateful to have passed the worst, and only have an inch or so of girth to accommodate.

"Hold it!" Lady Hartington snapped, and presented the glistening ball of the vaginal plug to the entrance to her feminine sheath.

"Go ahead," she commanded when it was in position, loosely held with the ball an inch or so within her pouting labia, and the girl let her weight fall back.

She had passed the point of no return now, she knew, and she could no longer control her own penetration. Oh god, it will split me in two, it feels as if it's in my gullet and going to choke me. I can feel my eyes bulging, she thought, as the flare at the dildo's root stretched her even further than the knob had done, and then she felt the nose pushing up seven inches into her belly. Indeed her eyes were bulging in their sockets with the strain of accommodating it and its comrade filling her vagina and swelling her belly in front, and her mouth gaped open in shock.

After a minute she had overcome the worst of the trauma, and Lady Hartington lifted her bound feet off the ledge and straightened her fused legs, securing them down and out in front of her by the strap attached under her feet, then returned to set the vaginal plug. Jenny gasped as the ball end clashed with the heavy knob in her rectum through the thin membrane separating the two.

All that remained now - and it was a big 'all' - were the two bunches of seaweed to cover her breasts, or at least the nipples and areolae in the interests of public decency. She had examined the fancy brassiere beforehand, had indeed tested it, but the sharp teeth, set in a crescent like a shark's jaw, still left her apprehensive. These were going to hurt, and she'd best prepare her mind as well as her teats. In the event her breasts sported hard, engorged, gristly teats, her usual reaction to fear and the anticipation of sexual torture, and the large nipples stood out like babies' thumbs, ready for the clamps to settle on their roots and start their painful work.

Jeez! It was far worse than she had remembered. No wonder Laura had made such a meal of it. She doubted if she could digest her own bitter portion with as much dignity. As she set the second in place she whined and snorted through her nostrils. The tears the first application of the asp-like bite had brought to her eyes had drained into her nose and now wet snot soiled her upper lip, and dripped from her chin.

"Don't make such a fuss, child," Lady Hartington admonished, "anyone would think you were going to be hanged; not be the star of the show."

"You don't know what it's like," she wailed in protest. "You haven't had to take a prong up your arse, and another in your belly, let alone have your teats cut off by a rat trap."

"Oh you girls," the Lady sighed, more in sorrow than in anger. "You seem to think that you're the first generation to have invented sex and sadism. I suppose it's always been so, though. I know my generation was the same, and my mother's before that. Goes all the way back to Eve, I suppose, made to suffer for seducing Adam. Let me tell you, young lady, if I were to drop my britches right here which, I might add, I have no intention of doing, you'd find me ringed and rimmed as tightly as any of you. I was writhing and squealing on old Doctor Gillespie's block, having my bum cut and stitched, while you were still sucking on your mother's teats, and we didn't have all Greta's modern refinements in my day either.

189

Took hours and we just had to grin and bear it."

All three girls looked at her in open-mouthed wonder, and a newfound respect for the still handsome aristocrat. So she was a Sexton wife too. Who would have guessed it?

Two down and one to go. While Lady Hartington moved off to get Renee into place, the first two to be mounted tried to adjust their bodies to accept the various pains and discomforts. The latest to settle pawed the air with her fingers, as if playing an invisible piano, fighting the almost irresistible urge to wrench the clips off her martyred teats but mindful of the awful punishments she faced if she disobeyed the explicit instructions she had received to leave them in place. Each of them wriggled on their seats, to try and accommodate their impalement better, and each fervently prayed that the teeth in their breasts would cease to bite so keenly and that the sharp pain would soon subside to a more bearable ache.

When Renee's gasps and cries had indicated that she too had been set in place, Lady Hartington visited them all again, wiping tear stained cheeks, dabbing a little powder on shiny noses, repairing bitten lipstick, brushing hair disordered by frantic head waving, as the waves of pain had hit them and been fought to a standstill. They received her attentions with gratitude and a new respect.

Gradually the viper sharp pain in their breasts dulled until it was a dragging feminine ache, matching that in their bellies, the neural paths of the female sexual system directing each to flow towards a meeting in their vulvas, where it could be sublimated into something other than agony. Now they could compose themselves enough to smile with apparent sincerity at the spectators they would meet on their route, smiles filled with an almost luminous inner feminine radiance.

First though they had to reach the village green. Tom drove carefully out of respect for their predicament, for he had not missed a moment of their agonising and degrading installation, or their woeful reactions to their various impalements and clampings. But the track was ancient and rutted and their progress up to the main road nearly undid all Lady Hartington's last minute repairs to their toilettes, as they had groaned and shaken on their seats and the tears had sprung afresh to their eyes. They all felt intense relief and gratitude for the relative smoothness of Tarmac under the wheels.

By the time they had reached the assembly point on the green, the girls had mastered their discomforts and were wearing apparently happy smiles, seemingly unconcerned at their near nudity among the teeming crowds of residents and tourists. George greeted them warmly, obviously proud of his charges, reaching up to kiss each of them chastely on the cheek, before returning to his table outside the Trident.

From somewhere, Tom produced baskets of flower petals for them to throw to the crowd. The band struck up, the banners advanced and the floats followed, processing sedately round the village, visiting each of its pubs, applauded all the way by a cheering throng.

The girls found themselves, despite their discomfort, entering into the spirit of the occasion, swept along by the tide of enthusiasm and goodwill.

It was a classic demonstration of the ability of nubile females to endure even the most unspeakable humiliations and discomforts, if they can exhibit themselves in public, preferably in a state of near nudity. One has only to watch the teens and twenties of the female gender spilling out of a disco in the snow, still barely covered while more sensible men will be fastening their windcheaters round their ears.

Their breasts still throbbed and ached, the malevolent invaders in their bottoms continued to contribute their dragging discomfort, every now and again the float wheels struck a too high paving slab, or a sunken drain, sending a jolt through them that played havoc in their bowels, but still they smiled bravely through, buoyed up by hot glances and

191

admiring comments from the crowd, repaying them with handfuls of rose petals scattered on their heads.

They even managed some good-natured repartee with the bold young men who took advantage of the slow speed of the procession to run alongside and pinch generous rolls of buttock flesh where it overhung the shallow moulded seats. By the time they returned to the village green, they bore crescents of black and blue bruises on their nether cheeks, painful but sincere tributes to their female attractiveness.

When they ran out of petals, they combed their long hair, attracting even more attention, the complimentary buttock nipping renewed with interest and responded to by oh's and ah's of half-hearted protest, though sometimes accentuated as an unexpected jolt disturbed their equilibrium. Finally the float drew up again before the Trident, while the panel of judges looked them over and discussed the finer points of their turn out and performance.

The half dozen men, drawn from all the villages taking part in the fertility festival, seemed to be having some difficulty coming to a decision. From time to time they would get up from their seats and move across to one or other of the half dozen floats that had been entered and take a closer look at the equipage and its riders. It may of course simply have been the natural male urge to take advantage of every opportunity to touch and admire bevies of such outstanding beauty as had been selected to take part, one could not blame them for that after all, but there did seem purpose in their fondlings and reason in their close inspections of the various sets of triple beauties they were observing so closely. One by one the floats were eliminated until only the Trident's Neptune and the trio of feathered 'birds' entered by the Cock and Hens pub from Foxis Mieux remained.

Renee was getting uneasy.

"I don't like it," she said doubtfully. "I think we may be about to dislike the next half hour intensely."

"What do you mean?" Laura asked. "It looks as if we're certain for runner up and we could easily win it. Personally I thought those half egg shells they used to cover their nips didn't hold a candle to our bits of weed."

"OK, so we could get second, but what if they call it a tie?"

Laura looked aghast.

"They wouldn't!" she gasped disbelievingly then, more doubtfully. "Would they?"

"I'm beginning to think so," Renee said glumly. "They seem to be going over and over it, first one float then the other. OK, some of it is just to cop a feel, after all that's part of the festival, but they seem to be stuck."

"Maybe they'll just declare it a tie, and share the prize," their redheaded partner suggested hopefully.

"Not a chance," Renee told her. "Quite apart from the fact it would go against the whole tradition, once they scent a tie-breaker in the offing nothing's going to cheat them of their fun."

"Oh, God, that last time I nearly died. I thought my tits would never recover. Don't tell me I'm going to have to put them on that damned table again and have them cut to ribbons like last time."

"With a bit of luck it won't come to that," Laura said. "That time was rather special. I haven't heard of a tit breaker being used at the festival before. No you can look forward to having your arse caned instead."

"Caned?"

"Yes. My guess is, we'll have to go up against the three girls from the Cock and Hens in a one on one caning comp," Renee said with continuing gloom. "That's how these things are usually settled, six each alternately until someone gives up. Ugh! I do hate canes."

As it turned out, she guessed correctly. The Chairman of the judges went to the microphone to announce a tie and that

193

there would be a tiebreaker:

"Nothing too demanding," he declared. "Just a simple caning competition. They're all experienced girls so they'll hardly feel it."

Renee snorted.

"Hardly feel it," she exclaimed disgustedly. "I'd like to see one of them keep bending for a girl to lay a rod across his bare bottom."

"No you wouldn't," Laura assured her. "It would offend your sense of what is proper, and quite right too."

"Yes. I know you're right," Renee said, resignedly. "But I do so hate that cane. I'd rather have anything else than rattan on my bottom. Of course that's why Tom sticks with it and it sure keeps me in line, but I can't help hating it."

"Well you'll have something to take your mind off it now," Laura informed her in an equally gloomy tone. "If we're going to pit our bottoms against those chicks over there we'll have to get ourselves off this float, and I think that's going to take all our concentration for the next few minutes."

She wasn't wrong. Lady Hartington soon had the hatches open, and their ball-ended cunt-stuffers loosened to allow them to pull themselves off them, but it was easier said than done. Just to move an inch cost a multitude of groans and moans as tortured flesh protested, while their limbs had stiffened during their long confinement, which made even small movements difficult. Slowly, painfully, they prised themselves off the horrid impalements, which exited their bellies with humiliating vacuum sounds, the anal plugs in particular emitting disgusting sucking noises as they came free. And some minutes later, when they were able to attain an upright posture again, there were even more humiliating parps and squelches as the trapped air in colon and vagina was expelled. Altogether they were both sore and red-faced before they could descend.

Once on the ground, their 'tails' discarded, there was the

small matter of their seaweed tit coverings. The rules of the tiebreaker, as explained with rather uncalled-for glee by the men, demanded that the contestants be quite bare, and the festoons of plastic weed covering their teats had to be discarded. A simple enough process and one ultimately to be welcomed, they were seriously sore by now, but the immediate future was bleak. All of them had had enough experience of this sport to know that their removal was an order of magnitude worse than their application. As each pressed on the vicious clip to remove a hated grip on her tender teat, she whined and writhed with the pain of the returning circulation, keeping up her tortured twisting for a minute or more before enough order had been restored to the mangled point for her to calm and think about facing the removal of its twin.

Eventually it was done and, red-faced, walking a little stiffly, for they were seriously sore inside still from the after effects of the ride on the twin dildos in their guts, they ascended the steps of the dais on which the judges sat. They were very conscious of the stares of the crowd and especially those strangers who had thronged in their hundreds to this otherwise secluded and neglected valley to see the famed fertility festival with its promise of female nudity and more. They were certainly going to get their money's worth this year, with a half dozen extremely nubile young women stripped naked and about to see who could lay the rod hardest across her opponent's bare backside.

The rules of the contest were simple, if the execution was arduous. Each girl on the team was to be paired off against one of the opposing side. Laura and Renee would go first, Jenny would go last as the least experienced.

"With a bit of luck you won't even have to try," Renee told her. "Laura and I should be able to see off those two soft bitches."

At first it seemed she might be right. Each girl had to

195

bend in turn and take six strokes of the cane from the other although, to keep it fair, the one who lost the toss and went first, only had to take half a sixer, before the cane was passed to her, and her rival had to present her own buttocks for a half dozen venomous cuts. From then on six of the best was the order of the day, until one either failed to come to the line, or rose before her tally was told.

Renee disposed of her opponent in a straightforward manner. She lost the toss but, despite her frequent and vehemently expressed dislike of the rod, took her three opening cuts without obvious difficulty. Perhaps, her redheaded teammate thought, she was putting up a heroic bluff to conceal her fear and loathing of the instrument. Allowed to stand, she took up the rod in a purposeful way that left her opponent yelping and kicking back her legs as the wicked rod cut into her soft buttocks six sizzling times. The battle raged without obvious advantage until each had received some thirty strokes but by then the blonde had had enough and failed to come to the line, shaking her head in denial as she clasped her sore and welted bottom, to indicate she was not prepared to put it up to be beaten any further.

Laura made a good start and soon had her opponent squirming and squealing but after three or four exchanges it becomes obvious that she, and most of the spectators who had plainly decided the girl from the Trident would soon be the winner, had been mistaken. Her opponent's movements had not been weakness, and the girl's accuracy and consistency was beginning to show in a solid narrow band of tumefied flesh under Laura's slightly fatted buttocks and a nasty patch on her flank where every cut seemed to terminate on the one spot, an ominously swollen bruise that threatened to burst at any moment.

Laura sensed her danger and whaled into the big soft bottom the girl from the Cock and Hens presented, but could make no significant impression on its plump cushions. Soon she was showing a very obvious reluctance when she was called to the line herself. Two rounds more and her tortured flank could not hold out and by the third stroke she was in agony with a thin trickle of red making its way down the side of her right thigh. She managed to hold out through the remaining three cuts, whining and writhing as the cane tip bit into an open wound, trying to turn her injured hip away, and made a final desperate effort to finish the match by using the last of her strength to punish the other bottom unmercifully, lashing into it with all her strength, but to no effect. This time her reluctance to bend again was obvious. There were tears of apprehension and pain in her eyes, which ran onto her cheeks as copiously as the rivulet on her flank. She held her ground for two fearful strokes and it looked as if she might master the third as well. For a moment she stayed bent, then slowly straightened, her hands going to clasp her ruined buttocks, while sobs visibly shook her whole body. Renee put her arms around the sobbing girl to comfort her.

So now it was up to Jenny. Well it seemed only fair. She had been a little hurt in any case to be treated as the weak sister, and now, willy-nilly, she would have to prove herself. With butterflies in her belly and an acute awareness of her nakedness and, especially, her bare tender buttocks, in front of a crowd of strangers from all over the county, she walked to the front of the dais and called as Tom tossed the coin. Tails! Ouch, she would have to go first. Still, it was only three, although that was a beastly cane the men had selected for the tiebreaker.

Long, lean and whippy, its honey coloured gleam spoke of more than mere sting on tender buttock flesh. Indeed, it was up to penal standard in all respects. She shuddered at the thought of a whipping of any length given by a man with such a stick. It was going to be bad enough with a woman's lesser strength. A sudden wave of fear and revulsion swept over her and she recognised that hatred of the cane that Renee had spoken of so bitterly. Now her own conditioning was approaching the point where she had only to see a rod to tremble at the sight of it, imagining it impacting her tender seat, raising thick hot welts on her defenceless rump which she would have to bare and bend so that it was totally exposed to the searing kiss. Now like Renee, and probably all the other Swives if she could only ask them, she found she dreaded the cane above all other instruments for the discipline of females. It cut, it stung, it sent waves of fire through her soft hinds as it struck, it left them stinging for an eon afterwards, it bruised her deep, so that she walked stiffly and awkwardly after a full correction, advertising her state under her skirt to any woman, and most men, she met in the village. It left her grunting and shifting on her chair when she sat, even days after she had suffered the actual cuts. No the cane was a beast among correctional instruments, tighter far than the strap or slipper, that spread their impact over acres of pneumatic posterior, allowing it to absorb the shock, or the friendly warmth of a masculine hand which, even at its horniest, was at least the human touch. Well, like it or loathe it, she was going to get the cane again, and in measure only limited by what she could endure. She prayed her opponent detested the rod with equal fervour and would not hold out for more than a couple of dozen strokes. Beyond that she was uncertain of her own endurance.

Well. She would find out soon enough. The last pair were being called to the front of the stage to perform their humiliating and painful pas de deux. As she took her place, back to the crowd, and bent to grasp her ankles, she felt more exposed and vulnerable than ever before. It wasn't as if she was unused to being naked in public, heaven knows a girl in Sexton went bare as often as clothed, or so it seemed, but that was usually confined to residents of the reclusive valley, where all shared in the knowledge of woman's position there and the girls all shared in the nudity. This was different.

Although not trumpeted abroad, news of the annual festival got around and there was a sizeable sprinkling of strangers among the crowd pressing up against the raised stage to catch a glimpse of female pudenda and flesh, voyeurs licking their lips over the girls' bare bodies and imminent immolation under the rod. She blushed crimson all over, a slight stirring of the breeze cooled her wet vulva and parted bottom crack, reminding her how totally and humiliatingly open she was to their hot gazes, how entirely exposed her pouting sex was between her spaced thighs, her anus still dilated from its rude impalement and rough ride on the float. She felt all buttock and bottom, quite apart from the threat of the rod that the girl from the Cock and Hens was swishing in fierce practice strokes that cut the air with an intimidating ripping sound and soon would be cutting her bare bottom flesh.

Thrrrrup! It caught her low on her cheeks, almost where they joined her thighs. She dug her nails into her ankles and bit off the cry that bubbled in her throat. This was a contest between girls, not a punishment from a master, and it would only encourage her opponent if she showed any sign that she was having any difficulty absorbing the stroke. Better to try and bluff her into thinking that all her effort was in vain.

Thrrrrup! Another beast but there was only one more to come before she could straighten and take her own turn on the right end of the stick.

Thrrrrup! The bitch! She was cutting low alright. Those three were all just where she creased under her bum, and they hurt like hell. Still, there was the blessed order to rise and she straightened painfully and held out her hand for the rod.

Her opponent, Beth, looked none too happy to hand it over but reluctantly let it go and advanced to take her place, bending and gripping her ankles, opening the crack of a well-developed bum, with slightly fatty cheeks and a wide pelvis that left a sizeable gap between her slim straight thighs. God she thought, looking at how the pose opened Beth's anal divide to the avid viewers, did I look like that? I must have done, I suppose.

The action of bending meant that everything Beth had was on view. Her vulva gaped and glistened, her cheeks were pulled apart by her pose and the rolled rim of her treated anus proclaimed her a Sexton wife as clearly as if she wore a placard with her status written on it. Even her breasts, with their turgid gold ringed nipples, showed through the wide vee of her legs, though pulled by gravity to show their soft white under-sides. A girl couldn't get more exposed than that.

Enough, she thought, I've got to get this bitch to say she's had enough and the sooner I lay some welts on that fat arse the better. She drew in a breath, and counted to ten slowly to settle herself after the waves of mortification that had swept her as she'd looked at Beth's degrading pose and recognised that she had made the same sexual spectacle of herself a moment before. Calmer, she eyed her target carefully, then wound up and let the rod fly in a sizzling arc into the ripe buttock flesh that Beth so generously displayed.

It seemed to physically shake the bending girl, lifting the soft cushions of the buttocks with its force. They shivered as they dropped back but, otherwise, the girl gave no sign of having been hurt. It appeared that two could play the confidence game. Methodically, leaving ten-second intervals between her strokes, she laid on the remaining five. By the end she had the satisfaction of hearing Beth grunt and gasp, and there were tell-tale twitches in the muscles of her inner thigh as she awaited each cut to her scalding bottom, but that was all. Now she would have to take a full six herself.

Grim faced she handed over the whippy cane and, once more, felt the shame of bending and presenting her bare buttocks and blatantly displayed vulval fig and rimmed anus to the avid gaze of strangers. It was an even more degrading experience this time, her mind's eye still filled by a picture of Beth's naked exposure and the knowledge that she was now the target of those eyes. Her embarrassment and humiliation did not last long however. Soon all such thoughts disappeared beneath the waves of pain and anguish that flooded her stretched bottom cheeks as Beth laid into her with a will born of determination and the desire for revenge for the hurt she herself had just suffered. As each cut burrowed into her cringing flesh she realised that Beth was working her lower and lower, and that she was taking the penal weight cane more on the tops of her thighs than in her actual buttock cheeks. Despite herself she was whimpering before the six were through and she offered tearful eyes to Beth as the latter handed over the cane prior to bending and presenting her own full seat to the rod.

Less than a dozen, and she was suffering. She'd have to make Beth feel every stroke if she was to have any hope of outlasting her. She increased her run by half a pace and dropped her shoulder to put every ounce of her weight behind each stroke. The rod was biting deep into Beth's generous gluteae, sending the thick slabby rump dancing with the shock of each cut, gratifying welts now standing proud of the pale skin. There were other signs too that she was hurting the girl, a certain urgency to her grunts of pain, the tight clenching of the buttocks after each stroke, white knuckles showing how she was gripping her ankles like a vice to keep herself from rising as the rod swept in each time to lacerate her bottom again. But as the last stroke sank in and she was allowed to rise, only a slight wetness around the eyes betrayed any real hurt.

Once more she had to bend and expose her cunt to coarse comments from lecherous visitors, though the embarrassment, while still strong, faded into less significance in the face of the imminent threat to her increasingly tender hinds. She had to hang on tight to slim ankles to stop herself

201

rising and running from the platform before the stinging rod impacted on her seriously sore flesh. Beth was still concentrating on her thighs, paying only token attention to her buttocks proper, laying the rod into what was fast becoming a single swollen belt of purple bruise, more on the tops of her legs than on her rump itself. One! Two! Three! Beth was laying them on with terrible precision on the tortured track. Jenny was whining and whimpering now, as she tried to absorb the searing cuts without conceding too much encouragement to her rival, but it was becoming increasingly difficult with the tumefied flesh, now swollen and tender, taking the full impact of that horridly stringent rod. She stuck it out without actually screaming her hurt aloud but when allowed to rise she did not at first take the proffered rod from Beth's hand. Instead she felt gingerly behind her, testing the hot raised bruise that decorated the tops of her legs. It stung like a viper's bite and pulsed and throbbed incessantly. Even the touch of her own probing fingers caused her to gasp in pain and she could feel the heat as she explored the wounded thighs, the merged welts standing proud, as thick as fingers, from the surrounding flesh.

It was obvious she could not take many more like these on this vulnerable strip of flesh. If Beth would only beat her on her padded bottom cheeks she knew she could hold out much further but this was getting too much for her. She considered appealing, complaining that it wasn't fair to keep whipping her there, off her bottom's limits as it were. But no-one had appealed before in the contest, nor in any other similar circumstance she had witnessed since coming to Sexton and it was pretty obvious it just wasn't done. She would have to grin and bear it but perhaps, she thought as she accepted the whippy cane that Beth still held out, she could try something of her own. She'd noticed from the first moment when Beth had bent and presented her own fatty hinds for the first dose of rod, that the girl had a wide pelvis

202

and slim thighs that left a marked gap between them. Now, as she took position, legs spaced to brace herself, buttocks lifted by her ankle gripping bend, her plump fig pouted blatantly between her thighs, set so low and with such meaty lips that it reached through the gap at the top of her legs and nearly projected beyond their limits. It was one of the most prominent quims she had seen on a woman and a cause of much comment from the crowd, some admiring, more merely obscene. Could she take advantage of Beth's possible weakness? Why not, she thought, the bitch is cutting my legs off. I'm entitled to whip her cunt if she sticks it out like that.

There were risks though. It was just possible, though unlikely, that Beth might appeal for a foul stroke if she tried it. More likely, she might respond in kind. Her own red haired pussy was pretty vulnerable to attack from behind, set as it was between equally well-spaced thighs. What the hell! She had nothing to lose. She couldn't go on taking them on her legs like this and a cut to the cunt might be almost a relief. Nothing could have illustrated her desperation more clearly than the latter thought. In that mood she gripped the vicious length of yellow rattan firmly and addressed her target, trying to keep the element of surprise by tapping gently on the right buttock, but keeping the point well on its fullness and much lower than she had been hitting. She shuffled her feet slightly backwards and drew back her arm. When it returned, with a belly clenching ripping sound, she had drawn her body back slightly and lowered her shoulder just a touch and the rod wrapped itself round the base of the left buttock and its tip, grazing the inside of the right cheek, bit unmercifully into the fatty labial plum, exactly as she had planned. Beth went rigid, her mouth opened in a silent scream as she realised what had been done to her, then she choked and gurgled in her pain, with her head thrown back, as its full intensity hit her.

Perhaps she had been too hurt to take it in instantly or

she put the horrible blow down to an error on her adversary's part; an unintentional miss-hit. Whatever the reason, she pulled herself together and dropped her head to ready herself for the next stroke. It was an exact replica of the first.

Now there could be no doubt among either victim or spectators about what was afoot, and a buzz of excitement ran through the audience, while Beth visibly cringed from the stroke to come. Already her plummy vulva had swollen alarmingly under the first two cuts. How would it hold up under four more? In the event the point was never tested. Beth held bravely on while the third stroke tore into her tortured quim, biting into the swollen labia and whimpered as the next approached. Her fear was intensified by the feel of cold air on the wetness of her vaginal opening, the swollen labia having parted and left it exposed to a direct hit from the searing cane tip. Her opponent had already spotted the opening and was not about to waste it. She belted the rod down, aiming for and finding the weakness in Beth's pathetic defences and the rounded end of the rattan rod disappeared into the pulpy gap in the labia and, as luck would have it, impacted directly on the tiny hole of the girl's meatus. Under the horrible bite into the mouth of her urethral tract her bladder gave way, and she collapsed to her knees in a small pool of her own golden urine.

Renee and Laura swept up the victor and bore her off to the bar.

"Do you think I cheated, hitting her like that?" the latter asked, still tearful but fortified by a stiff drink.

"Oh, darling, of course not," Renee reassured her. "She was the one making it a no holds barred match, whipping you on the legs like that. If she wasn't prepared to whip your bottom like a Gentlewoman she deserved all she got."

There wasn't time for more discussion, as their men bore them off in triumph to the Bay Tree for a victory dinner. When they placed their still naked charges on their knees beside them, to be fed delicacies from their own plates and dosed them liberally with the best wines in the restaurant, it was not an act of discipline, as so often the case when a naked Swive knelt docilely by her man, but an act of kindness. None of the three would have liked to put her wounded bottom on a chair of any sort, not even if padded with a pair of cushions.

The next day though they were sent to clean their mounts. Their pinched vaginal linings and trapped clits still ached in mute testimony to the abuse they had suffered on the rocky ride through the villages and country lanes that connected them. They blushed to see that not only the vaginal plugs but the seats as well, were encrusted with their female secretions, flowing freely in response to their publicly naked display, and the masculine attentions they had received. Despite the pain and discomfort that had accompanied them on their humiliating outing, their vibrant female natures had triumphed again.

"That girl of yours has come on remarkably well, Henry," the tall man nursing the large brandy and soda remarked in a conversational tone, "I'll be the first to admit I had my doubts when you first brought her to Sexton, but these last three years she's shown a remarkable adaptation to the life. And she's such a stunner. I haven't got over the weekend you lent her to me to fill in for Meryl. She was quite delicious."

"Nice of you to say so," Henry replied. "Anytime you'd like a repeat visit, just let me know and I'll send her over."

"Oh, I wasn't angling for favours," Richard assured him, "just commenting on how you never can tell with women. She was so sure of herself, so confident in her profession, such an altogether twenty-first century woman, it was difficult to imagine her not just submitting to a man, but revelling in it too."

"Don't know about that," Tom contributed, coming out from behind the paper he had been studying. "It's my experience that that's just the type that does go overboard. Your little milk and water soft feminine type is often the most difficult to tame; too selfish and self centred by half beneath that weak woman exterior. The career girl appears the harder nut but once you've cracked her, she makes the best kind of woman to serve a man's needs. Perfect pets. Just look at Renee, Laura and Henry's girl. They all came from that stable and what a fantastic threesome they make."

Richard raised his glass in salute.

"I'll drink to that," he declared but Henry seemed to have reservations.

"Sometimes I think we've been almost too successful," he remarked thoughtfully. "My girl has thrown herself into the part so thoroughly she sometimes seems to be leading me, rather than the other way around."

"Ah!" sighed Richard. "That's what it's come to has it?

Well cheer up old chap. You're not the first man to come up against that particular difficulty. Serious, I grant you, but it is curable. A good formal flogging will usually pull them back into line. Quietens them down no end you know."

"Oh, she gets beaten hard and regular," Henry answered him, "I'm sure you've noticed the results on Friday nights. I don't think that it's going to change anything much if I just take a whip to her back, instead of a rod to her bottom."

"Quite so, not you!" Richard hastened to explain. "No, you mustn't do it yourself, that'd never do. What you have to do is send her for a proper judicial flogging. Meryl got that way once, making demands on me to satisfy her needs rather than mine. Sent her to Marindorra to be flogged and she came back transformed. No trouble ever since."

"Marindorra? What else goes on there then?" Henry enquired.

"Oh, they have an excellent house of correction for women over there," Tom informed him. "That vicious Doctor Greta, you know, the German bitch who does the business with Sexton wives, she's the medical superintendent there."

"Didn't enquire into any of the details of the process when mine was done," Henry admitted, "just interested in the results. A house of correction you say?"

"You bet. Some sort of ancient Episcopal foundation I believe," Tom replied, "provided for the needs of the principality and did a brisk business as well in the erring wives and daughters of European aristocratic houses. Quite secular now but still provides the same service for the remaining independent minor states in Europe and still takes in sinful females from the families of the rich and famous."

"They get imprisoned there?" Henry enquired.

"Mainly short sharp shocks," Tom explained. "Months rather than years, so that their absences from society can be glossed over and scandal avoided, but plenty of stick to compensate. A tight caning on a bare bottom before breakfast every day for the more minor offences; public drug and alcohol abuse, unsuitable boyfriends, that sort of thing, with bare-backed floggings in the chilly dawn for those who have really let the side down; disobeyed their men, caused any kind of open scandal that has disgraced the family name. You know the sort of thing."

"And they'd take a girl from outside for a whipping?" Henry asked

"No problem," Richard assured him. "As I told you, I sent Meryl up a few years back. I could let you have the Company jet to fly her there one afternoon, they like to have them in overnight ready for the dawn parade, and she'd be back here the following evening. Make it a Friday and she could be the centre of the usual gathering in the Trident."

"Sounds good to me," Henry admitted, "and would answer one of her outstanding requests very appropriately I think. It's just about three years since she became a Sexton wife and she's been dropping large hints, almost nagging you might say, about doing something very special to mark the occasion. A judicial flogging in a prison yard might be just the thing."

"Yes, I think so too," Richard assured him. "Meryl was as supple as a glove after her visit."

"Then that's it then," Henry said decisively, "a bloody back for my lady in a cold yard. Quite Judge Jeffreys when you think of it. Thanks for the offer of the jet, Richard. That way, not only will we all get the benefit of her back while it's still hot, but I won't have to endure an empty bed for too long. I miss it when I don't have that hot little body against mine."

"Oh that's the least of your worries," Tom laughed, "Renee will be available, any time you like. Just give me the word; I know you've always fancied her. Actually, you'll be delighted with the substitution, I think. She fucks beautifully while, as to the back door, she's as sweet as a nut and as agile as a

208

monkey. I'm prepared to believe she'd get a dead man to attention and milk him dry, if she could just get him started between those satiny arse cheeks of hers."

"That's extremely kind," Henry said gratefully. "But what about you?"

"Don't worry about me," Tom said with a grin of anticipation. "Bernard is away until the end of the month and he's asked me to keep an eye on Cleo for him; see she doesn't lack for anything while he's away. I'll wrap a nice whippy rod round that pert tight bum of hers to keep her lively for him and make sure she doesn't forget how to satisfy a man before he comes back."

"It's a deal," Henry replied.

As a result of this conversation, Jenny found herself, only a couple of days later, sitting with her hands cuffed behind her in the back of a prison van being driven up the long winding road to Marindorra by two smartly uniformed women guards.

Henry had given her but the briefest of details.

"I've always wanted to have you take a Judicial flogging," he had told her, "I'm given to understand that they still take a very tough line up there. They flog at dawn and I'll lie with Renee and think of you being put through it."

She'd talked at greater length with Renee.

"Promise me," she'd said, "that at dawn you'll roll on top of him and get him inside you. It won't be difficult; he'll be erect in seconds with your tits dangling in his face and your hot cunt swallowing his prick."

"Yes, I know Sexton wives aren't meant to do things like that," she had replied, when Renee had protested that it seemed a bit forward, "but he can whip your bum for you afterwards to pay you for that. It'll be nothing compared with what I'll be going through."

She hesitated a moment. "How many do you think I'll get anyway?" she asked.

"Not sure," Renee replied. "The last person I remember being sent for a flogging was Meryl, and she got two dozen. I think that would be about right."

"Jeez! As many as that? Alright, here's what you do. You wank on that rampant prick of his with that educated vagina of yours and see if you can get him off in twenty-four twitches, spaced out slowly like my flogging. You can do it, even after the kind of night you two will have spent together. Bring him off right on the last, just as I get my last lash. Promise?"

Renee had given her the promise she had begged for, and she had gone off to meet the plane Richard had so kindly lent to take her to her fate.

It was uncomfortable in the back of the windowless van, with her hands fastened behind, and the journey seemed to take forever but then they were pulling through the high arches of the massive medieval gatehouse of the forbidding house of correction, every corner of its cold stone mass designed to impart an appropriate sense of doom to the sinners consigned to it.

Released from the van, she was marched, still cuffed, into a wing of the grim establishment with no delay for baggage as she'd been sent with nothing more than the clothes she stood up in. The guards knocked at an office door, marked Superintendent, and pushed her through it to stand before a heavy desk at which another uniformed woman sat working at papers. After a short pause the woman looked up to give the prisoner a searching glance.

"Are you the girl to be flogged?"

When she admitted she was, the official asked her a series of more or less routine questions, name, age, place of birth, etc., and the name of the person who had referred her to the correctional establishment.

"And what is the reason for your referral to Marindorra?"

She hesitated a moment. How did one describe the

210

circumstances when they were not totally clear, even to herself?

"Preventive conditioning," she replied, "Mr Maltravers and I have been together for over three years now, for two of them I have been a Sexton Wife and it seemed an appropriate measure, given my demanding nature. Also," she added with a somewhat incongruous blush, given the circumstances, "I wished to make him a present."

The Superintendent looked up at her from her papers.

"Hmm," she remarked thoughtfully after a short period of reflection, "a trifle presumptuous on your part, I would say. Still no harm done. We can arrange for the fault to be corrected as part of tomorrow morning's proceedings."

Somewhat abashed Jenny asked if she night ask a small favour.

"I'm listening."

"When is dawn tomorrow, please?"

The Superintendent consulted a diary.

"0648. Why?"

"Mr Maltravers and my friend Renee will be thinking of me at seven. I would be grateful if it could be arranged that that is when I... that is... if it could actually be happening then. It would help if I knew they were lying there with me in mind."

"No problem. Now go with the sergeant. She will see to your preparation and medical. After we get the result of that you'll be informed of your sentence. You'll get some supper and then be put away for the night. You'll be called shortly before dawn."

The medical of course brought Greta, who grinned at her in recognition. Made to strip, her clothes taken away, Jenny lay on an icy cold plastic covered examination table while Greta minutely examined every inch and orifice of her body, before sending the sergeant off with a form for the Superintendent. While they waited, Greta gave her a coarse

211

cotton gown, which, she gathered, would be her only clothing during her stay in Marindorra. The returned sergeant held yet another official form.

"The prisoner, being certified as fit in mind and limb, is sentenced to twenty-four strokes of the whip on her bare back. Sentence to be carried out at dawn tomorrow."

The officer consulted the paper afresh and spoke again. "In addition, to punish the presumption displayed by the prisoner, the whipping will be taken crotched, the size and nature of any additional features to be at the medical officer's discretion."

She had just time to observe Greta literally licking her lips in anticipation as she was marched from the room to her solitary cell.

Dawn in the High Pyrenees came cold and dull, the sun not yet over the mountain rim that surrounded Marindorra. She was roused by the clang of the iron barred door as it was opened to allow in her early morning visitors, the guard and Greta.

The doctor carried a small bag which she laid on the plank bed that had served for the prisoner's night's rest.

"Get your gown off, girl," she ordered, "and come and stand here, with your legs apart."

Obediently she swung her legs off the bed, wincing at the feel of the icy flags under her bare toes and stripped the coarse garment over her head to stand quite bare where Greta indicated.

From the bag appeared two glistening yellow objects, rubbery looking, two-inch long, torpedo shaped horrors. She recognised them instantly as the twins of the horse suppositories she had had to endure on the 'treasure hunt' all that time ago.

"I won't be needing those," she protested, conscious that their use would mean immediate humiliation as the only toilet facilities in the bare, stone-walled chamber, more dungeon

212

than cell, was an enamelled bucket over which she would have to squat with Greta and the guard looking on.

"When you're screaming under sergeant Liebvicz's leather you'll shit, just so long as you've an ounce of shit in you," Greta assured her. "Believe me girl, they all do, and I'm not having you mess up the place if I can help it, so bend over and pull your cheeks apart for me."

Defeated, she bent over from the hips, reaching behind to grasp her tight twin buttock halves and pull them apart to reveal the rimmed and partly open anus that Greta herself had created there. She tried not to react as the first of the deadly inch-diameter suppositories pushed its way past her reluctant sphincter but couldn't quite suppress an involuntary clenching of her buttocks.

"Keep still," Greta growled, rewarding her with a stinging slap on one tender cheek.

Both barrels loaded, she was set to exercises designed to make the burning fluid washing her guts out as quickly and effectively as possible. And only when her sphincter was almost turning itself inside out in its contortions, was she allowed to run to the bucket and void the contents of her bowel noisily and humiliatingly into it.

By the time she had mastered her spasming belly, Greta was holding a solid leather belt with a chain and other daunting objects hanging from it. She had enough experience now to know that this was a crotch strap, and that she would be wearing it for her whipping.

It was not an ordinary - if such a term was justified - instrument either. The crotch chain itself was not unusual, that is to say it was a chain with medium sized square links which, she was very aware, would cut into a girl's tender parts like a knife if pulled really tight. With Greta applying it, she was quite certain it would be. The rather less common feature was the pair of plugs through which the chain was threaded. The anal plug was short, thick and smooth, little to complain of for a girl of her experience with an educated sphincter, well used to accepting some very significant male organs, but the vaginal plug was a different matter. Apart from its size, which was considerable, it was covered with a series of short studs. Not sharp, it was true, and unlikely to cause any serious injury of themselves, but obtrusive enough to guarantee considerable pain when trapped against the fat dildo in her rectum. Unless she could remain totally relaxed under the whip, she was going to come away from Marindorra with a sore belly as well as a sore back.

Obediently she parted her legs and bent her knees slightly to allow Greta to nose the horror between her plump labia, unaccountably glistening with female dew already, despite her knowledge of her coming fate or, could it be, because of it? She grunted sharply as Greta began the slow and painful process of driving it deep into the tender but muscular tube. When it was home, she bent forward submissively to grant Greta easier access to her rimmed rear crater, pulling the cheeks wide apart once more to accept the monstrous intrusion of the anal plug equally deep into her rectum. Plug and studs jostled each other deep in the hot humid reaches of her belly. If she thought she was suffering then, it was twice as bad when Greta hoisted the crotch chain as tight as a clipper's forestay, adding the pain of its angular links cutting into her soft vulva to the current and potential anguish in her guts.

Greta smiled evilly at her handiwork and invited her to resume her gown.

"It's time," the guard said, pinioning her arms behind her again, then pushing her through the door of the cell.

It was a long, cold walk in bare feet down the icy stone corridors that led to the prison yard, and not a particularly comfortable one. With the monstrous plugs churning within her gut and the cruel chain chaffing on her clit and her coccyx, she could only move in a painful shuffle, legs wide spread and waddling, urged on by the guard pushing on her back to hasten her progress. The yard itself was even worse; first cobbles, then cutting gravel that had her wincing at every step until she could reach the relative safety of the platform around the post to which she would be fastened to be whipped.

The welcoming party was as sparse as the yard was Spartan. The Superintendent and a male official, at least she assumed he was an official; in this strange world he might just as easily have been a merely curious spectator come to enjoy the invigorating sight of a woman flogged naked at the post. Did he perhaps have a woman of his own for whom he was contemplating such treatment? Besides these two, the only other person awaiting them was a large woman with brown skin, a prison officer it would seem, since she wore a regulation skirt and boots but, for this occasion, only a very skimpy singlet top, behind which her huge pendulous breasts swung freely even when she was at rest. Jenny could imagine how they would fly as the woman did her duty, for the thick black leather snake she was drawing through the fingers of one hand told without doubt just what her duty would be at this dawn execution. This monumental member of the female sex could only be Sergeant Liebvicz, under whose leather girls screamed and shat themselves. Springing from the platform by her side was the tall thick column of the whipping post itself, black oily looking timber, greased by the sweat and tears of the innumerable females who had pressed their tender bodies against its rough sides under the agony of the lashes to their naked backs.

As Jenny stood panting from the exertion of climbing the steps while cuffed, and handicapped by the bruising columns thrust up her vagina and rectum, the Superintendent formally recited her name, offence and sentence.

"...preventive conditioning... twenty-four strokes... naked back... crotched."

215

"Is the prisoner fit and ready?" the Superintendent enquired of the white-coated doctor.

"Fit for all punishment," Greta replied, "with an anal plug and vaginal discipline."

"You're a rigorous cat, Greta," the Superintendent said indulgently, "but it's within your rights. Very well, we may proceed. Carry on Sergeant."

Liebvicz stepped forward and removed the steel manacles, substituting wide leather cuffs with solid steel rings through which a length of tough rope was threaded. She passed the rope through an iron ring, set high on the post, and hauled on it until her victim was forced up onto her toes. With the rope cleated fast to hold the straining girl in position, the Sergeant bent and fastened the cuff of a spreader bar to one ankle, then drew the other ankle out to the far end of the bar, forcing Jenny to strain even higher on her toes. With the bar now dropped into a clamp at the foot of the post, the figure to be flogged was stretched as taut and trim as on a classic triangle.

There remained only one further act before the execution could proceed. The coarse prison gown was held at the shoulders by two studs. Sergeant Liebvicz unsnapped them and peeled the gown down to the victim's waist, leaving her whole upper body bare, her unprotected breasts rubbing on the rough surface of the post, the nipples hardening instantly with the combination of the freezing chill of the dawn air and the harsh frictioning of the grainy wood. She moaned softly at this new soreness to add to the anguish in her belly from the clashing dildos in her bowel and cunt.

"Ready Ma'am!" the Sergeant barked.

"Proceed."

As if on cue, the prison clock, set high above the great gateway, struck the hour. As the first chime rang out the lash fell across her straining shoulders.

It was incredible, unbearable, quite unlike anything she

216

had endured before, a line of fire across her back, pure pain with no sensual element to relieve its awful bite. A woman can always, even in the worst extremity, commute some of her agony into sexual stimulation if the whip is applied to her buttocks, so intimately connected to her genitals and the seat of her sexuality between her legs. But the lash of leather on her bare back is pure punishment, with no mitigation. Even a thrashing on the breasts, sensitive as they are, can hold an erotic element to take some of the edge off the agony but a flogging, the whip laid across her naked shoulders, is hard for even the most experienced woman to endure.

She choked on her pain, swallowing the scream that strove to escape, letting only a strangled gasp bubble from her throat. Her body tensed with the pain, and the spiked shaft within her vagina reminded her instantly of its presence.

As she waited in rising pain for the next blow to fall she had a sudden mental picture of Renee climbing onto Henry's rampant prick, taking it into her body and milking it with strong contractions of her well-trained vaginal muscles. When the leather cracked across her shoulders the second time, she clenched down deliberately against the spikes, imagining herself in Renee's place, the beloved penis deep inside her. The wave of pain she provoked seemed to cancel out some of the worst of the lash by tapping into the sexual charge building in her belly.

Sergeant Liebvicz was working her way slowly down the stretched white back, laying the strokes on in shallow vees from alternate sides. The first strokes had been high up, traversing the whole width of the shoulders, the weight of the blows throwing the victim against the post, her breasts slapping on the rough timber. When it was new the post itself must have been an instrument of torture, its rough hewn surface driving evil splinters into the soft defenceless breasts driven against it by the heavy blows of a judicial flogging. Even now its surface was ridged and grainy. Before the countless girls who had preceded her on this penitential pilgrimage had removed the splinters with their bare breasts, each touch of the wood must have been agony itself and the pain of the spiteful punctures an enduring torment for hours or even days until they could be removed from the tender tit flesh. The slight abrasion they now caused was almost welcome in its sensual connotations.

As Liebvicz progressed downwards more tender meat came under attack. First the tip of the thick leather thong burrowed into the opened and defenceless armpits, provoking even more anguish in the hanging girl, then the breasts, even though they were pressed against the post, were vulnerable to a leather serpent curling round her side, and leapt and juddered under the searing bites. Angry splodges of dark bruise soon sprang up on the tender sides of the vulnerable mounds even touching the turgid nipples on occasion and dragging sharper grunts of pain from the hanging girl.

Clinging to the picture she had conjured up of her beloved Henry thinking of her, as Renee pumped his cock in time to the lash, she kept to her own rhythm of contractions on the spiked dildo, trusting Renee to be keeping time with her. Her friend had suffered under rod and whip so often it would be instinctive for her to know at just what pace the pain would reach its apogee, that point when an expert whipper would strike again.

The light was strengthening now, the weak rays of the morning sun falling across the taut tormented back, throwing into relief the rapidly rising welts that ran across them. The bruises were darkening and swelling until they stood proud of the whipped flesh, the purple of the blood from crushed capillaries brightening in places where ruby specklets appeared on the traumatised weals.

She had clung on to her cries until now, merely grunting and gasping, whimpering softly as she waited in between, but the next caught a nipple, cruelly abrading the tender teat and she could hold it in no longer. As the scream passed through her throat she caught it and converted it into a word, shouting out the name of her lover who had condemned her to this torture.

She fell into a pattern, trying to ride the flogging rather than resist it, screaming Henry's name to each blow, clenching down hard on the studded shaft and accepting the pain it generated into her belly to sweeten the bitter lashes to her back and sides. She was strong and determined but the lash was heavy and enervating and she could feel her strength slipping, even though the heat in her belly was rising. She was losing count in the trauma of the whipping and could not guess how much more she must endure. She hoped Renee was keeping better score. As the final blow fell and she croaked Henry's name for the last time, a hot red glow erupted in her belly, a red mist fell over her eyes and she hung in her bonds, barely conscious that it was over.

Back in Sexton, Renee also lay slumped. Henry had not lasted the course as well as his love. Two dozen of Renee's vacuuming clutches were more than he could endure and on the twenty-second he had groaned and shot his load of hot sticky jism into Renee's convulsing cunt for, perfectly trained as she was, she automatically entered her own spasms at the same time as the man she served. As the flogged girl collapsed against the post that held her, the turgid teats of Renee's firm bare breasts were already pressed tight against the soft curly hair of Henry's chest as they lay together, spent.

Meanwhile the girl, whose imagined cries and writhings under the whip had sparked their fierce explosive ejaculations, was taken down from the post on which she had been so cruelly thrashed. Instinctively she wrapped her arms around her wounded breasts, covering the lumpy contusions that disfigured their sides and cradling the twin pointed peaks, one so distorted, where the whip had caught it, as to be unrecognisable. Her back was the worse for wear as well; not open splits and freely flowing blood, the institution was too careful of its charges to inflict lasting damage, but the welts oozed stickily in a dozen places, where the stroke had been too much for the underlying vessels, and specks of blood had found their way to the surface through the pores of the skin. Weak and in pain, hampered by the cruel dildos still distending her rectum and vagina and the angular links of the sharp steel chain digging into her vulva, she could hardly walk, and a guard had to support her on either side to get her back to the preparation room.

Greta took charge of her once again. Stripped of her gown, her waist belt was removed and the chain drawn out of her flesh. She whimpered as it was withdrawn, the links having bitten deep and the crushed tissues beneath them protesting violently at the return of circulation. The removal of the dildos from anus and cunt, those twin punishments for her 'presumption', drew more squeals and gasps as the studs rasped the tender lining of her vagina on their way out and the anal plug tried to suck the rectal tube inside out on its exit. At last she lay, gasping but unencumbered, face down on the examination table.

Greta looked over the thick dark weals with evident satisfaction.

"Liebvicz did a good job there," she pronounced. "Made you feel them, I'll wager, but you won't have any permanent scarring to speak of. Maybe some faint marks to carry around for a while but she's laid them on beautifully symmetrically and they won't diminish your attractions. Still, they'll be the better for a little attention. Hang on in there. This may sting a little."

If she had been a little more aware, and not still wrapped up in her pain and thoughts of the distant Henry, savouring her sacrifice, she would have flinched from Greta's promise of a little sting. When that icy hearted maiden admitted there might be pain involved in the treatment, a girl had better look out. As it was she squeaked in shocked surprise, and writhed as Greta applied a caustic solution to the broken skin of her back, and squealed again as the fingers reached beneath her to anoint the battered teat.

"Don't make such a fuss girl," the white-coated doctor admonished. "It's just styptic to close the skin. Time's running out and you'll have to get dressed. You don't want your clothes sticking to your back."

Minutes later a guard arrived to summon them to the Superintendent's office. They found the officer once more at her desk.

"Will she live?" she asked the doctor, ironically.

"She'll do," Greta confirmed. "Superficial scratches only. Tough, healthy one this. Could take a flogging every month without too much damage."

"Well, one's enough for now," the official declared, "though any time your man thinks you'd benefit..." She left the invitation hanging in the air.

"Anyway," she continued, "the van is here to take you to the airport. You'll need these before you go," and she pushed a small package and an official looking envelope across the desk.

"Eh, thank you Ma'am, what are they?" the whipped and still wet-eyed girl asked.

"Your certificate of correction to confirm the number of strokes, the conditions under which they were applied and a video as evidence for your master of your behaviour under correction," the Superintendent informed her. "You should hand them over as soon as you return. Meanwhile, I'll wish you good-bye. The van is waiting."

The journey back seemed at least as long and arduous as the trip from the airport, less than twenty-four hours before. Was it really only that long since she had come up this way, manacled in the back of the black van? At least she was not handcuffed this time, and she as able to kneel on the seat with her back to the driver, her arms clasped round the back of the seat, wincing from time to time as the jolting of the van bounced her wounded breasts on the hard moulded plastic of the utilitarian chair.

At the airport she found the company jet that had brought her waiting to depart and was led on board and handed into the care of the tall, sophisticated attendant without delay. With great reluctance she allowed herself to be sat in her place, the seat belt fastened, her throbbing back against the meagre upholstery of the seat.

Once airborne however, things changed. She had left Marindorra with adequate medical attention, but no chance to take any care of her appearance, other than to resume her own clothes. Even that was a strain as, against her wishes, she had been made to put a bra around her sore breasts and aching sides. Her face was still streaked with tears and the sweat of her agony, her hands stained similarly with her perspiration and the oily residues left on both post and manacle cuffs by the generations of women who had been flogged there. None of this seemed to faze the stewardess and she rapidly came to believe that the girl had seen more than one woman returning in this state from a judicial flogging in the principality. For all Jenny knew she may well have made that painful progress herself at some time. In any case, she took in her passenger's state without batting an elegant eye-lid and produced soft hot facial towels, hairbrush and comb, and even some basic make-up. She had recognised at once the soft and docile state the girl had been reduced to by her ordeal and took over completely, brushing her hair, wiping her face, hands and neck, applying make-up with skilled and practised care.

She was not unaware of her patient's discomfort either. She had noticed the painful flinching as the girl had set her back to the seat and had come up with a small padded roll to place at the base of her spine and a horseshoe shaped neck pillow which, between them, served to keep her welted back from pressing on the seat. There seemed little doubt after that that she understood exactly what her passenger had endured in Marindorra, and her condition under the dress that covered her. She even offered an analgesic tablet to ease the pain but, though still putty-like in other respects, Jenny shook her head.

"It wouldn't be appropriate," she explained.

The hostess smiled understandingly and took the tablet away.

A chauffeur driven car awaited her at the airport to take her home, where the driver waited outside, saying he had instructions to take her on when she was ready. Still in acquiescent mood she didn't argue but went inside to find a note telling her to change and come as soon as possible to the Trident where Henry and Renee would be waiting. Her clothes were waiting for her.

She found them laid out on the bed and thought she recognised Renee's hand in their selection. Very much the bare minimum. High heeled pumps, not quite her tallest, but quite enough for her weakened condition, hold-up stockings and a soft clinging dress. No underwear but she hadn't expected any under the circumstances. A punished girl at the Trident always went without panties and bra for the good of her soul and to give the other women a view of what might be laid on their own buttocks if they fell below perfection. Except that this time, it was not her buttocks peeping knickerless beneath some pelmet of a skirt that would bear witness to her correction. The dress had the simplicity that shouted big bucks, a slinky sheath, reaching down to her calves, but not quite revealing her nipples. What there was of it in front was supported by two silken strings that crossed behind her neck and ran on down to meet the sides of the deep wide opening at the back. Indeed, the gown did not have any back as such, being scooped out to her sides, and

223

down to a fleeting glimpse of the top of the crack that divided her pert buttock halves. Only the tension of the two crossed laces kept it from sliding off altogether and every inch of her hot raised purple welts was blatantly on display, even to where the sides of her breasts exhibited the blobby bruises where the sergeant's leather had wrapped and bitten deep. There was just one more part of the outfit and, she was sure, it was that which had made Renee choose it. It was a modest, almost puritan, fitted jacket, of the same turquoise silky material, that came to her wrists, dropped to the ledge of her buttocks behind and rose demurely to her collarbones in front. With the jacket closed, she was completely covered and ready to attend the most conservative gathering, with it off she was as near naked as made no difference, given that all attention would be on those parts of her where her flogging showed.

The Trident was as crowded as ever on a Friday night, when few residents of Sexton Hinds resisted the impulse to watch corrected femininity, its bottom still hot from the rod, writhing on its seat. A loud cheerful hum of conversation filling the bar. It stopped as if switched off as she appeared in the doorway and every eye in the place turned to see. For a moment she stood tall, quiet and graceful, glowing with an inner light, then slowly peeled off the jacket and laid it over her arm. A hiss of surprise rose from those nearest her, a sound that spread along her path as she began slowly to walk across the full width of the large room to where Henry and Renee awaited her.

With the jacket gone, there was nothing to hide the vivid plummy ropes of the thick dark welts that ran, ladder-like, down her back, from nape to waist. She carried herself stiffly, in obvious pain, her complexion a little pale beneath the make-up, but with dignity and poise, as if making a statement, not of defiance but the opposite to that sinful weakness. Softly radiant she emitted an aura of total femininity devoid of all harshness and belligerency. Slowly she crossed the space

224

separating her from her lover and dropped on one knee to take his hand in hers and press it to her lips. Henry watched her come with pride and affection, received her homage and, as her warm lips left his hand, drew her very gently to her feet and, careful not to press her too hard across her wounds, placed his hands on the twin juts of her swelling buttock cheeks and kissed her long and hard on the mouth she tilted up to him. The whole room burst into loud applause.

When Henry finally released her, half swooning, from his passionate embrace, she found herself in a pair of equally loving female arms, two firm breasts pressing on her own as Renee took possession of her lips.

"Oh, darling, how lovely to see you back," Renee breathed into her wet and warm mouth. "Now turn around and let me see what they did to you."

"In a minute but, first, I've something for Henry."

She took the certificate and cassette from the pocket of her jacket and gave them to her lord and master.

"We'll watch it together sometime," he said.

"And me too, please," Renee begged.

"Hmm. I understand you may well have one of your own soon," Henry answered her with a sly grin.

Renee flushed and turned back to her friend.

"Come on darling, let me see."

"I'm not stripping right here for you to gloat," came the answer but, all the same, she turned and let Renee see the full impact of the damage to her back. Immediately another woman stepped up to share the view and, from that moment on, she existed in a daze of admiration and questioning. By the time it was time to eat she was nearly fainting from tiredness. She had been roused at dawn, purged and penetrated by devices designed to torture a woman severely on their own. She had had to endure them while under the sergeant's whip, flogged virtually to the blood in a chilly dawn, then rushed back to her friends so that they could see,

225

and benefit by her condition, while the welts were still hot and fresh. Exhausted, she sank into her seat.

Food and wine did a little to revive her and she pressed Renee for details of her night with Henry and, especially, how she had milked him that morning at the same hour that she was suffering on the post, the sergeant's leather cracking methodically on her bare back, the studded dildo playing havoc in her tortured vagina.

"I tried my best," Renee assured her, after an almost blow by bow account of her passionate night with Henry, "and I really thought he would go the distance and hold up for the full two dozen but, well, I was pretty excited thinking of you myself, and I think I must have got carried away a little. I'd just counted to twenty-two when I felt him spurting inside me. I couldn't stop him so I let go myself and joined him. I hope you don't mind."

"Of course I don't," her friend assured her, "I'd have done the same in your place."

"You may get the chance sooner than you think," Renee said, a fleeting shadow crossing her beautiful face.

"What do you mean?"

Renee hesitated a moment.

"Tom was so impressed by what you've done, and so jealous of this," she added, kissing her again, and this time thrusting her tongue deep into her mouth, to make quite clear she referred to the Sapphic rites they increasingly shared, "that he's suggested I should go out next month myself."

"And what did you say to that?"

Renee had the grace to blush.

"Oh," she said demurely, "I just said, 'you're the master and, of course I shall do exactly what you say'."

For the first time since her arrival at the bleak doors of the House of Correction in Marindorra, twenty-four hours before, Jenny was able to raise a genuine smile.

And now for the beginning of next month's title: "Naked Deliverance" by *Lia Anderssen.*

Chapter 1

Kathy Cooper brushed back her dark locks as she made her hurried way across the yard toward the shower block. As she walked, she glanced about her, as if anxious she might be seen in her brief, somewhat inadequate bathrobe, the short hem threatening to expose her buttocks at every step. She hugged it to her body, wondering momentarily if it might not have been wise to leave her underwear on before heading for the bathroom.

At least it was a warm night, she mused. In fact it was positively muggy, the conditions typical of this part of the southern United States, the incessant chirping of the insects reminding her how far she was from her English home.

The shower block consisted of a low building, set about a hundred yards from the small accommodation area of the motel. As she neared it, she eyed the low, dirt-streaked wall with some trepidation. She would have much preferred a hotel with en-suite facilities, but out here, in this remote and hilly area, there had been nowhere else to stay. The next motel might be miles away.

The entrance to the block was a narrow doorway with a single naked bulb dimly lighting it, the sign announcing 'Showers' hanging at an odd angle. Kathy glanced back at the row of rooms behind her. Only her own showed any sign of life. It appeared that she was the sole guest. As she watched, the green neon sign announcing the motel to the world flickered and went out. Clearly there would be no more visitors tonight.

She opened the door and stepped through into the shower block. She found herself in an open courtyard. Opposite was a low, squat building with the legends 'Men' and 'Women' painted by hand onto two doorways that stood side-by-side. She made her way across to the women's block and pushed the door.

It was dark inside, and she groped along the wall for a light switch. When she snapped it on, she thought for a moment that it wasn't working. Then there was a flash, and another, and the fluorescent strip came to life, emitting a low buzz.

Kathy glanced about her. It was certainly Spartan, she mused, but then this wasn't exactly the smartest motel she had stayed in since arriving in the United States. It was, however, the only place in town, she reminded herself.

She tested the shower's controls. Why was it, she wondered, that these always seemed so complicated? She pulled at a lever, twisted another, then the pipes gave a rattle and a gush of water sprang from the showerhead, soaking her robe in an instant. She cursed her clumsiness, wrestling with the controls until she managed to turn the stream from cold to lukewarm. Deciding that this was the best she could hope for, she shrugged off her sodden robe and stepped back under the cascading droplets.

Despite its coolness, the stream of water playing over Kathy's naked flesh felt good, and she turned her face up to it, letting it wash the sweat and grime of the day from her slim, young body. There was a bar of soap in a dish on the wall, and she managed to work up a lather, spreading it over her firm breasts, the large nipples hardening to solid buds as she caressed them, enjoying the sensation of her hands on her soft orbs.

She washed herself all over, soaping her smooth, pale flesh and letting the water run over her. By the time she had finished, she felt cool and invigorated.

It was only when she stepped out of the cubicle that she realised that she didn't have a towel with her.

Kathy's heart sank as she remembered the towels lying at

the foot of her bed in the motel room. She had completely forgotten to bring one with her, accustomed as she was to in-room facilities where the towels were always to hand.

She looked at her robe. It was saturated. Besides, it was made of thin cotton, cut short so that it barely covered her pert, round backside. It would have been of little use even if it hadn't been wet, she decided. Her best bet would be to allow herself to dry off naturally.

There was a long mirror attached to the wall of the shower room. It was old and somewhat discoloured, but she moved across and stood in front of it, eyeing her body critically.

Kathy was barely out of her teens, but her puppy fat had long deserted her, and her slim body was almost perfectly proportioned over her small, five foot three inches. Her breasts were not large, but firm, like small, ripe oranges. The nipples pointed slightly upwards, the tips still hard, like small, pinkish-brown nuts. Her waist was slim, her stomach flat, her neat belly-button drawing the eye down to her pubis, covered in a neatly-trimmed triangle of short, dark hair. Her sex was prominent, unusually so, the cleft running up so that the thick lips were perfectly visible. Now, as she parted her legs slightly, she felt a familiar frisson of excitement as she glimpsed her large clitoris peeping through the slit of flesh at the top of her valley.

She continued her inspection, twisting round and admiring the curvature of her spine, and the plump cheeks of her beautifully rounded bottom, letting her eyes run down her shapely legs to her neat ankles.

She turned to face the mirror again. It always gave her a thrill to admire her naked body. There was something exciting about being here, in this strange place, completely naked. Tonight, she resolved, when she was safely tucked up in bed, she would masturbate.

The thought made her shiver slightly with anticipation, and she gazed into her own soft, green eyes. There was a hint of crimson in her beautifully sculptured cheekbones as she contemplated her wantonness, and she smiled slightly, her rosebud lips parting to reveal her perfect white teeth.

Almost unconsciously she ran her hand up her flank and squeezed her breast from beneath, licking her lips as she felt the tingling sensation in her nipples. She let her other hand stray down between her legs, stroking the short hairs on her mound before going further, easing her nether lips apart and teasing the already swollen bud of flesh out from between them.

She began to rub it gently, a low, almost inaudible sigh coming from her lips as she responded to the delicious sensation her caresses were bringing her. She gazed at herself once more, wondering at her ability to become aroused so quickly and easily. She had always been sensitive to sexual caresses, and was no stranger to the pleasures of masturbation. Now, in this strange place, she was enjoying her own nudity, and the sight of her fingers penetrating her bare crotch was suddenly very stimulating indeed.

She glanced across toward the door of the shower block. It had been some time since she had had the pleasure of stimulating herself in the open air, and all at once she felt the desire to do so.

Kathy's predilection for exhibitionism had developed soon after she had discovered that her body aroused the desires of men. Normally a modest youngster, she had, since the age of about seventeen, realised that her lovely young form drew glances from all about her, and that this was something that brought her extraordinary pleasure.

She had begun wearing the briefest of bikinis on the beach, flaunting her body and revelling in the attention she drew. Later, even this had not been enough, and she had started fantasising about showing off her naked body. Sometimes she would drive to remote spots, where she would strip naked and walk through woodland, high on the arousal she got from the danger of being seen. Indeed, she was nearly spotted on a number of occasions, crouching down in the bushes whilst people went by, revelling in the possibility of exposure. Always she would end these little adventures by masturbating to orgasm, before returning guiltily to her clothes.

Now, she realised, was a perfect opportunity to stand nude under the stars and pleasure herself. There was nobody about, since she was the only guest, and the walls about the ablution block would hide her from view. Besides, she told herself, her body would dry more quickly in the open air.

Her heart pounding, she made her way toward the door. She paused by it, briefly summoning up her courage, then slowly pushed it open. Outside was quiet apart from the sound of the insects. Kathy moved through the door, revelling in the sensation of the night air on her bare skin. She stepped onto the grass and glanced about herself. There was nobody around. At once her hand dropped to her crotch and she began once again to gently rub her swollen love bud, a low moan escaping from her lips as she felt the pulses of arousal flow through her lovely young body.

She made her way across to the wall, still moving her fingers back and forth between her legs. When she reached it, she turned and leant back against it, the hard, cool surface feeling oddly stimulating against her naked flesh. She shivered with excitement, spreading her legs and pressing her pubis forward, exposing her prominent crotch as she continued to rub herself down there.

Kathy was suddenly overcome by arousal, the desire to come in this harsh, open place, almost overwhelming her. She glanced down at herself. Her pale, naked body was in stark contrast to the dullness of her surroundings, her dark nipples erect and pointing up toward the starry sky. All at once, the youngster's mind was filled with erotic thoughts as she slipped her fingers into the hot, wet cavity of her vagina.

Though she found it hard to admit it to herself, it was the prospect of being caught like this that thrilled her most of all. She knew in her heart of hearts that she would be mortified if anyone saw her and she dreaded the thought of her wicked desires becoming known to anyone else. Still, it was this fantasy of being discovered that spurred her to pump her fingers even harder into her open sex, her breathing coming in short gasps as she felt the onset of her orgasm.

Then she heard the door to the yard open.

Kathy's heart almost stopped beating as the creak of the hinges reached her ears. She froze where she was, legs spread wide, her fingers still inside her, though no longer moving. She was standing against the wall only a couple of yards from the entrance to the courtyard. Paradoxically, this was what saved her from being discovered, since the hinges were on her side, and she was temporarily screened from view by the opening door.

Her heart in her mouth, Kathy watched as a figure walked into the courtyard. She recognised him at once as the motel owner. He was about forty, a heavily built man with a balding head. Less than an hour before she had been signing his guest book. Now she was naked only a few feet from him.

She felt certain that he must see her, but he didn't glance in her direction, heading instead for the shower rooms. The door to the ladies' room was still open, and for a moment his figure was silhouetted against it. Then he pushed open the door to the men's shower and stepped inside.

Kathy knew she had only seconds in which to act. She began to move toward the women's shower room, but almost at once she saw the other door open again and knew the man was about to emerge. She stepped to one side, pressing herself into the corner between the courtyard wall and the shower block, hoping that the shadows would be sufficient to conceal her.

The man stepped out and closed the door. Kathy watched, scarcely daring to breathe, as he went into the ladies' convenience. Moments later he snapped out the light and she saw him cross the courtyard and exit, banging the door behind him.

The youngster breathed a sigh of relief on finding herself alone once more. She stayed where she was for a full minute longer, listening hard for any sound of the man, before finally easing herself away from the wall and heading toward the shower room. She reached for the handle of the door, turning it and pushing.

It didn't move.

She pushed harder, putting her shoulder against the peeling paint, willing it to open, whimpering softly as she applied her full weight to it. But her efforts were in vain. There was no doubt about it, the door was locked.

Kathy gave a little cry of despair. It hadn't occurred to her that the man might be locking up for the night. Now she was alone and naked in this strange place, her bathrobe out of reach.

She stood for some time staring hopelessly at the closed door, her mind a whirl. What could she do? There were no windows on the block apart from small barred ones set high up in the walls, and there was no way she could force the door. There was nothing else for it, she would have to try to get back to her room without being seen.

Cautiously she made her way across to the door of the courtyard. To her relief it was unlocked, and she pushed it open, peering through it anxiously. All was quiet. There was no sign of the man and no lights were showing.

Her heart pounding, the naked girl stepped out onto the hard gravel path that lay between the shower block and the motel rooms. She glanced guiltily about her as she made her way toward her accommodation, only too aware of the paleness of her bare flesh, and how visible she would be to

235

anyone nearby.

It was about twenty yards to the long porch that ran the length of the front of the motel, and she covered it quickly, her breasts bouncing as she hurried along. She reached the door to her room and turned the handle.

Then her heart sank yet again. The key to the door was in the pocket of her bathrobe.

She leaned her head against the door and cursed her ill-fortune. Just feet away from her was her suitcase, containing bra, pants and dresses, yet she couldn't reach it. She was nude, and quite unable to get at any article of clothing. What on earth could she do now?

She crept along the porch, searching for anything she might be able to use to cover herself, a discarded tea towel maybe, or a piece of curtain material, but there was nothing.

As she rounded the end of the porch, a light came into view and she stepped back instinctively. The light was coming from the window of a small bungalow that stood on its own in the motel grounds. This, she guessed, must be where the proprietor lived. She stared across at the building. It was the only sign of life. If only she could find something to wear, she mused, she would at least be able to go and ask the man for help.

Slowly if began to dawn on the hapless beauty that, with or without clothes, the motel owner was her only chance to get out of this mess. Short of smashing a window, she really had no choice but to seek his aid if she wanted to get at her clothes and regain her modesty. He alone held the keys that would give her access to her luggage. She glanced down at herself, at her bare, jutting breasts and her prominent pubic mound and gave a little sigh. What would he think when he saw her?

Then something unexpected happened to Kathy. All at once, the prospect of being discovered in this unclothed state sent an odd shiver of excitement running through the young beauty. This perverse reaction shocked her, though she knew there was no reason why it should. After all, it was the exhibitionist inside her that had got her into this situation in the first place. Now, for the first time, her secret was about to be discovered, and she would be forced to expose herself to a complete stranger. Suddenly she was reminded of the pleasure she had been giving herself before the man had appeared in the shower courtyard and, almost instinctively, she moved a hand back down to her crotch, gasping slightly as she gently caressed her clitoris with her fingertips.

She looked across at the bungalow once more, her fingers moving in small circles about her love bud. She was about to expose her naked charms to a complete stranger, just as she had in her masturbation fantasies and the thought sent new tremors of excitement coursing through her.

Slowly, still gently frigging herself, the pale, naked young girl began to walk toward the building.

To be continued.......

The cover photograph for this book and many others are
available as limited edition prints.
Write to:-

Viewfinders Photography
PO Box 200,
Reepham
Norfolk
NR10 4SY

for details, or see,

www.viewfinders.org.uk

TITLES IN PRINT

Silver Mink

*UK £4.99 except *£5.99 --USA $8.95 except *$9.95*

All titles, both in print and out of print, are available as electronic downloads at:

http://www.adultbookshops.com

e-mail submissions to:
Editor@electronicbookshops.com

TITLES IN PRINT

Silver Moon

ISBN 1-897809-16-6	Rorigs Dawn	*Ray Arneson*
ISBN 1-897809-17-4	Bikers Girl on the Run	*Lia Anderssen*
ISBN 1-897809-23-9	Slave to the System	*Rosetta Stone*
ISBN 1-897809-27-1	White Slavers	*Jack Norman*
ISBN 1-897809-31-X	Slave to the State	*Rosetta Stone*
ISBN 1-897809-38-7	Desert Discipline	*Mark Stewart*
ISBN 1-897809-40-9	Voyage of Shame	*Nicole Dere*
ISBN 1-897809-42-5	Naked Plunder	*J.T. Pearce*
ISBN 1-897809-43-3	Selling Stephanie	*Rosetta Stone*
ISBN 1-897809-46-8	Eliska	*von Metchingen*
ISBN 1-897809-47-6	Hacienda,	*Allan Aldiss*
ISBN 1-897809-48-4	Angel of Lust,	*Lia Anderssen**
ISBN 1-897809-50-6	Naked Truth,	*Nicole Dere**
ISBN 1-897809-51-4	I Confess!,	*Dr Gerald Rochelle**
ISBN 1-897809-53-0	A Toy for Jay,	*J.T. Pearce**
ISBN 1-897809-54-9	The Confessions of Amy Mansfield,	*R. Hurst**
ISBN 1-897809-55-7	Gentleman's Club,	*John Angus**
ISBN 1-897809-57-3	Sinfinder General	*Johnathan Tate**
ISBN 1-897809-59-X	Slaves for the Sheik	*Allan Aldiss**
ISBN 1-897809-60-3	Church of Chains	*Sean O'Kane**
ISBN 1-897809-62-X	Slavegirl from Suburbia	*Mark Slade**
ISBN 1-897809-64-6	Submission of a Clan Girl	*Mark Stewart**
ISBN 1-897809-65-4	Taming the Brat	*Sean O'Kane**
ISBN 1-897809-66-2	Slave for Sale	*J.T. Pearce**
ISBN 1-897809-69-7	Caged!	*Dr. Gerald Rochelle**
ISBN 1-897809-71-9	Rachel in servitude	*J.L. Jones**
ISBN 1-897809-72-2	Beaucastel	*Caroline Swift**
ISBN 1-897809-73-5	Slaveworld	*Steven Douglas**
ISBN 1-897809-76-X	Sisters in Slavery	*Charles Graham**
ISBN 1-897809-78-6	Eve in Eden	*Stephen Rawlings**
ISBN 1-897809-80-8	Inside the Fortress	*John Sternes**
ISBN 1-903687-00-4	The Brotherhood	*Falconer Bridges**
ISBN 1-903687-01-2	Both Master and Slave	*Martin Sharpe**
ISBN 1-903687-03-9	Slaves of the Girlspell	*William Avon**
ISBN 1-903687-04-7	Royal Slave; Slaveworld Story	*Stephen Douglas**
ISBN 1-903687-05-5	Castle of Torment	*Caroline Swift**
ISBN 1-903687-08-X	The Art of Submission	*Tessa Valmur**
ISBN 1-903687-09-8	Theatre of Slaves	*Mark Stewart**

UK £4.99 except *£5.99 --USA $8.95 except *$9.95